BOLLYWOOD ROULETTE

Inside the Struggle!

BOLLYWOOD ROULETTE
Inside the Struggle!

Rahul Bajaj

INDIALOG PUBLICATIONS PVT. LTD.

Published in July 2007

Indialog Publications Pvt. Ltd.
O - 22, Lajpat Nagar II
New Delhi - 110024
Telefax: 91-11-29835221/29830504
www.indialog.co.in

Copyright © Rahul Bajaj

10 9 8 7 6 5 4 3 2 1

Printed at Print Tech, Darya Ganj, New Delhi

All rights reserved. No part of this book may be reproduced or utilized in any form or by any means, electronic or mechanical, including photocopying, recording or by any information storage or retrieval system, without the prior written permission of the publisher.

 ISBN 81-8443-011-6

Contents

Prologue: *Naatak!* 11

Chapter 1: Love 15

Chapter 2: Lust 29

Chapter 3: Friendship 52

Chapter 4: Action! 74

Chapter 5: Reaction 94

Chapter 6: Joy 115

Chapter 7: Desperation 143

Chapter 8: Trap 166

Chapter 9: Anger 190

Chapter 10: Loss 204

Chapter 11: Gloss 228

Chapter 12: Tears 248

Epilogue: *Hope*! 283

Dedicated To:

The *Deserving!*

DISCLAIMER

This is a work of fiction. Names, characters, places and incidents are either the product of the author's imagination or are used fictitiously, and any resemblance to any actual persons, living or dead, events or locales is entirely coincidental.

Acknowledgements

As an aspiring actor, I had once fantasised (as I suspect all actors have at some point or another), about delivering a thank-you speech at the Oscars. The Oscars have not worked out for me; nevertheless, I do have many thank-yous to give. These thank-yous are not necessarily directly linked to the writing of this book, but are perhaps more indirectly linked in letting me have those experiences that made this book possible and in making me the person that I am. (Is this sounding like an Oscar acceptance speech already?).

I would like to thank my father for encouraging me, supporting me and inspiring me. At times, he was the only one standing by me – steadfast in his faith in me – sometimes perhaps even more faith than I had in myself. My mother, wise and strong, is my greatest strength. Nanaji and Naniji, thank you!

I am forever indebted to the teachers and staff at Modern School, Vasant Vihar, New Delhi, who made me and prepared me for life. Professor Marilyn Reizbaum of the English Department at Bowdoin College, I thank you for teaching me the nuts and bolts of writing. Professors Denis Corish and Scott Sehon of the Philosophy Department at Bowdoin, I thank you for opening my mind to new intellectual vistas. Professors John Fitzgerald, Michael Jones, Jon Goldstein, John Holt,

Deborah DeGraff, Allen Tucker, Bill Watterson and Andreas Ortmann, many thanks for making my years at Bowdoin an intellectual treat. At the London School of Economics, I remain grateful to the late Professor Morris Perlman, who, as a holocaust survivor, in addition to Economics, taught me the importance of being fearless in the critical pursuit of all things – a quality which, I suspect, has something to do with the writing of this book.

Megha Subramanian, Executive Producer with UTV, Mumbai, thank you for giving me a major break by casting me in the main lead of *Kabhi Hero Kabhi Zero*. Sandiip Sikcand, Creative Director at Balaji Telefilms, I thank you for casting me in *Kahaani Ghar Ghar Kii*. All the executives at all the other production houses that offered me roles, I thank you all.

Barry John, my guru, I thank you for putting me back in touch with the monkey-within-me and also for encouraging me to write. Kishore Namit Kapoor, Vidur Sir, Mohit Sir, Shakur Shaikh (the greatest dance teacher in the universe) – thank you all.

Shinie Antony, my editor, friend and guide, I can't thank you enough. At Indialog, I am grateful to Mr. Basant Pandey and Mr. Gagan Das for their near-missionary zeal for discovering and promoting new literary talent in India. More power to you! Thank you Krishnadasan Nair for producing a kick-ass cover! Kunal Mahajan and Jeff Treut thank you for your suggestions. Sandeep Kumar, Ishwar Das and everyone else at Indialog who played a vital role in production, many thanks.

Any media product is incomplete without the participation of YOU – the audience. In a world of ever-expanding infotainment possibilities, dear reader, thank you for choosing this book.

PROLOGUE

"Why is a play called a *play?*"
None of the students in this new batch in Bollywood's famous Anil Taneja Acting Academy knew the answer to Guruji's question.

"You have all come here to learn drama, to become actors, but what is this thing that we call *drama, naatak*? As an actor, or even as a layman with an interest in dramatic arts, you must know the answer to this question."

Blank looks shot back at Guruji.

"In the *Natyashastra,* drama is compared to sport. Drama and sport have the same ingredients. The same tension, the same grip, the same what-will-happen-next feel, the same joy, the same thrill…" Guruji paused as he noticed some students yawning.

"A play is called a play because dramatics is like sports. A theatrical play is called a *play* because it is just that – *play! Krida! Khelna!* Acting and playing have a deep connection. Your acting training will begin today with an exercise that you have probably done before – we are going to play a game – a children's game. *Aaj hum khelenge.*"

Shiv Shankar Pandey, an obvious Bachchan fan going by the *Zanjeer* cowlick on his forehead, shot up an excited hand. "Sir, I can speak dialogues like Amitabh Bachchan. Should I show sir?"

"Be quiet," Guruji snapped.

Pandey's obsession with Amitabh Bachchan had reached fever pitch. He could recite every single Bachchan dialogue backwards, and had trampled over his Brahmin father's hopes of succeeding him in the family business of priesthood by running away from his hometown Benaras to Mumbai with ambitions of becoming the next Amitabh Bachchan.

"Today, we will play. *Krida!* The name of the game is dog and the bone." Guruji announced to the class.

This damn Guruji is not giving me a chance to show my talent, Shiv sulked. Shiv had not run away from Benaras and paid Rs. 40,000 for this acting course – money, which, by the way, he had raised with great difficulty by surreptitiously selling the family buffaloes the day before he had taken the train to Mumbai – to play children's games. He wanted to do Amitabh style dialoguebaazi, fighting, dancing … No! Instead, *aaj hum khelenge!*

Guruji whipped out a handkerchief from his pocket. He divided the class into two groups, gave each member of the two groups a number, and then started the game of dog and the bone. When he announced a number, two players from opposing teams whose numbers corresponded with that number came up to a central point where the handkerchief was placed, and like two dogs meandering around a bone, they circled the handkerchief in an attempt to quickly pick it up and run back to their side. If a player picked up the handkerchief and ran back to his team's side without being touched by the opposing team's player after he had picked up the handkerchief, he won his team a point. If the opposing team's player managed to touch him while he fled to his side, the point would be lost. So, both players (dogs) circled the handkerchief (bone) in an attempt to swipe it and return to safety without being touched out by the other player. The team first to reach a score of ten points would win.

"Four," Guruji called out.

Meghna, who was number four on one team, and Amrit, who was number four on the opposing team, simultaneously ran from opposite ends of the classroom to the handkerchief placed in the centre of the class. Meghna's team was on nine points, and so was Amrit's team – the team that won this point would win! Both circled the handkerchief like keen dogs, observing the movements of the other. Meghna had to win this point. She was not used to losing. She had ruled every other class she had ever been in. Today was the first day of classes at the Academy and she wanted to set the same winning standards here too. The tall and athletic Amrit, himself a winner in all endeavours he ever undertook, was also keen to win. They both circled the handkerchief staying alert to the other making a move. From the looks of her opposing player, Meghna determined that physically she was no match for him – for the six-footer from Amritsar did outgun her. She would have to use some cunning if she were to win this point.

"Oh hi!" Meghna gestured to an imaginary person behind Amrit's back.

Amrit fell for the trick, and looked back. Before Amrit could realise that there was nobody behind him and that Meghna had used the oldest trick in the world to distract him, she had picked up the handkerchief and had made a dash for safety. She was quick, a former track and field champion from her school days. She had managed to distract Amrit and was now on her way to safety with the handkerchief in her hand. With this point, Meghna's team would win. Not to be outdone, Amrit leapt into the air like a panther on a kill and shot out a long, outstretched hand to touch Meghna, landing flat on the floor with a loud thump, but managing to get a tickle on Meghna's back before she could reach safety.

"Out!" announced Guruji.

Amrit had won the point, in an all-out effort to win the game for his team, but he had hurt his chin slightly. There was a round of applause from everyone for his athletic display.

"Are you hurt?" The beautiful doe-eyed girl on his team who reminded Amrit of Audrey Hepburn asked with a concerned look on her face.

"No, I'm fine. Thanks for asking!" Amrit beamed back.

"I'm Sapna." She held out a hand and smiled back. "You have lovely dimples."

Amrit's dimples deepened as he smiled embarrassingly. It was love at first sight.

CHAPTER 1

Amrit was sprawled on the bed with his face buried in the pillow. Sapna stared at his back, bared by the bedsheet and thought – *My boyfriend!* – proudly eyeing Amrit as he lay on his tummy, jaw open, arms spread out wide in deep slumber on this pre-monsoon Mumbai afternoon. Sunlight was streaming in through the half-drawn curtains. The ceiling fan creaked noisily as it spun intermittently, providing cover for Sapna as she tiptoed into the one-bedroom flat. She was quiet as she moved across the room; her intention, to surprise Amrit. Sapna dropped the extra key to Amrit's apartment back into her handbag. The key made a metallic clicking sound as it landed on some coins in her purse. Sapna froze. Thankfully, Amrit showed no signs of waking up. He had been working late the previous night, finishing off the last bits of a software programme he had been writing till three in the morning.

With a mischievous smile on her face, Sapna advanced into the room, pulling off her t-shirt, unhooking her bra. Now she was ready for her prank. Positioning herself at the base of the bed, she dived on to Amrit's back and landed with a thud.

"What the hell…" Amrit drooled.

"Wake up Amrit! *Jaldi karo!*" Sapna was all excited, her hands vigorously shaking his shoulders.

Amrit turned around rubbing his eyes, still groggy with sleep, and immediately focused on Sapna's well-formed breasts. His eyes widened, his spirits rose. "Am I dreaming?" he muttered.

"No baby! These are real! Here – touch and see." Sapna took Amrit's hand and placed it on her breasts. Amrit was now fully awake. This was better than a dream.

Sapna hit Amrit with a pillow. "Oye Amrit from Amritsar, before you get any ideas, let me tell you this was just a prank. Don't you get fresh with me…" Sapna knew Amrit got horny everytime he saw her breasts. Once he had got to her breasts, they would almost invariably end up having sex. Today, though, she was in a hurry. There was no time for sex.

Amrit turned her around in a flash and was on top of her.

"Amrit!" Sapna protested. Amrit picked up the pillow and hit her back.

"Revenge! You want a pillow-fight?" Amrit smiled, and playfully hit her again with the pillow. Sapna struggled to push him off but, couldn't; Amrit was much stronger.

"Amrit, get off me! Or…" Sapna demanded.

"Or what…. Aaaaahoouuccch…" Amrit felt a sharp pain on his belly where Sapna had just pinched him.

Amrit turned over and let Sapna escape. She didn't seem like she was in the mood for sex. He looked at the spot on his stomach where Sapna had pinched him; it had turned red.

"What *yaar*…" Amrit tried to reach out for Sapna's breasts, but she had already left the bed, picking up the bra that dangled from the bedpost.

"Not fair. I am already turned on. Come *na!*" Amrit unsuccessfully tried to protest, as the breasts disappeared from view, the bra coming on.

"Oh Mr. Amrit from Amritsar, at least sometimes stop thinking with your dick. I have some good news to share. Listen up. Do you know that toothpaste ad I had done?" There was excitement in Sapna's tone. She had auditioned for and managed to get cast in an advertisement for a leading brand of toothpaste. The ad had been running on all television channels for the last few weeks. Amrit was not paying attention, still sulking.

"I got called for a film audition because of that! The producers say that I have been shortlisted. They really liked me in the toothpaste ad. They say they are most likely going to take me. The audition is at three at a studio in Bandra. C'mon get dressed and take me there."

Amrit was in no mood to hurry up. He had had a very late night working at his laptop, which Amrit noticed, was still on. Sapna was not giving him any lovin'. He must have been really tired, because he normally never left his laptop on at night. Besides acting and Sapna's breasts, the other thing Amrit was passionate about in life was writing computer software. In fact, had Amrit not been so driven to 'try-out' to become an actor in Bollywood, he would have been working at a desk-job in a prominent computer software company in Bangalore, writing software code for American clients, rather than be a struggling actor in Mumbai. Amrit was more of an actor than a techie, or so he thought. Others at home in Amritsar didn't share his view. Acting in college plays was one thing, but choosing acting as a profession was a complete no-no as far as his parents were concerned for their computer engineer son. But Amrit knew he just had to come to Bollywood. The joy he had experienced when performing on stage at college festivals was scintillating. He held that joy above everything else in life. Even above warnings of prudence that his brain would sometimes issue him: "Take the software job, Amrit! Don't be foolish. Acting is risky business." Like many who had come to Mumbai to try out their luck in Bollywood, Amrit had thrown caution to the winds. He had said no to the venerable job at the big software company in Bangalore that had recruited him from campus. Instead of going to Bangalore, he was here, in Mumbai, in Bollywood. He just *had* to be an actor. He was in it for the passion of acting. Passion was still running high after many months since the Golden Temple Express train had brought Amrit from Amritsar to Mumbai. He had excelled in the acting course at Anil Taneja's Acting Academy, had circulated his photographs to all the prominent film producers, casting agents and television production houses. Yet, he awaited the elusive 'big break.'

Luckily for Amrit, he was also a damn good software programmer, and made enough money freelancing as a software programmer over the Internet. Financially, he was not dependent on anyone, for he made roughly 500 dollars every other week, and when converted to rupees, that was adequate to get him through comfortably, even in an expensive city like Mumbai.

"Did you hear what I said, *oye* Amrit? Stop fiddling with your computer. Audition time." Sapna snapped her fingers, as Amrit gave the shut down command on his laptop. He still wished Sapna had not put on her bra.

"Why don't you move-in with me, Sapna?" Amrit suggested, as he put on a t-shirt.

"Amrit, my Colaba*wali* aunt, she is very conservative, don't you know. If I don't live with her, she will send a telegram to Jaipur and the whole bloody Rathore family will be up in arms. They still think they are rulers of their fictitious princely state, and think I ought to live by certain norms. You know ... a princess should be like this, a princess should be like that!" Sapna mimicked her royal relatives. Amrit could tell Sapna didn't like her aunt in Colaba with whom she was forced to stay. It was a precondition set by her father, Maharaj Ranasingh Bahadur Rathore, for letting her come to Mumbai and trying out in Bollywood.

"That aunt of yours, why don't you poison her? She's a royal pain in the arse," Amrit said, half-serious.

"Anything for a regular supply of sex, huh?!" Sapna eyed him dismissively.

Amrit mumbled something under his breath. Sapna's Colaba*wali* aunt was coming between him and a healthy sex life. There was no point. He had tried earlier. Sapna's family was anal like this. They were all bankrupt drunkards, but still pretended to cling on ferociously to some ancient moral code that existed only in their heads. They still felt like they were medieval maharajahs or something. Sapna, the second daughter of the eldest son of the Rathore clan, was expected to comply.

"Okay baba, tonight for sure, *pukka*. You'll get what you want. Now can we go please...my audition remember..." Sapna was getting impatient.

Excited at the thought of getting sex tonight, Amrit hurried up. Sapna waited while Amrit got dressed, her eyes scanning the walls of Amrit's room. The walls were covered with posters of Amrit's favourite movies. Most of them were Hollywood classics – only a few Bollywood movies, the good ones, made the cut to be on Amrit's walls.

"Amrit! The *Pyaasa* poster is torn…" Sapna pointed to the poster of the classic black and white Guru Dutt film just above Amrit's bed.

Amrit immediately leapt to the rescue, smoothening the end of the poster that was slightly torn. *Pyaasa* was one of Amrit's favourite Bollywood movies, 'a classic,' he would often tell Sapna, whom he had forced to watch the movie three times already.

"You know I spent a whole day in Chor Bazaar looking for this poster. I don't know how it got torn." Amrit took a piece of scotch tape and mended the tear in the poster.

"I remember. You had dragged me along too." Sapna said with disdain.

Amrit noticed Sapna rolling her eyes.

"I can't imagine how you *can't* be passionate about a movie like *Pyaasa*. It's movies like this that inspire me to be an actor. It beats me that you want to be an actress with so little passion for that which is good and classic in Bollywood." Amrit shook his head.

"Okay, okay I have heard this lecture many times! What to do, I am not up there with you *baba!* I like the mindless, senseless, masala Bollywood films, fine? Now please, hurry up or I'll miss my audition for a mindless, senseless, masala Bollywood film. They don't make movies like *Pyaasa* any more." Sapna did not want to engage Amrit in a debate right now. She wanted to make the audition on time.

"That's the problem, my princess." Amrit combed his hair. "That they don't make movies like that any more." Amrit noticed in the mirror that his biceps looked smaller today. He made a mental note to work out harder in the gym.

"Hey! Have my biceps shrunk?" Amrit asked Sapna for a second opinion.

"If you write software programmes all night long, don't eat right, surely they will," Sapna said adding, "But it doesn't matter for you, you want to do art films, you don't want to be like bodybuilder Bhola."

"Bhola does have a fabulous body, I must remind you." Amrit eyed himself carefully in the mirror. "In today's Bollywood, being a bodybuilder has become so important. It sucks but it's true."

"Riz is not a bodybuilder." Sapna said.

"Yes, but Riz is a star-son. He doesn't need to be a bodybuilder. His dad, superstar Sandy Khan, is there for him. The lucky bugger has the whole film industry at his feet." Amrit made a face in the mirror.

"Oh please hurry up, will you. You look just fine." Sapna was now really impatient.

"Have you heard from Riz? Isn't he shooting for his launch movie?"

"I spoke to Meghna on the phone the other day, she told me he's gone to Los Angeles to get plastic surgery on his face, to get rid of his double chin, before he begins shooting for his first movie."

"Hmmm..." Amrit was now ready. "By the way, how is Meghna? Has she managed to get any decent break? Haven't spoken to her for ages. I am so not in touch with my classmates."

"I'm going to go visit her tomorrow. Will ask her and let you know." Sapna was looking down, and was suddenly serious.

"What now? What happened?" Amrit asked.

"Oh, nothing. Come on please *na jaldi baba*! We're getting late." Sapna was irritated.

Just as they were about to head out, Amrit's cellphone rang.

"Amrit. Hi! This is Seema; I'm casting director at Jai Jai Productions. I got your photographs. We're conducting an audition for a major role in our daily soap *Saas Ka Sindoor*. The audition is from 10 am to 9 pm on Friday, at Jai Jai House in Andheri West. Do you know where it is? Good. Come around noon. See ya!"

Amrit did a celebratory jump in the air after hanging up with Seema. Just the thought of working for Jai Jai Productions sent Amrit's adrenaline pumping.

Amrit picked up the pillow lying on his bed and hit Sapna.

"What was that for?" Sapna protested.

"I got an audition call from Jai Jai Productions!" Amrit dropped the pillow and hugged Sapna, lifting her off the ground and pecked her on the cheek.

"Come, let's go my princess!"

Amrit looked up at the sky as they stopped outside the studio. Dark clouds seemed to be gathering. It looked like the monsoon rains were finally going to break, bringing an end to a long and hot summer.

"Sapna, I'll wait outside, if that's okay with you?" Amrit parked his Yamaha RX100 motorcycle and looked out at the sea. The studio was on a road facing the Bandra seafront, and Amrit felt like hanging out looking at the sea for some time. Growing up in the landlocked heartland of Punjab,

Amrit always found the boundless expanse of the sea spectacularly mesmerising.

"But it looks like it's going to rain. You'll get wet." Sapna said with concern.

"Relax sweetheart. This is the best place to get drenched in the rain … by the sea! You don't worry about me. You focus on the audition. Good luck!" Amrit beamed back. Sapna hugged him and ran off. Amrit saw her disappear in the studio, and then strolled off towards the promenade, where he could hear the waves crashing against the rocks.

The transition from hot to cool represented by the first monsoon showers in Mumbai is nothing short of dramatic. After a long scorching summer, the first droplets of cool, monsoon rain are manna from heaven for Mumbai dwellers. Suddenly, the collective mood of the city lifts. The temperature drops to comfortable levels, with cool breeze blowing in the dark moisture laden clouds from the Arabian Sea. The sky is darkened with thick smoke-like clouds that sail in like huge galleons. The trees are swept violently from side to side by lashing winds, and then, at one precise moment, the clouds burst, releasing sheets of rain pounding the roads and the pavements and the buildings, which, not long ago, were simmering hot in the blazing tropical sun.

The best place in Mumbai to experience the first rains is on the seashore. The ocean, already swollen from the rains falling further out at sea, like a giant grey-skinned python that has just gorged a humongous meal, lifts and roars. Massive cargo ships are tossed up and down like tiny warts on the surface of the gyrating swollen serpent; the waves crash noisily and with added fury against the big, black igneous rocks; the army of menacingly-grey clouds heavily pregnant with moisture continue their march inland like a mighty invasion force, ready to bombard the hinterland of a subcontinent that has been baked bone dry by months of hot incessant scorching sun.

"Guess who?" Sapna said in a mock old-woman voice, her palms cupping Amrit's eyes.

"It's my princess. You're back quickly." Amrit turned to face Sapna.

"Yes … they were waiting for me. It didn't take long. They just wanted to see how I looked on camera."

Just then there was a cloudburst. The first droplets of monsoon rain pelted down upon the two of them. Sapna closed her eyes and let the rain fall on her face.

"So, do you think you'll get the role?" Amrit asked.

"I don't know. They'll get back to me soon." Sapna was enjoying the raindrops playing on her face.

"Whooooo..." she let out a cry of joy. Amrit hoisted her from the waist and lifted her up towards the sky, as if offering her to the rain gods. Sapna spread out her arms, to catch it all – the rain, the mist of salt-water from the violent waves crashing on the rocks below, the gust – letting out another continuous cry of "Whoooooo…," drowned out by the sound of the loud crashing waves. Amrit brought her down and now picked her off her feet, and held her in the cradle of his arms, holding her like a little baby, her legs dangling. Her eyes were looking straight at him, smiling.

"Sapna … you know … you have the gift of being able to smile with your eyes."

"I'm smiling because I'm happy Amrit. I am so happy and content in your arms. I just want this, nothing else. This is heaven!" Sapna spread out her hands like a bird.

Amrit lowered his neck and kissed her on the lips. She

smiled. *Those smiling eyes.* They drove Amrit crazy. They were both madly in love with each other.

"If you ever leave me, I will drown myself." Sapna said, raising her eyebrows and pointing to the sea.

"How will you drown yourself? There is no water in Rajasthan, my princess. Not even rivers." Amrit teased.

"I will drown myself right here, right at this spot," Sapna said seriously, pointing to the ocean.

"Shut up! Don't have bad thoughts. Or I will drown you myself, right now!" With those words Amrit broke into a sly smile, his dimples on full view, and playfully attempted to launch Sapna towards the hungry sea. Sapna protested, "Stoooppp!!! Amrit stop! Amrit, put me down, right now!" poking a finger into his dimples.

"Ouch! Your nails hurt!" Amrit complained. She loved poking his dimples. And she loved it even more when he complained.

"They hurt?" Sapna quizzed playfully, as she put her arms around Amrit's neck, and kissed the spot where her finger had poked his cheek.

"Does that help?" Sapna asked, naughtily. *Those eyes!* Amrit looked deep into Sapna's eyes. They were both serious again, as they looked eye-to-eye. Sapna moved forward and kissed him. Amrit kissed her back. The rain had intensified, drenching them as they remained locked in a deeply passionate kiss. Their wet clothes clung to their bodies like wet paper. As they held each other tightly, they could feel the contours of each other's bodies, as though they were completely naked. The rain became heavier and the wind and waves lashed them from all sides – but the two lovers stuck together in a magnetic hold – the rain only hammering them tighter into an embrace.

"Do you want some grilled corn?" Amrit asked.

"Yes!" said Sapna.

They walked hand-in-hand to the old lady at the corner of the street who ran a *bhutta* stall. It was a makeshift shack made of crate-wood planks and transparent plastic sheets used as a canopy; and the old lady, holding a large black umbrella to protect herself from the lashing rain, was grilling the corn over red-hot coal embers that crackled every now and then. Sapna and Amrit stood there, holding hands, waiting for the corn to grill, happy.

Amrit's RX100 motorcycle zipped onto the Goregaon-Malad link road, towards the relative seclusion of Madh Island. They drove onto the narrow road that connects the island to the mainland over the salt-water estuary. A left turn would have taken them to the various beach resorts and bungalows that dot the seaside, and towards the Indian Navy area, which was off-limits to civilians. Amrit took a right, and headed towards a secluded sandy beach that he knew. He had come here one morning, to meditate, and it was one of the last remaining untouched beaches of Madh Island. The secluded beaches of Madh Island had in the past been notorious as landing spots for gold smugglers. With the opening up of India's economy, the gold smuggling had ended, but these beaches had become major tourist destinations, and were mostly overcrowded and dirty. A few unexplored gems still remained, and Amrit and Sapna sped towards one.

A full moon peeped out of the clouds as they lay down on the sand. There was a gentle breeze blowing, and it blew Sapna's hair into her eyes. As she pulled her strands back, she could see what a beautiful sight it was. The waves washing up the sands, silking their way up the gentle gradient – the ocean looked magical silvery-blue as it shimmered in the moonlight. The moon was full and bright, like a giant bedside lamp showering an ivory white glow. It was a picture postcard scene. And it was so silent, the only sound being the gentle washing of the waves against the sand in a pleasurably soothing rhythm, and the occasional ruffling of the coconut palms by the sea breeze.

Sapna and Amrit lay there on the sand, taking in the mesmerising spectacle, amazed to find such calm and peace in a city like Mumbai. Such peace, such calm, such beauty. This could have been in any other place but Mumbai – the Caribbean, or Thailand, or an atoll in the Pacific – unbelievably, they were in Mumbai.

"The tourism people should make a film of this beach and promote it. Wow!" said Amrit.

"Why? So that crowds of tourists come and take it over like locusts? This is our place, our private beach!" said Sapna, looking up at Amrit with a glint in her playful eyes. Amrit noticed how Sapna's teeth glowed pearl-white in the moonlight, and he smiled back at her, his dimples showing. Sapna put her fingers in his dimples, poking them till Amrit protested. "Sapna! Your nails … they hurt!"

"Oooh my macho man … it hurts, huh!" Sapna teased, grinning ear to ear. They were looking into each other's eyes, and whenever they did, something magical happened to both of them. They suddenly stopped giggling and became serious. Sapna's eyes darted as she stared into Amrit's eyes, alternating her gaze on each of his eyes. Amrit just looked, mesmerised and completely in love with her.

Just then the wind blew a strand of hair from Sapna's brow across her eyes, blocking her vision. Amrit raised his hand to smoothen the hair back in place. Sapna's hair was so smooth to touch, as he continued to caress her head, while the two were locked in eye contact. Suddenly, Sapna moved forward and buried her head in Amrit's chest. Amrit rested his chin on her head while his arms curled up around her in an embrace. The sweet smell of her perfume filled his nostrils like fragrance from a thousand wild flowers and intoxicated him. Amrit shut his eyes. Sapna embraced him tighter. Gently, they both reclined out on the sand, holding each other. They lay there blissfully, their hearts beating in unison, as the ocean provided the rhythm. Sapna raised her head and looked up at Amrit. Their eyes met again.

"I love you," said Sapna.

"I know."

They kissed; and sank into a deep embrace. The sand, the sea and the moon bore witness as two souls that were meant to be one, became one.

CHAPTER 2

"Aaachoooo!" Sapna sneezed.

"Is that why you wanted to see me urgently – because you're getting a cold?" Meghna sounded offended.

"No, no. I'm not getting a cold." Sapna wiped her nose and took another sip of the hot tea Meghna had made for her. "Just got wet in the rains yesterday with Amrit, that's why the sneezing. There is a more serious medical reason why I wanted to see you Meghna. A gynaecological reason."

"Sapna, you know that I don't practice medicine anymore," Meghna replied curtly. "I can refer you to a good gynaecologist friend if you like." Meghna was about to scribble something on her pad when Sapna held her hand.

"Meghna, I can't risk it. You're the only one I trust. If word gets out to my aunt in Colaba, and you know how well-connected she is in South Mumbai social circles, that I went for a pregnancy test to a doctor, there will be an earthquake in the Rathore family in Jaipur." Sapna pleaded with her former classmate. "I can't risk it. Please. Meghna, you're the only doctor I trust."

Meghna looked away. Meghna Aggarwal, or more aptly Dr. (Mrs.) Meghna Aggarwal, had not practised medicine for many months now – ever since she had decided to enrol as a student at the Anil Taneja Acting Academy – and had vowed never to take it up ever again. Medicine, Meghna believed, was the reason for her downfall.

The problem with Meghna was that she had always been an overachiever, and now she suffered from a deep sense of underachievement. Meghna had always excelled at everything she had done in life. She had been an ace student throughout school. Her academic and athletic records still remained unbeaten at Mumbai's premier Cathedral and John Connon School. She had never done anything wrong or taken a single misstep. In school, she was the kind of girl who was both loathed and held in awe by her classmates. Teachers loved her. She was a model student. An all-rounder, her principal had announced while appointing her Head Girl. She would go places, everybody had said. She had stood first in the medical entrance examination for a coveted spot at the All India Institute of Medical Sciences, New Delhi, the toughest medical college on the planet to get into. There, while studying, she had met her husband, Raman, who too graduated with her and they had then settled down in Mumbai. Meghna and Raman had a lovely flat in South Mumbai's posh Peddar Road, a good medical practice and a comfortable life.

Yet, Meghna was deeply unhappy. She felt like a failure. Nobody *knew* her. She never appeared on Page 3, the gossip page in newspapers (though some of her famous patients did). *Dammit! If she was run over by a bus tomorrow, nobody would even notice her absence.* Oblivion is the worst thing in the world. A life of oblivion and anonymity – albeit one of worldly comforts – *naah!* She was so upset at where she had ended up in life that she couldn't sleep at night. She would lie awake in bed, dreaming with her eyes open. Dreaming that one day she would be a *somebody;* that she would rise above the teeming masses of nobodies who wake up every morning and go to work and get back home and go back to sleep and then wake up the next morning and repeat the drill. She wanted to become someone *special* – someone *known* – be recognised when she walked out on the street. Oh, the thrill of being recognised on the street! It sent shivers of excitement down her spine! Oh, having to make an effort to conceal one's identity, wear shades or a balaclava and be hounded by the paparazzi! To open the morning papers and see one's photograph on Page 3. To be invited to give interviews by journalists and TV hosts; to be invited to cut ribbons and give lectures – to be a *celebrity!*

The word *celebrity* is a very strange word. A *celebrity* is a *celebrated person* – celebrated for ostensibly some great quality or deed done by that person. Meghna was a medical practitioner and she was very good at it – she cured patients. Yet, she was not a celebrity. Society did not *celebrate* her for what she did. *It is so frustrating!* All her life she had done things right, blazed a trail, done extraordinarily well. Still she was in a dark hole of anonymity. She was a *nobody.* She had fallen behind in the rat race of life. Maybe she had taken the wrong path altogether. A doctor was just a doctor – nobody cared about one. Sleep didn't come to her, only these thoughts did. So Meghna decided to go to the kitchen for a drink of water. She opened the newspaper lying on the granite kitchen counter. It only infuriated her further. *This whole bloody society has a lopsided way of viewing things.* It was breast cancer awareness week and the newspaper had a special report on it. They had interviewed a host of celebrities to get their opinions on breast cancer – two models, one actor, a director, one social activist and one business tycoon. Nobody had asked *her?* And she knew more about this topic than all of them combined! There – staring her in the face from the pages were smiling photos and comments of all and sundry *celebs* on breast cancer. Meghna Aggarwal, MBBS, MD, had hit a new low. Tears rolled down her cheeks as she sat there on a bar stool in her ultra-modern chic kitchen. *This is just plain simple unfair.* She composed herself and returned to her bedroom. Raman was in deep sleep, like a baby, on his stomach, his face buried in the pillow. *How could he sleep so soundly? How could he be so satisfied?* She certainly wasn't. Ordinariness. Anonymity. These were sounding worse than breast cancer. Could she let life pass her by like this, while others got all the limelight?

Not being famous was killing Meghna. She had to do something. She shut her eyes. And imagined. She was at a Page 3 party, surrounded by all the familiar faces she saw on TV and in the papers; mingling with them, on first-name basis, joking, blowing kisses, being photographed by the paparazzi. *Oh …this is life! What if she were a Bollywood star?* The thought struck through her head like lightening. *Yes!* That would be her ticket. *Hurrah! Now there was hope!*

Meghna's problem was that nature had endowed her with more than one gift. She was mighty intelligent. She was also mighty good looking. A classic beauty who had always underplayed her looks and let her brains define her. Now, it was time to use her other gift. If she were ugly, she would probably be happy being the great doctor that she was. It was as if nature was playing games with her, confusing her – it had given her two boats to embark on for her voyage of life – one named Brains and the other named Beauty. There she was, poor soul, switching from one boat to another on the high seas. She shook Raman and woke him.

"What? What happened?" An understandably shocked Raman mumbled, rising from deep slumber.

"Raman, I want to tell you something."

"What? What happened? You okay?" Raman looked worried, as he rubbed his eyes.

"I am giving up my medical practice. I want to be an actress. I am joining acting classes."

"Meghna! Meghna!" Sapna's repeated calls broke Meghna's chain of thoughts and brought her back to the present moment. Meghna turned to her former acting academy classmate.

"Are you going to help me or not? Please!" Sapna pleaded.

"Okay Sapna. Just this one time I will make an exception. Wait here while I get my kit." Meghna went to get her medical kit to perform the pregnancy test on Sapna.

After a few minutes of examination, Meghna finally announced.

"Relax. You are not pregnant."

"But ... but what about my periods this month?" Sapna asked, almost disappointed at the diagnosis.

"Sometimes they get delayed. Nothing to worry. I'll prescribe some pills. They will regulate your periods."

Sapna smiled. "Thanks Meghna. I really appreciate it. I know you've given up medicine. Thanks for doing this. I really could not trust anyone else. You know Amrit and I are not married, and if word gets around…" Sapna looked down, avoiding eye contact with Meghna.

"Hmm…. Just this one time, so you better be careful; I won't do this favour again … and say hi to Amrit. Tell him he's a bad boy. He should have been here with you." Meghna put away her medical kit and then continued. "Anything happening on the acting front? Your toothpaste ad seems to be all over TV."

"Yes! Just auditioned for a movie role. Actually it was the toothpaste ad that got me noticed. Keeping my fingers crossed, let's see! How about you?" Sapna asked.

"Have auditioned for a few TV serial roles. Nothing materialised yet. Have distributed my photos around; keeping my fingers crossed too." Meghna cocked her head. "It will happen; I will become famous." There was steely determination in Meghna's voice.

Amrit stood at the massive sign announcing that he was at Jai Jai House, the headquarters of Jai Jai Productions. Jai Jai Productions was a premier television production house in Bollywood, with a commanding position over all prime slot TV shows across all the prime channels. Founded by Vinta Malhotra, Jai Jai Productions Limited, Bollywood's largest television production company, ruled the tube. Vinta, termed the soap queen of India, had become a legend, both loved and loathed by aspiring actors in Bollywood. Vinta's father – Kuku Malhotra, the retired filmstar, who was most famous for bringing the Elvis Presley look to Bollywood, is still remembered for his bellbottoms and standing hair, gyrating, Elvis-like, to one particular Bollywood number that had a hundred extras moving in sync behind him on the beach. That number, which became an instant hit, Kuku Malhotra's moment of crowning glory, is still his lasting legacy. Mention Kuku Malhotra's name to anyone from that era and they will be quick to recall the famous beach dance in bellbottoms. Vinta, weighing in at an obese one hundred and fifty kilograms, had decided against becoming a Bollywood heroine, when her father had offered to 'launch' her. Instead, she had expressed a most unusual interest in setting up a television production company that would specialise in family dramas, or soap operas. The television industry in India was at a nascent stage at that time, and Vinta's request had sounded strange. However, as time would show, Vinta had been a visionary and a leader. Today, Jai Jai Productions Limited was listed on the Bombay Stock Exchange and was a blue chip wonder. At age 33, Vinta had achieved more that what most girls in Mumbai could dream of. She had single-handedly steered the Jai Jai ship from a one-woman setup to the mammoth media house it had morphed into. Today, Jai Jai's shows ruled the airways. Credited with taking family melodrama to a new height, Vinta's shows were a huge hit with womenfolk, the dominant television watching audience in India. It had also brought her great riches, half a dozen BMWs to her garage, and a stock market capitalisation of half a billion rupees to her company.

From an actor's point of view, Vinta Malhotra had launched many a career. Unknown actors who had been given breaks by her in her early soaps were now household names. These soap-stars would have been nowhere had it not been for Vinta and Jai Jai Productions. Yet, actors also hated Vinta for her totalitarian ways. Bollywood was rife with stories about how Vinta ran her company as a complete dictator, with utter disdain for anyone else. Jai Jai Productions was the Third Reich, and Vinta Malhotra was the Fuhrer. Every totalitarian regime has its doctrine, and for Vinta and Jai Jai Productions, that doctrine was religion – more specifically, the cult of the Hindu goddess Kaali. Every aspect of Jai Jai Productions was touched by an obsession with goddess Kaali. Vinta, ever since a teenager, had been a devout believer in the cult of Kaali. There were rumours that even as a teenager, she had performed strange ceremonies and sacrifices, slitting a goat's neck and letting it bleed to death in the middle of a full moon night. Eighty per cent of India watched Vinta's soaps, making many believe that it was Vinta's obsessive worship of goddess Kaali that brought her such spectacular success. She was a character in herself; someone no newcomer wannabe actor could ignore, wanted to work for and also feared.

It wasn't just stupendous success that made Vinta a curious specimen. It was also the way she had achieved it, and the way she lived her life, which itself had become a parallel running soap opera. Still unmarried, Vinta's obsession with Kaali worship had become a point of novelty. There was a mini Kaali temple constructed in the driveway of Jai Jai House – the corporate headquarters of Jai Jai Productions – complete with a massive six feet tall black-granite statue of goddess Kaali, sprinkled around which were marigold flowers, and a continuously burning electric *diya*. The idol was always garlanded in fresh flowers and there were incense sticks always burning at its feet. A large brass multi-lamp also stood before the statue, with split coconuts and rose petals scattered on the temple floor. The temple was raised a few feet above the ground level, and fenced in with a black marble *jali* wall. Next to the temple were always parked a fleet of jet black BMWs, announcing that Vinta was in her office. Black was the colour of goddess Kaali, and black was Vinta's favourite colour. Passers by always paid respects at the Kaali temple before entering the glass cube office building that was Jai Jai House. Some would even tap the brass bell hanging outside the temple, ringing it to seek blessings from the goddess. Paintings and statues of goddess Kaali could be found all over Jai Jai House, and even in all the studios and outdoor locales where multiple crews of Jai Jai Productions shot for their various soaps day and night.

The cult of Kaali pervaded even the work culture at Jai Jai Productions. The first shot of every team's shoot, every single day, would be that of an *aarti* being performed before the photograph of goddess Kaali. Most Jai Jai crews had a spot boy or someone similar who also doubled as a priest for these daily *aartis*, chanting Vinta-prescribed *mantras* in Sanskrit. All cast and crew were expected to participate in this 'first-shot' *aarti*, like children in Catholic schools begin every day with mass in the church. Anybody who might resist this, as much as even utter an oblique comment that may be anything but fully compliant to this practice of daily *aartis*, risked being sacked by Vinta. Vinta was rumoured to have spies everywhere on the sets – from spot boys to executive producers to even cast members – Vinta had eyes and ears everywhere, her secret SS, keeping her empire together. Consequently, the atmosphere on the sets was mostly chilly when it came to anything to do with Vinta or her policies. People on the sets were very,

very cautious – aware that even a single non-complimentary word they might utter would travel directly to Vinta's ears. People would laugh and joke about almost any topic – but when a newcomer or a naïve fool uttered something like, "Why do we have these strange rituals every day?" or "Vinta shouldn't force us to do this," suddenly, there would be pin drop silence and everybody would look the other way or just get up and leave. Most were happy to be a part of Jai Jai Productions, and didn't want to do anything to jeopardise their position. They knew they were lucky to be there; thousands were vying for their position, willing to replace them at any moment. Vinta knew that too, and that's why she could afford to be autocratic. "One job, a thousand candidates, and all replaceable – you get the picture." "I am the only star of my TV shows. Everyone else is replaceable." Vinta would announce at her late night meetings. All her meetings were conducted late at night.

Vinta's day began in the afternoon and ran into the wee hours of the morning; during the day, she slept. That had been her routine ever since she had founded Jai Jai Productions. Every afternoon, Vinta personally performed *aarti* at the Kaali temple, before heading upstairs to her office on the top floor of Jai Jai House to begin her day. Vinta was believed to have a perpetual bleeding finger – her left pinkie. Every day, she would puncture her finger with a needle, letting blood flow onto the feet of the goddess' black granite statue. The blood thus blessed by goddess Kaali would then be mixed in a rich saffron paste and applied to Vinta's forehead in a long *tika*. Vinta would never be seen without her *tika*, the bright ochre-red line marked vertically across her forehead. This was her daily ritual. It was believed to give her power and invincibility.

On full moon nights, it was rumoured, Vinta would walk barefeet to a seaside cremation ground, not far from her house in Juhu, and sacrifice live chickens by slitting their throats and letting their blood flow into the sea, in an act of sacrifice to goddess Kaali. Her legendary success – with all her soap operas hitting record popularity – were rumoured to be a result of her tantric practices. One leading woman's magazine had called her a true Indian feminist, bringing together the best feminist practices of the ancient past and those of modern times. Others had described her as a power hungry lunatic suffering from perpetual PMS.

Feminist or not, there was no doubt that Vinta was a dominant person. "An actor or an actress is just a daily wage labourer. Nothing more. Like those guys digging ditches. Let the bastard or bitch dig – if he or she gives trouble, fire their ass. As simple as that." Vinta had famously remarked during an interview about her management style in dealing with dissent from actors and actresses in her soaps.

Notwithstanding all this, every struggler in Bollywood had wet dreams about receiving the golden call from Jai Jai Productions. For the chance to work in Vinta's soap could mean a major boost for any actor. Overnight, an unknown face, featured in Vinta's soap, would be beamed across millions of television sets across India, and to the Indian diaspora abroad, turning him or her into an instant somebody. The call for audition was the first step. Most who were invited to Jai Jai Productions did not make it any further. Thousands were auditioned for *one* single spot. Competition was fierce.

Amrit passed the massive gates of Jai Jai House, with its army of private security guards who, after patting him down thoroughly, finally let him through. In the massive driveway were parked three black BMWs. Everywhere that Amrit could see, there were actors. On the lawns, leaning against the BMWs, pacing up and down the driveway; like inmates inside a prison complex, these fellows seemed to be everywhere. Actors with sheets of paper with lines scribbled on them could be found spilling all over the place furiously memorising their lines and rehearsing. In alleyways, in corridors, in the bathroom, on the roof – like worms that spawn after the first monsoon showers, these aspiring actors were everywhere. They all had this look on their faces that said that they knew that the odds were desperately against them. For a single decent role in a prime time television show, hundreds, if not thousands, of actors would be auditioned. A ninety-second audition is all that the poor aspirant got to showcase what he or she had to offer. Hence, the ferocity of preparation evident in the faces of these aspirants.

Amrit instinctively folded his hands and uttered a prayer as he passed the Kaáli temple. Everywhere he could see, there were actors – lost in a world of their own as they pushed themselves to the limit in preparing for the audition. Faces convoluted, foreheads frowned, eyes intense, voices modulated – Jai Jai House and its environs had turned into some sort of circus-like tradeshow for actors. Snatches of the same dialogues could be heard uttered in hundreds of different ways – each actor rendering his own version or experimenting with different versions as he went about his preparation. Everything they had learnt in acting school was going to come in handy now. This was ultracompetitive, trial by fire.

Amrit tracked down Seema, the casting director, who was in the basement of Jai Jai House, conducting auditions. Between takes, Seema handed Amrit a page-long script.

"The role is of a poor college student, who comes to Mumbai from a small town and falls in love with this super rich girl. Go through the lines and sign up on the call sheet. You'll be auditioned by your number. We are at number one hundred and twelve right now."

Amrit took the script from Seema and signed up on the call sheet. He was number one hundred and seventy-nine. There was plenty of time to prepare his lines. With this kind of competition, he would have to pull out all the stops. Amrit found a quiet little spot and read through the script. It was a breezy scene, where the protagonist was trying to convey his love to his beloved. He read it again. And again. And then began his preparation. Within twenty minutes, Amrit had worked out three different variants of performing the scene. Then, he zeroed-in on one variant that he felt best conveyed the meaning of the scene. For the next two hours, till his number was called, Amrit was lost to the world, as he prepared the scene with a fanatical zeal. When number one hundred and seventy-nine was called, Amrit had ceased to be Amrit, and had become the poor college student who had come to Mumbai from a small town and had fallen in love with the super rich girl.

The effort paid off. The audition went well. Amrit was happy.

"Thanks. We'll be getting back to you shortly." Seema seemed happy too.

Amrit smiled his dimpled smile and made his way out of Jai Jai House, bowing his head to goddess Kaali as he walked past the temple.

"What else? Are we done for tonight?" Vinta announced, sitting at the head of her magnificent mahogany table. For the last many hours, Vinta and her team of various creative directors had gone through their usual daily rigmarole of tweaking the plots and storylines of half a dozen Jai Jai Productions' soaps. Vinta liked to sign off on all the twists and turns that her team of creative directors came up with. She kept tabs on what was happening in all of her soaps, and micro-managed the storylines down to the last detail.

"One final thing," Nandini, Vinta's senior most creative director said. "We've auditioned for the new character we are introducing in *Saas Ka Sindoor*. I have shortlisted about ten possibilities out of about eight hundred that we auditioned. We need to finalise who we're going to take." Nandini had gone through all the audition tapes and narrowed the list down to the best ten. The final choice in picking the actor for the role, as always, would rest with Vinta.

"Okay, play the audition tapes." Vinta announced, like an empress before her court.

Nandini went over to the gigantic plasma screen attached to the wall facing Vinta and pressed a button on the video player. The audition tapes began rolling. Everyone turned their chairs to face the screen and watched. The ten auditions short-listed by Nandini rolled out. Once they were all viewed, everyone turned to Vinta, waiting for her decision.

"That 6th audition … what's his name … tall guy…" Vinta looked towards Nandini to help her out.

Nandini looked down at the audition call sheet in her file.

"Number six. Amrit."

"Yes, Amrit." Vinta said, yawning. "I like him. Take him. He's got spark."

The matter was settled. Amrit, who was fast asleep at this hour, had just been finalised for a major role in *Saas Ka Sindoor*.

"Anything else?" Vinta asked. She seemed eager to get over with the meeting.

Everybody nodded negatively. There was nothing else left to discuss.

"Well then. The meeting is over. Good night." Vinta announced, as she glanced at her black Rado watch. It was 4 am. This was the last meeting for the day. She always scheduled Nandini's group for the last. Every night. As usual, Nandini left Vinta's office with the creative team of her show. During the meeting, she had received an eye signal from Vinta. They were on for tonight. Nandini left Vinta's office and headed to the attached toilet. There, she changed out of the conservative salwar kameez that she was wearing the whole day, and into a black low-neck dress Vinta had bought her from Paris. Nandini adjusted her dress straps in the large bathroom mirror. She pulled out the rubber band holding her hair together in a conservative plait and twirled her head to reveal a thick mane of long silky-black hair. Nandini could look very attractive if she wanted to.

Nandini was Vinta's right hand. Whenever a show was in trouble, which generally meant lower than usual Television Rating Points, or TRPs, Vinta would turn the show over to Nandini. Nandini's creative suggestions had twisted the plot of many a languishing Jai Jai show back to healthy TRPs. By having a character killed off to generate sympathy, or another raped, by making someone pregnant, or someone else lose their child – Nandini was an ace at convoluted twists and turns – the show could be brought back on track. Soaps are strange things. The whole purpose of a soap is to keep the audience coming back day after day, and during a telecast, coming back after each commercial break. The more twists and turns, or 'hooks' as Vinta called them, that could be introduced, the more it was likely that the viewer would come back. Nandini had mastered the knack of knowing which 'hooks' worked and which didn't, what would make the show compelling and addictive, to pull the housewife back to it after the commercial break, and not drift away to another competitive channel or get lost serving dinner or cleaning the dishes. The biggest hook of them all had to come at the end of the day's episode – a big 'whodunit' or 'what happens next?' – to get the viewer back the next day. Higher viewership, measured by higher TRPs, meant more advertisement revenues, which meant happier TV channel executives and more business for Jai Jai Productions. Anything for eyeballs – nothing is too dramatic or nothing too ridiculous – Vinta would say.

Nandini pulled out her eyelash highlighter and ran it through her lashes. Vinta liked her with her eyelashes done up black, and with heavy mascara under her eyes. "All black," Vinta had slipped a secret note to Nandini during the meeting. As she ran the highlighter through her lashes, Nandini tried to think when professional admiration had turned to something else. For Nandini hadn't been a lesbian always. In fact, she was voraciously heterosexual. As an 8th grade school girl at St. Stephen's School, Chandigarh, Nandini had lost her virginity to the school's cricket team captain in the back of his Maruti 800 car. From then on,

Nandini had bedded about half a dozen boys by the time of her wedding night. Nandini's parents, middle-class government servants, had set her up with an NRI businessman's son in Canada in an arranged match. Nandini, when agreeing to him, had calculated that being an NRI brought up in Canada, the fellow wouldn't be like the other MCP Indian men who want a virgin bride on their wedding night. She was so wrong. When Nandini did not bleed in agony on her first night, and rather kind of enjoyed the romp, hubby dear Mr. NRI became furious. "How dare you're not a virgin!" he had shouted at Nandini. "Bloody MCP!" Nandini had shouted back. The marriage was over in two weeks, and Nandini was back in India. Partly for a change of scenery, and partly to get away from the chattering aunts and grandmothers of Chandigarh, Nandini had decided to move to Mumbai, and pursue a master's degree in mass communication. The cosmopolitan and free spirit of Mumbai, plus the anonymity that came with a big city made her decide to stay on in Mumbai after the completion of her course. She spotted an ad in a local newspaper for an assistant at the then fledgling Jai Jai Productions. That's when she first met Vinta. Since then, the two had not looked back, and had gone from one success to another. As Jai Jai grew, so too, did their intimacy. Perhaps it was Nandini's hate for her ex-husband that turned into a general hate for men; and into love for Vinta. Nobody quite knows how these things work.

Vinta had eased a bit and was now sitting with her head down on the mahogany conference table. She looked tired. Nandini came up from behind Vinta and began massaging her neck. Vinta moved in her chair, her large frame shifting slightly. Nandini began kissing the back of Vinta's neck. Vinta was now beginning to get turned on. She turned her neck back and her lips met Nandini's. Their tongues met and both locked arms around each other and settled down for another night of woman-to-woman love.

Bhola strutted into the lobby of the posh J.W. Marriott Hotel in Juhu. It was a typical balmy night after the first few monsoon showers, and Bhola was dressed accordingly in a blue floral Hawaiian shirt spread out over tight fitted Armani jeans with brown leather cowboy boots to match. Three buttons of the blue floral shirt were undone, giving a glimpse of Bhola's muscular and bareshaven chest, which was still pumped from the bench presses he had done at the gym an hour ago. All those years of arduous workouts and a steroid-rich diet had indeed given Bhola a fabulous body. Biceps and triceps made the floral shirt look tight around the arms, and a size smaller, but it was really his correct size. Even though Bhola was not barechested, a simple glance towards him revealed that he had a bodybuilder's body. The cowboy boots knocked down on polished granite flooring making a click-clock rhythm as Bhola sailed through the lobby towards the elevator bank. With over-sized purple coloured shades wrapped around his eyes, Bhola looked all smart and dandy. But he was no showstopper. People in Mumbai are so accustomed to seeing even the greatest stars breeze by nonchalantly that they seldom turn to give someone of a much more mediocre stature as Bhola as much as even a second glance. Dandies are a dime a dozen in Mumbai, especially in the *filmy* areas stretching from Bandra to

Lokhandwala. So, in relative anonymity, Bhola slipped into the gleaming brass-bodied elevator and pressed the button for Floor 6.

"Ting!" The elevator announced its arrival on the 6th floor. Cowboy boots met a carpeted corridor this time and the click-clock sound of heels hitting hard surface was conspicuously absent. Bhola felt that he had vanished, no reassuring sound to remind him of his own presence. Passing a large, teak-framed mirror, he adjusted his shirt and ran his fingers through his curly, short black hair. For a moment Bhola thought he was sitting under a shady peepal tree staring at an ordinary one foot by one foot mirror hung from the bark. As a little boy growing up in Bihar, Bhola had had all his haircuts from the village barber who practised his art under a shady peepal tree. His saloon was simple – a high seated wooden barber's chair, a one foot by one foot mirror hung from a nail hammered into the trunk of the tree, an empty brown sherbet bottle refilled with water and attached with a metallic sprayer to wet the hair, and a small jute bag that the barber hung from his waist. After the haircut, which at that time cost two rupees, a lot of money in poverty stricken Gaya district of Bihar, schoolboy Bhola would run his fingers through his curly black hair to make sure it was a good cut. He had always been obsessed about his looks, which is what had attracted Bhola to bodybuilding in the first place. After watching the barechested Sylvester Stallone's impressive torso in *Rambo*, which he had watched at a rich landlord friend's 14th birthday party on a rented VCR, Bhola had taken up bodybuilding, spending as much as four hours a day exercising at a local wresting club. At the age of 17, Bhola was the fittest man in the whole of Bihar.

Representing Bihar at the All-India Under-18 Bodybuilding Championship brought Bhola to Mumbai. He didn't win the title, but won some admirers in the crowd. Tanuj Mal, the famous fashion designer, offered Bhola a spot in his next fashion show; and ever since then, Bhola had become a permanent fixture on the fashion ramp. Hoping to turn his modelling success into Bollywood success, Bhola had enrolled at the Anil Taneja Acting Academy. Models in India all aspire to be Bollywood stars. So did Bhola, as he now checked his overall appearance once again.

Flashback over, Bhola realised he was no longer in Bihar, but in Mumbai – in Bollywood – in the corridor of a posh hotel, about to meet a very posh person. Reassured, Bhola made his way to Room 611. Three knocks and the door opened. Falguni Iyer stood with her hair open, wearing a flowing pink silk nightgown. The window in the room was open, facing the side that overlooked the Arabian Sea. A wind tunnel had developed that brought a gust of air into the room from the sea-facing window and towards the open door where Bhola stood. Falguni's frail figure was pushed forward and her hair blown towards Bhola by the strong draft from behind. Steadying herself, she placed a hand on Bhola's shoulder. Falguni Iyer, wife of coffee magnate Nagaraj Iyer, and herself a socialite and permanent fixture on Page 3, was quite attractive for her age. Nobody knew what her actual age was, with all the plastic surgery and the regular spa treatments, she had maintained herself well – but people close to her had ventured to put it anywhere between forty-five and fifty years. She was thin and delicate and had sharp, attractive features. She had been a former ramp model, which is where Nagaraj had spotted her, and the glory of those days had not completely faded from her body.

"Where have you been, naughty boy?" she said to Bhola, pressing her hands over his shirt and moving them towards the open buttons.

"Oh, was at the gym. Gotta stay fit, no?" came Bhola's answer, consciously trying to mask his natural rustic Bihari accent with a put-on upmarket Americanised drawl he had picked up from the video jockeys on MTV. One of the reasons Bhola had loved ramp modelling so much and had been so successful at it was because it never gave away his background. On the ramp, his body did the talking for him. In the sphere of acting, he knew his rustic Bihari accent would be a problem, and he was working hard on trying to mask it.

"Fit as a fiddle!" Falguni commented in a refined South Mumbai accent, suddenly moving her hand from Bhola's shirt and grabbing his crotch tightly. She too preferred his body to do the talking.

"Let me come in first." Bhola closed the door behind him as he entered the room. It was a really well appointed room. Bhola could still remember the first time he had been in a room in a five-star hotel. He had been so overwhelmed by the luxurious appointments that he had even forgotten about the job at hand. He had never been inside a five-star room until then. He had gone absolutely berserk in the bathroom, not knowing how to operate the knobs and mixers in the shower, and then, after a good fifteen minutes of fiddling around and drenching the whole place, once he had figured it out, he had gone nuts showering for over forty minutes in the running hot water, causing a minor flood by the time he was done.

The hotel plumber and engineer had to be called to fix the problem. Now, of course, he was well accustomed to such luxuries, having been in fine, five-star environs on hundreds of occasions. This is the best job in the world, Roxy had told him. Initially, he had been reluctant, not sure if his uncouth Bihari ways would be acceptable by such a discerning clientele. "Relax." Roxy had told him. "They're only after one thing. Your cock. For conversation and other fine things they have their husbands and their hi-fi social circle. You give them what their husbands can't." Roxy at that time had been the number one male model in India. The young Bhola, fresh from Bihar and just drafted into fashion modelling, had walked the ramp with the great Roxy. Roxy had noticed him in the dressing room, noticed his well worked out body, and invited Bhola to join the *trade*. Like a bull in high demand, Roxy was getting more offers than he had the nights for. So, he wanted to draft a partner who could share the workload and also the profits. Of course, that was five years ago, when Bhola had first arrived in Mumbai. Roxy had retired from modelling since, and was now running a chain of fine Italian restaurants in South Mumbai. Bhola thought of Roxy's words as he made himself at home in Room 611. *This is the best job in the world!*

Falguni wobbled along to the dresser, the alcohol in her system too much for her petite body to handle. *I should start cutting down*, she reminded herself often but never followed through. She had just been to the opening of an art gallery in Juhu, where champagne and caviar were served. Four glasses of bubbly later she had asked her driver to bring her to the Marriott. Leaning against the dresser, she tried to stay upright, fiddling with her alligator skin

Coach bag. She pulled out a wad of thousand rupee notes from the bag and placed it on the bed.

"This is for my fit as a fiddle stud boy." She pointed to the money and then to Bhola's crotch, pointing a finger and shutting an eye, as if taking aim at Bhola's groin with an imaginary gun. A very shaky aim. Bhola could see that she was really inebriated today and would pass out soon. He wouldn't have to do much.

"Now come here and make me happy," Falguni said as she undid her silk nightgown, revealing one of the better bodies Bhola had seen in his gigolo career. Tossing the nightgown to the chair next to the bed, the coffee baron's naked wife slipped into the sheets. Bhola followed suit like an obedient boy.

CHAPTER 3

It was Amrit's third knock that brought Bhola to the door. Bhola stood there at the door, barechested, with shaving foam spread all over his chest and a razor in his hand.

"Bhola, what are you doing? Shaving your chest *paagal*?" Amrit exclaimed, stepping into Bhola's flat.

"Hi Amrit! Come in *yaar*. You should do it too. It's the in-look these days, the shaven chest – the *chikna* look – smooth smooth, nice nice." Bhola said as he ran the razor over a patch of foam on his chest.

"I prefer the classic look. A man should have hair on his chest. Like James Bond. The *chikna* look is too gay for me."

"Here!" Amrit thrust forward the box of sweets he had brought for Bhola.

"What is this? *Mithai?* You've become a father or what?" Bhola stared at the box of sweets in Amrit's hand.

"No *saalae,* better than that! I got a role in Jai Jai Productions' serial *Saas Ka Sindoor.*" Amrit clarified. Bhola took a piece of *mithai* and put it in his mouth.

"Congrats man! That's good news. It's a really popular TV serial. You'll get noticed. Good break! Now movies are not far." Bhola gobbled up the piece of *barfee* and put out his hand for another piece when Amrit pulled the box away.

"Don't eat too much. You'll get fat." Amrit teased. "I'll put the box in the fridge, eat later, spread out over a week."

"I worry though…" Bhola said as he licked his fingers, "You're not the serials type, and *Saas Ka Sindoor* is a hardcore *saas bahu* serial…"

"So you think I can't do it?" Amrit was slightly offended.

"*Abbae nahin,* that's not what I meant. Everybody knows you were the best actor in our batch. I didn't mean *that*. I meant you're not the serials kind … you're more the film kind, and that too the *arty farty* film type … I doubt you'll like acting in *saas bahu* serials."

"Like it or not, I have to do it. It's the only break I have. Besides, as you yourself said, it'll get me visibility. Everybody and their dog watches *Saas Ka Sindoor*."

"True … even Shah Rukh started off with serials … *Fauji* and *Circus* … it's the way to go for us outsiders. *Lage raho!*" Bhola snatched a piece of *barfee* from the box and ran into the bathroom.

"*Achcha* give me five minutes. I will quickly wash off and then we can go to the gym." Bhola's voice boomed out of the bathroom. Amrit dropped into the comfortable leather sofa in Bhola's otherwise modest flat and picked up a Bollywood film magazine that was lying on the floor. There was a photograph of Riz on the cover page. Amrit turned to the article. It described how Riz Khan, the son of Bollywood superstar Sandy Khan, was soon to be launched in a big-budget movie that was going to be shot in Switzerland. There were some exclusive photographs from the *mahurat*.

"Let's go." Bhola appeared from the bathroom, clothed in his workout outfit. He noticed Amrit was reading the article about Riz.

"It is such an unfair world!" Bhola shook his head. "This sisterfucker Riz – who can't act, has no body, can't dance – was the worst student in our batch – look at the kind of launch pad he is getting. Not fair!"

"Don't worry my friend; if we work hard, we'll make it too! There is god up there watching. We can beat him. But we have to work ten times harder than him, because we have no father or godfather in Bollywood." Amrit stood up from the sofa.

"Talking of which, I need to pump up man. My biceps are stagnating at sixteen inches; I need to cross the eighteen inch mark." Amrit said, flexing his biceps to show Bhola.

"Amrit, I've told you before. If you really want a bodybuilder's body, you've got to take supplements. Look at this – you don't get a body like this without supplements." Bhola peeled off his t-shirt and flexed his muscles. Bhola had the finest body going of anyone from their acting class. Unlike Amrit, who was more into fitness, Bhola was a true bodybuilder. Though not an especially good looking man, Bhola had worked hard on his body, gatecrashing the handsome category. Where he lacked in natural good looks, he had made up in building a body that looked like it was out of a muscle magazine. He had it all – bulging biceps, triceps, a well-formed chest, six-pack biscuit abs, deltoids, thighs, calves – the works.

"Wow!" Amrit exclaimed. "I'll have a word with the trainer at the gym. See what he says." The two ran down the stairs of Bhola's apartment block and took off on Amrit's Yamaha RX100 motorcycle in the direction of Olympus gym.

The sprawling reception of Olympus gym looked more like the lobby of a five-star hotel than the reception of a gymnasium. Two pretty girls were seated behind a gigantic cider-wood desk, which curved stylishly to match the curve in the cider-wood panelled wall that ran all around behind them. Large bronze statues of human figures with perfect bodies stood on the Italian marble floor dotting the entire reception area, illuminated with warm yellow spotlights that shone from the false ceiling above.

"I need to renew my subscription." Amrit said as he noticed that the expiry date on his membership card was only a week away.

"Hey Bhola, don't want to sound rude, but how do you afford this place *yaar*. Do you make that much from your modelling? I am thinking of switching to a cheaper gym." A truly five-star gym, Olympus also charged a five-figure membership fee. It blew a hole in Amrit's budget every month.

"Just like you, my dear friend, I have a side business too. But it isn't software programming. I am not brainy enough for that." Bhola chuckled a little and then continued seriously. "Let me know if you want to ever get involved. There is always scope for expansion."

As they passed through the automatic glass doors of the gym, Amrit felt he was in a foreign land. He got that feeling every time he entered Olympus gym, no matter how many times he had come there before. The gym was absolutely state-of-the-art, with the most advanced imported machines everywhere – treadmills, rowing machines, cycles, cross trainers, body toners.

"Hey Samson!" Bhola extended a hand to the gym's owner cum head trainer. The beefed-up, dark complexioned man with his trademark shiny, shaven-bald head and silver earrings shook Bhola's hand.

"Bhola, how are you buddy?" Samson turned to him wearing a bright white smile. Then he turned to Amrit. "Hi Amrit."

"Amrit here wants to seriously bulk up." Bhola declared. "Samson, why don't you suggest something? I've tried. He doesn't listen to me. He's *pussy* about taking supplements." Bhola winked at the gym trainer.

"So far I have been more into fitness and athletics, not so much bodybuilding. I guess in Bollywood muscle mass is also important." Amrit admitted, slightly sheepishly.

"No problem, you can bulk up if you want to. I'll have a detailed chat with you about it later." Samson winked. "Have a good workout."

"Twelve ... Thirteen ... Fourteen ... Fifteen." Bhola pushed back the rod on the bench press. "Now you go."

"Bhola dude, you lift like a maniac," said Amrit. Bhola was on his 4th set on the bench press, and had pulled through fifteen reps with a heavy load with great ease. He was solid as rock.

"I have been bodybuilding for the last ten years. You too will be able to if you go on for that long. Remember, it is all about exercise and diet." Bhola said, flexing his chest in front of a mirror on the wall. In the mirror, he noticed a familiar figure. It was Riz Khan, working out on one of the toning machines.

"Well! Well! Well! Who do we have here! Riz Khan! I thought you were in Los Angeles? Come and work out with us here, won't you?" Bhola called out to his acting school classmate.

"Oye Bihari...first learn how to pronounce Los Angeles properly!" Riz snapped back. Bhola's blood boiled, his biceps twitched. Bhola was always trying hard to mask his Bihari roots, always insecure about them. Amrit held Bhola's arm in a gesture to calm him down.

"So Riz, nice job on the chin. You're looking sharper." Amrit quipped.

"Who told you about the chin job?" Riz was aghast. His plastic surgery to get rid of his double chin had been top secret. How did word get out?

"A little bird told us!" Bhola said, pronouncing "bird" as "bard." He had just picked up the expression and was happy to get to use it in conversation.

"Bihari, you are fluttering your wings too much. Better behave like a little *bard*...or you will be sent packing back to Bihar." Riz was angry that his little secret was public knowledge.

"Relax dude." Amrit patted Riz's back. "He means well. C'mon, we're all batchmates. Like brothers! No need to be pissed off with each other. Let's go work out together. I am sure Bhola can give us some tips on bodybuilding."

Riz agreed grudgingly and the three of them went to the free weights section of the gym.

"So, you've been working out regularly?" Amrit asked, trying to change the subject.

"Dude I only come here because dad says I have to. I hate this bodybuilding crap; besides, what's the need?" said Riz.

"Well, if you have to make it in Bollywood, you need to have muscle plastered all over your body. It's a pre-requisite nowadays. With the likes of Salman and Hrithik, the bar has been raised sky high." Bhola declared.

The bar for the quality of bodies to be had by Bollywood men and women had indeed been rising with each passing year. In Bollywood today, men are supposed to be international-standard bodybuilders, while women must be lean and supple divas. Gone are the days when a chubby Shammi Kapoor, the darling of the 1960s and 1970s Bollywood era, could romance the equally plump Asha Parekh and still appeal to audiences. Bollywood actors are now expected to be beefy Sylvester Stallones and the actresses' skinny Jennifer Anistons.

To some extent, it was the young aspirants who had really pushed this trend so far. Every new aspirant to Bollywood wanted to outdo the current lot in order to have a leg up. They worked harder and harder in the gym, and obsessed with their diets. Women were on the edge of anorexia. An arms race developed in bodies. A good body became not only mandatory but also the only currency an aspirant could trade on, especially one from outside the film fraternity. Those who didn't have anything else, at least had their body. Many would even risk permanent damage and take anabolic steroids to get that fab body – it was the only thing they could do. Kill a portion of themselves, gamble on their health – all for the big, elusive prize – Bollywood stardom.

"Bhola, even with a great body you won't be able to make it in Bollywood. Bollywood is closed for outsiders my friend, closed," Riz announced pompously.

"That's not a nice thing to say, Riz." Amrit shot back, as he finished his last set of exercises.

"Let's go and sit down at the bar and I'll explain to you two newbees." Riz pointed to the in-house bar that served fresh fruit juices and all sorts of protein shakes.

"The way Bollywood works, newcomer wannabe lead-actors need a 'launch movie' to launch them into the orbit of stardom." Riz sipped his carrot and wheat-germ blended juice, seated across a stylish metal-top table from Amrit and Bhola.

"Once stardom is achieved, only then do they get real offers for main leads. This is the star system. Why is it so difficult to break? Well, let's see the dynamics and economics of filmmaking." Riz continued.

"A movie producer has profit foremost in his mind. He wants to maximise the return on his investment. The way a producer generally makes money is by producing a movie at the cost of, say, five crores. Then, he hopes to 'sell' the movie to distributors, who are the exhibitors – and the music rights, television rights, oversees rights, all of these rights for the movie, at a higher amount – say, ten crores – he's made his five crores on a five crore investment, a return of hundred per cent, and he is happy."

Bhola took two large gulps of his double whey-protein milkshake.

"Now, the distributors are the buyers of the movie – they too are businessmen and their only aim is profit. The distributors will only buy movies that have brand name stars in them. Because brand name stars draw the audiences in and give the film a big opening at the box-office – which reduces the risk. A fantastic movie with a cast of newcomers and with no big-name branded actors will entice very, very little interest from the distributors. They don't want to take a risk. On the other hand, a mediocre, run-of-the-mill flick albeit with a big name Bollywood star cast in the main lead will be picked up by the distributors in no time – maybe even before the movie is finished, sometimes even before filming begins! As long as the big names are on board, distributors will open their purse strings. So, if you were a producer who wanted to make money in Bollywood, and had no interest in the art of filmmaking and only cared about profit, what would you do?"

Riz looked at Amrit and Bhola as if the conclusion was self-evident.

"Would you risk your money on a newcomer hero and heroine? No way! You would sign up a branded star pair in the main lead, get some good music, get a decent director, some foreign locales and bingo – you will have a hot product to sell to the distributors. Script, storyline, content, message, etc. are all secondary. It's all about the *money*, honey!" Riz took another sip of his carrot drink.

"There must be some exceptions to this, isn't it?" Bhola asked, with a look of despair in his eyes.

"None! Bihari! None!" Riz continued. "At times, movies are even scripted in reverse. That is, the main lead actors are finalised first and then a writer is commissioned to create a script for it. A typical brief given to a writer in such a case would be something like this, with the producer saying to the writer:

'Hello writer! I have signed on Star A for the main male lead and Starlet B for the main female lead. Star A has agreed to give me thirty-five days of dates at a stretch and Starlet B has agreed to give me twenty days now and then another twenty days after three months; so we have about twenty days when both Star A and Starlet B's dates overlap, and then I have Star A solo for fifteen days and Starlet B solo for twenty days after three months. I would like about six songs in the movie, two to be picturised in Switzerland, I have got a great deal with the Swiss Tourism Department, two in Malaysia and one song that should be an 'item number' to be performed in a cabaret-like setting which we'll shoot in a studio here in Mumbai. One song can be a slow, sad number. I have signed Villain X to play the main villain in the movie and I would like a few good fight sequences in the script too. Comedian K will play the hero's sidekick so make sure there are lots of funny moments too. Oh, and yes, kissing scenes are very popular these days – try to see how you can add a few without making it difficult for me to get the movie through the censor board. Be clever about it, so that we can say it is artistic or something. Now, make a script for all of the above. I want a complete family entertainer masala film that should be ready for release around the Diwali and Eid holidays. We begin shooting next Monday ... we are taking the Sunday night flight to Malaysia to picturise the first song ... fax me the script by Friday night. Thanks.'"

Bhola took two more large gulps of his protein shake. Riz continued, looking at Amrit, who had a disbelieving look on his face.

"Producers are not stupid. There is good reason why they don't take newcomers in their movies. Unless, of course, you are the producer yourself and are putting your own money on the line, like say, my family will do for my launch film. For the rest of the thousands and thousands of strugglers doing the rounds of producers' offices in the hope that they will land a lead role – I have some news for you, *don't waste your time.* Simply put, a new face does not sell. And Bollywood is a business, like any other business."

Riz took another sip and then continued.

"Launching a movie star in Bollywood today is serious business. It is like launching a brand. The brand launch has to be supported by big money. It may take several attempts to get it right – so I'm talking of seriously big money here – even more than launching a FMCG brand, like say a toothpaste. No wonder then that you see only certain type of actors making it. Ever wondered why is it that star children, industrialists' kids, politicians' kids and NRI-businessmen's kids are the ones you see in movies these days? It's because they are the ones who have the funds to back films starring their children."

"It can't be like that!" Amrit protested. He was not happy about the dire picture Riz was painting before him.

"It is *that*, my friend. You don't know how the system works. You're not even aware. *Chale aatae hai muh uthake hero bannae.* This is Bollywood. It appears all clean and nice from the outside, but it is a viper's pit on the inside. Things are done in such a closed and clubby manner that very little in known about what goes on in those wheelings and dealings. Complex payback schemes are arranged, almost always involving unaccounted for black money and favours of the kind you can't even imagine." Riz had a naughty look in his eyes.

Amrit still seemed unconvinced as he shook his head.

"I'll give you an example." Riz now tried to provide concrete evidence.

"Did you know that my father, Sandy Khan, campaigned for Bandhoo Kumar's Loktantra Party in the last elections?"

"Yes, we saw him on TV. Your dad was at all the Loktantra Party rallies. He was a huge crowd puller," Bhola recalled.

"Well, what you *don't* know is that my dad, in return for campaigning for Bandhoo Kumar's party in the last elections, secured a ten-movie deal for me, from Govardhan Motion Pictures, on whose board Bandhoo Kumar sits." Riz was grinning from ear to ear.

"What?" There was a gasp from Amrit.

"Unbelievable!" Bhola said, making a gurgling sound with his straw.

"My dear friends, this is business. Bandhoo Kumar's party got what it wanted. They won the elections. And dad got for me what we wanted – a ten movie deal. It's quid pro quo. Here's another story for you." Riz took another sip.

Bhola and Amrit were all ears.

"Do you know the famous actress of yesteryears, Seema Kumari?"

"Yes."

"Well, did you see her in Dharmesh Sharma's last blockbuster?"

"Yes. She played the hero's mother's role." Amrit had seen the movie recently on DVD.

"Indeed she did." Riz said with an arrogant tilt of the head. "What you *don't* know, is that she didn't charge Dharmesh Sharma a single penny for that role. Instead, she got a promise from him."

"What promise?" Bhola looked on suspiciously.

"Seema Kumari's daughter, Gauri, is turning nineteen next year, and Seema wants Dharmesh Sharma to launch her in his movie. Simple. Mother works for free in Dharmesh Sharma's movie, and Dharmesh Sharma casts daughter in his next blockbuster! Quid pro quo." Riz took a long sip, finished his drink and pushed the glass to the centre of the table.

"Now, how can you match that, tell me? Could you snatch a role from me or from Gauri, even if you are the best actor or best bodybuilder in the whole universe? No chance. All you strugglers in Mumbai don't get it. The doors to Bollywood are shut. It's a closed circuit. You are wasting your time." Riz now stood up, and stretched out his arms, which seemed to have stiffened after the weight training, and then settled back on his chair.

"Amrit, most of these people you see, these *strugglers*, they all think they have something special in them, something that would soon be 'discovered' by some producer or director or whoever it is who 'discovers' new talent and will be given that dream role and shot at making it big. To some extent, this is a myth that is convenient for one and all to believe in and propagate. The establishment – the acting academy people, Anil Taneja especially, the production houses, the entire auxiliary industry that feeds off people coming to Mumbai to 'try-out' to become actors – all of them propagate this myth because it is good business for them to do so. Trainloads of young boys and girls arrive in Bollywood every week to become stars relying solely on this myth. Those who come also believe in this myth because it gives them hope. Hope – it is often *all* they have – hope. Propelled on hope, they just keep coming … and trying and trying and trying ... until most of them finally realise what it is – a myth. Bollywood is closed for outsiders. There is no 'discovery process.' Ninety-nine point nine per cent of those who get breaks are in my category – star-sons or star-nephews or star-somethings. Talent and ability are secondary. Or tertiary. Actually immaterial."

"That is not true Riz. I just landed a role in a television serial. And I didn't know anybody there. I just went and auditioned. Purely on merit." Amrit countered.

"Television is an exception *yaar*. It's somewhat of a meritocracy, I agree with you." Riz admitted. "But do you want to know why? I will tell…" Riz stopped mid-sentence as he felt a tender hand on his shoulder.

Udita Usgaonkar was a sight to watch as she stood there, body tilted suggestively, with one hand resting on Riz's shoulder. Not that she was exceptionally pretty. It is what she wore. Or rather what she didn't wear. A knitted white blouse dipped below her neck deep enough to reveal a well-formed cleavage. Below the blouse she was wearing a black bra – the kind that props up the breasts and presents them pushed-up like two buns jutting out of a bread basket. The black outline of the bra was visible between the knits of the blouse – and so was her wheatish-brown moisturised smooth skin. Her hair was medium length and jet black, worn open. The ends of her hair were tied to small threads that had little round bright red beads attached to them, so that her hair looked like a kind of black curtain held down by tiny cherries. Her face was round – very round. Udita had large saucer-like eyes – brown, and very enchanting. She had done up her eyebrows so they looked more pronounced and added to the impact of her impressive eyes. She had a small, stub nose, which added to the overall round feel of her face, and voluptuous lips thickly smeared with cherry-brown lipstick. Around her waist Udita wore a large, stylish belt embellished with semi-precious stones; one end of the belt dangled from the buckle in a fashionably casual way. Below the belt was a pleated white skirt, not much wider that the belt above that. Udita had smooth, wheatish-brown tan legs that were visible from her upper thighs down to her ankles. Those were nice legs. She had waxed them well and they had a shine to them.

"Hi Riz! How are you?" Udita said excitedly to her classmate from the Anil Taneja Acting Academy.

All male eyes in the room were on Udita Usgaonkar. She was not what you would call a classic beauty. She would never make it to the top hundred prettiest women of India list. Maybe not even the top one thousand list. She was sexy as hell though. She gave out "fuck-me" vibes that reached the crotch of every man around; but she was not the kind of girl a boy would want to take home to mamma. She was a toy to be played with, and she had invitation written all over her.

"Oye *chammak challo*, we also exist in this world. *Hi hi!* Say hi to us also! We were also your classmates. *Bhool gaye?*" Bhola let out a low whistle. Udita did not like it. She did not want to fraternise with the Bihari. Seeing her cold reaction, Bhola winked at her.

When a man comes across a woman like Udita, there is only one thought running through his head. Two great boobs glaring at you, almost ready to meet your face if you craned your neck ever so slightly; mesmerising round eyes, a glimpse of a bellybutton, a loin-cloth of a skirt and then miles and miles of deliciously smooth gleaming brown legs. With such a display, it was just impossible not to be thinking sex when you saw Udita. You might not be turned-on by *her* per se, and a lot of men were not – they found her too crass and in-your-face and even outright disgusting – but Udita had the ability to at least compel you to think in the general direction of sex – even if it is not her that you would want to ever have sex with.

Udita ignored Bhola's advances, as if they hadn't happened. Udita could stand calmly in the company of men, apparently oblivious as they often swarmed around her and ogled her. Male attention, even of the nasty kind, didn't seem to bother her. She had an almost Buddhist detachment to the whole thing, as if she couldn't perceive all the attention she was drawing. She would respond to small talk initiated by men who buzzed around her like flies, seemingly oblivious about the fact that all those men were totally uninterested in her talk and wholly interested in just her assets. They just wanted to fuck her. Right there and then. Yet they would converse about all sorts of unrelated things.

Bhola winked again. Udita smiled. It was an act. Udita was no fool. She had deliberately turned herself into a walking-talking female sex-billboard and made quite an effort at that. Waxing those legs to perfection took time. Doing up the hair and dressing up like a tart was effort consuming. Yet – there she stood, half-naked in a culture and society where men are hardly exposed to live woman-flesh in a non-controversial setting – behaving as if it was totally normal. Of course it is *not* normal. Not in India. Not even today. And she knew that. She had perfected the art of putting herself on display without making a big deal about it or being affected by the attention it drew. She had done it often enough. It was like water on a duck's back now. Men thought she was dumb. Or loose. That she didn't cover up or turn away when they continued to stare directly at her and giggle incessantly in her company encouraged them even more. Morally correct Indian girls are expected to be demure virgins guarding their modesty and bodies from the view of strange men, even when fully clothed from head to toe. Any girl departing from this norm was a slut. Udita was labelled "friendly." "She likes men." Attention was even more forthcoming.

Udita wanted just that. She was the one who was actually playing them. Attracting attention via skinshow was her chosen strategy of making it in Bollywood. She knew she wasn't beautiful enough to draw attention standing fully clothed in traditional, conservative Indian attire. She had to put herself on display if she was to have any chance of being noticed and progressing in Bollywood. She certainly succeeded in getting noticed. How far she could go beyond that – well – that was another matter. She had thought it all through, and even had a backup plan. In case Bollywood didn't work out for her and she couldn't make it as a heroine, she would ensnare a big fat Mumbai businessman as a husband. Bollywood heroines have a tradition of picking up rich businessmen and NRI husbands in the twilight of their careers. What better trophy wife can a successful Indian man have than a Bollywood diva? Udita would probably not be in the running to bag the real big fat cats – that she knew – but she could certainly pick up a small to medium level player who himself wouldn't have the reach to pull a true A-list Bollywood heroine. Right now, however, she was not thinking of her backup plan; her target was Riz Khan. There could be no better catch for her than Riz. Besides, he was well connected in the industry.

Riz made a gesture of acknowledgement towards Udita as she settled down on the chair besides him.

"Don't let Bihari bother you sweetheart. Come, let me tell you also what I was telling these fellows. Let me give you also some *gyaan*." Riz placed his hand around Udita's shoulder. She smiled. Progress.

"The only place you strugglers have a chance is in television – because television is the only part of Bollywood that is closest to what you may call being corporatised. Most Bollywood TV channels are corporate entities, or owned and governed by corporate entities. Corporatisation imposes disciplines and controls that cut through the largesse and bullshit otherwise possible in lesser-controlled environments. Bean counters at TV companies want every single rupee to be squeezed to maximum effect. If a TV show costs Rs. 5 lakh to produce, the bean counters, the corporate accountants, would want to push that figure down. They want to cut costs anywhere and everywhere possible and increase efficiency as much as possible. Since TV production houses are downstream from TV channels and TV companies, they too have to comply with the corporate ethos and get super efficient. They too need to squeeze maximum mileage out of every resource. As a result, and this is what you, as an actor, need to be thankful about: TV producers, in their mad rush to lower costs, are always looking for good talent as cheap as possible. Aspiring actors, and directors, editors, scriptwriters ... everybody across the spectrum – anybody and everybody who is willing to work for less than the previous guy, is welcomed. So the only entry point that talented aspirants in Bollywood have is television. If you are good and willing to work for peanuts, you are welcome in television."

"Wow!" Udita said with a look of amazement on her face as she heaved her breasts forward, offering her cleavage to Riz, "You speak such *satasat* English. Wow!"

"But remember," Riz glanced at Udita's tits and then continued, "The moment a TV actor becomes even slightly established and starts demanding a fair remuneration for his or her services, he or she is shunted out." Riz made a cut sign with his hand. "He or she is immediately replaced by the best from the next crop of aspirants."

Udita was yawning.

"You bored darling? I'm sorry." Riz apologised.

"Udita, nice workout clothes! What body part are you working out today? Chest?" Bhola teased, sticking his tongue out to point to Udita's breasts.

"I am not here to work out. Riz is taking me to meet a producer. I am dressed for the producer's meeting." Udita said proudly, looking at Riz with great expectation.

"That's right baby! Let's go." Riz continued, "Okay guys, I've gotta go. I'm off to Switzerland tomorrow; to begin shooting for my launch film. I will let you know when the premier of the film is. You guys must come. Bihari you especially. Come Udita." Riz walked off with Udita in tow, leaving Amrit and Bhola alone, still trying to digest the meaning of Riz's words.

"*Chutiya* is just trying to scare us, that's all." Bhola declared, opening a pouch and emptying it in his remaining protein shake. "Don't believe all that he says."

"Yes, but he's really connected in the industry. He knows what he is talking about. What's that?" Amrit asked, pointing to the pouch in Bhola's hand.

"Nothing. Just vitamins. I like to supplement my protein shake with vitamins." Bhola stirred the powder into the thick concoction of low fat milk, designer whey-protein powder, egg whites and a banana, all blended together.

"How long have you been taking supplements *yaar*?" Amrit frowned.

"For many years now. First I just used to eat six egg whites for breakfast and small, high protein meals every three hours. But then I discovered that supplements are really what juice up the body. And look, what they do!" Bhola spread out his arms in an eagle-spread pose, his muscles bulging ferociously.

"But aren't you worried about any side effects?"

"Not to worry. Nothing will happen. Except, of course, your muscles will grow like mad!" Bhola flexed his arms once again, and then glanced at his wrist watch.

"Oh god, I'm late; I have to go. Client meeting. Will see you later. And thanks for the *mithai*." With this, Bhola downed the contents of his glass and got up and left in a hurry.

As Amrit was about to get up to leave too, he heard Samson call out.

"Amrit! Here! Could I have a word with you?" gesturing with his fingers for Amrit to come to his room.

Amrit followed Samson into his room, which looked more like a corporate CEOs office than the quarters of a gym trainer. Amrit settled down in one of the fully upholstered leather chairs across from Samson, placing his hands over the glass table that separated them.

"You have a good body my friend, and you lift decently. I saw you lift." Samson pointed to the bank of CCTV monitors that lay behind his desk. Cameras caught every single square inch of the gym and Samson could watch all the action seated right here in his office.

"Very high tech!" Amrit was impressed.

"You know, rarely do I see someone who *looks* like he deserves to be a Bollywood star. *You* do!" said Samson, flashing those white teeth at Amrit. "You have the looks, the height and the body."

"Thanks," Amrit said.

"But I think you should really go for the kill." Samson frowned his temples, looking like a philosopher about to deliver an important message.

"You should set the standards as far as bodies are concerned. Don't get me wrong. You have a terrific body as it is. You could be a star just with what you have. But I want you to be fantastic-mindblowing-outofthisworld!" Samson's eyes were popping out as he gestured with his hands. "Superlative body!"

"Thanks. What do you think I should do?" Amrit bent forward, looking forward to some gymming tips from the pro.

"Steroids. You have to take anabolic steroids. They will give you an outofthisworld body. Superlative!" Samson repeated the gestures.

"Steroids ... but ... but aren't they dangerous? I've heard they really damage the body internally and screw up the hormonal balance?" Amrit responded. He had been offered steroids at his gym in Amritsar, and after doing research about them on the Internet, had decided against using them. Liver damage, kidney damage, heart problems, internal haemorrhaging, hormonal imbalance – the list of potential disastrous side effects of steroid use seemed long and deadly.

"Oh not really. Only in some cases." Samson said with scorn, using his hand to make a dismissive gesture. "Everybody is doing it. Look at Sallu's body. Mindblowing. Do you think you can get that without steroids? Ha! No chance. Even your friend there ... what's his name ... Bhola ... he uses them. No big deal. Here, I have some." With that Samson picked out a sachet from his desk drawer similar to the one Bhola had emptied into his protein shake. "This is deca durabolin. Affectionately called deca by bodybuilders. You take this baby, and you will make Sallu look like a scraggy dog."

"Thanks, but no thanks." Amrit said this as politely as possible, trying hard not to offend Samson. Samson's expression changed, the white smile vanished.

"Look, there are more chances of you being hit by traffic on the streets of Mumbai than this causing damage to your body." Samson pressed on.

"I appreciate it, Samson. But I rather not. Thanks." Amrit stood up to leave.

"Your choice." Samson flashed those pearl whites again, as he replaced the pouch back in the drawer. "See you tomorrow."

CHAPTER 4

On the first day of his shoot for *Saas Ka Sindoor*, Amrit's nerves were a little frayed. No matter how much training an actor has had or how much preparation he has done, the first day is the first day, and there is no escaping that.

The man who took a bit of the nerves out of Amrit was an unlikely character. Not more than four and a half feet tall, Chotte Laal was in his sixties, had short cropped white hair, his teeth were all gone except for two incisors that dangled miraculously like two tiny tusks on his upper gum-line, with enough gap between them to poke three fingers through. They were golden yellow, not from years, but decades of paan chewing. How Chotte Laal ate his food, without the assistance of any workable teeth, seemed like a miracle.

Chotte Laal was a real old timer. Born in Itawa, Uttar Pradesh, he had run away to Mumbai in his early teens. He had joined a circus group, and then graduated to a film studio, specialising as a dressman. He had been a dressman for over forty years, putting clothes on actors before shots, and then taking them off and putting them back into large iron travelling chests for later use.

"*Baba*, what scene do you have?" Chotte Laal asked Amrit.

"Emh ... I'm playing Sonal's boyfriend." Amrit replied, slightly nervous. Amrit was an outsider to the world of Bollywood. He had never been on a set before.

"College student. Okay." Chotte Laal announced. "Jeans and t-shirt." With that he disappeared, returning a minute later with blue jeans and a t-shirt in his hand.

"Wear this." He handed them over to Amrit. Amrit complied.

"Wow! Exact size. How did you know my size?" Amrit exclaimed. The jeans and t-shirt fit perfectly.

"Oh *baba*, my whole life has been spent doing this only." Chotte Laal smiled, the two tuskers dangling.

Amrit instantly liked Chotte Laal. He was a cute old man.

"You know *baba*, I have been around so long, I think even my ghost will come back and work here as a dressman. Fashions come and go, heroes come and go, I am always here." He chuckled.

"Really, which heroes have you seen come and go?" Amrit asked.

"Oh *baba*, so many. Raj Kapoor, Rajender Kumar, Dilip Kumar, Rajesh Khanna, Dharmendra, Amitabh..."

"Who was the greatest of them all?" Amrit asked.

"All were great *baba* ...but my favourite is Rajesh Khanna ... the greatest!" Chotte Laal's eyes had a distant look.

"Really? What was he like? I mean Rajesh Khanna?" Amrit enquired.

"Just like you." Chotte Laal was looking straight at Amrit, smiling.

Amrit smiled back, and then blushed. He looked away, but his confidence was swelling. Chotte Laal had managed to get rid of all the butterflies in his stomach, with that one single comment comparing him to Rajesh Khanna. Amrit was now ready to face the camera.

"I will tell you more about him later. I have to get the other actors ready." Chotte Laal winked at Amrit and left.

Chotte Laal was part of that army of behind-the-scenes folks who toil day and night to make Bollywood work – for years, for decades – without acknowledgement. Lightmen, cameramen, assistants, dressmen, spot boys, make-up artists, junior artists … so many of them. They have all come to Mumbai from somewhere. They all earned a pittance. Many lived in abject squalor and in the poverty of slums. They are the invisible workforce of Bollywood. The hidden army of workers that props up the world's largest film and television production industry.

Amrit and Chotte Laal instantly developed a bond. Both became fond of each other – it was in the eyes of Chotte Laal – the way he looked up to Amrit – with awe, respect and expectation – and the way Amrit reciprocated, with warmth in his eyes, and a genuine interest in his past, an acknowledgement of his contribution, now and in the past – and that's all Chotte Laal needed. Chotte Laal to Amrit was a legacy – the living history of Bollywood – an elder, deserving of respect.

One of the Assistant Directors, or ADs, as they are usually called in Bollywood lingo, arrived in the makeup room where Amrit was getting his makeup done.

"You're playing Sonal's boyfriend? Here. Go through it. Shot in one hour." The AD dropped a script in Amrit's lap and left. After reading the script, Amrit was relieved to see that his scene for today was not a crying one. It was a romantic scene! Romance was Amrit's forté. Now, if only he didn't let his nerves get the better of him. *Just keep your head down and do the job at hand* – Amrit kept psyching himself. All his training was going to be put to test now. *Now! It was showtime!* What he did today would be broadcast to the living rooms of hundreds of millions of people on primetime. *Phew!* Amrit felt the butterflies coming back. He shut his eyes, concentrating on his breathing. He had to slow his mind down, stop thinking about everything else except the scene at hand. *How should I tackle this scene? What did Guruji say? Magic If? That's right. Magic If!* Amrit's mind jogged back to the Magic If lesson at the Academy.

"Today, I want to talk about emotions." Guruji announced to the class. "Ordinary people add words to emotions; actors add emotions to words."

Shiv Shankar Pandey could not contain his excitement, and shot up an arm, "Sir! I can say emotional dialogues very well. Especially those dialogues when Amitabh Bachchan is dying in the arms of his mother in the movie *Deewar* after his brother has shot him…"

"Be quiet Shiv Shankar and listen to what I am saying." Guruji cut him off or Shiv would certainly have leapt into the dialogues from *Deewar*.

"When people in ordinary life feel something, they express it in words. The feelings, the emotions come first, then come the words. As actors, we are expected to do the reverse. We are given words – in the form of dialogues or a script. We are expected to deliver them with the right feelings or emotions. How will we do it successfully and convincingly?"

Guruji paused, his eyes scanning the class.

"Luckily, for actors, there is a key to do it! Stanislavsky and the Method School of acting call it the 'magic if'. What it really means is that if you can put yourself in the position of the character, in his or her shoes, and feel the way the character ought to be feeling, then your emotions will automatically come out right."

Shiv Shankar Pandey looked thoroughly confused. All this went totally over his head. He longed for the fight classes to begin so that he could show some Amitabh Bachchan fight moves.

"Feel the way the character should be feeling, and the right emotions will automatically be triggered from within. Let's talk about life first; then we'll come to acting. In life, does anybody ever tell you to produce a certain emotion?"

Guruji paused. There were a lot of blank looks around the class.

"Shiv."

"Yes sir." Shiv replied back nervously. He wondered if he had done anything wrong. Usually, whenever Shiv had been called on by the teacher in a classroom setting, it had meant bad news for him.

"In real life, do you produce emotions deliberately or automatically?"

"Ummm ... deliberately ... no ... automatically ... no no no deliberately," stumbled Shiv. There was spontaneous laughter in the classroom.

"Exactly. Everybody just laughed." Guruji said out loudly with an animated expression on his face. "Did I tell anyone to laugh? No! Yet you all laughed, automatically. In real life, nobody tells you to laugh; yet you do laugh. If I were to fart right now, you all would laugh, no?"

Guruji shifted his weight and actually let out a loud fart.

There was collective smirking.

"See! It happens automatically."

He let out another fart. More laughter came from the students.

Guruji waited for the laughter to die down, and then he continued.

"In real life, nobody tells you to cry. Yet, we cry. When feelings become overbearing, we burst into tears."

"Our reactions in real life are triggered by the way we feel. Now, as actors, we must be able to produce the right reactions in reel life by feeling the right way. Let's work with an example here. Suppose I went home today to find my girlfriend in bed with another man. How would I feel?" Guruji looked at Amrit, eliciting an answer.

"Very angry!" Amrit answered.

"Exactly! I might say something like: *'You bitch! You fuckin' bitch! You've been cheating on me! I don't want to ever see your face again; get out of my house you whore!'* Notice that the emotions came first here and then the words. I got angry, and then that anger worked itself into the words automatically in the right way. The words will automatically carry the appropriate emotions to the listener."

Guruji paused again, waiting for the point to sink in.

"Now suppose I am a movie director and you are the hero of my film and the scene is that the hero is a soldier who comes back home after the war to find his wife in bed with a strange man. On seeing the wife in bed, naked with another man, you, the hero of the movie, are to say in anger and disgust the following lines:

'You bitch! You fuckin' bitch! You've been cheating on me! I don't want to ever see your face again; get out of my house you whore!'

As an actor, how would you say these lines? Notice here that the words are being given to you, in the form of a script, and as an actor, you have to add emotions to them. As I said before, in life, we add words to emotions; as actors, we add emotions to words."

Shiv shot up his hand. Guruji nodded. "Sir, I know how I would say these dialogues."

"Like Amitabh Bachchan!" snickered Riz.

"Quiet. Let him speak," was Guruji's sharp retort.

"Sir, I would make my face like this," said Shiv contorting his face by pushing his eyeballs out from their sockets, exposing his clenched teeth, and breathing heavily through his flared nostril, "and say very loudly, looking angry, yeah! Like Ravana in *Ramleela*." Shiv then went on to say the lines, heaving and panting and contorting his face in several different ways to exhibit anger.

"Ladies and gentlemen, what Mr. Pandey just demonstrated is called hamming or fake acting. Ninety per cent of the actors in Bollywood use this technique. They don't feel; they just pretend to feel. If the lines are to be said with anger, they will screw up their faces, like Shiv just did, raise their voices, gesticulate wildly, and deliver the lines – there you have it, Mr. Director, anger for you! Bollywood directors will be mostly quite happy with this type of an output from an actor. In fact, many Bollywood directors will often guide actors as they perform – more anger, more anger sir, turn up the volume, make the face more angry, grind your teeth, yes, yes ... that's right, anger – good! This, I'm afraid, is not acting. This is hamming.

Here the actor is pretending to be angry. He is not really, deeply, truly angry, as he should be. He just adorns a mask of anger – enough to fool the audience and get the job done – but the emotion of anger never really touches him while he is speaking those lines."

Shiv looked depressed. He had played the role of Ravana in a local enactment of the *Ramayana* many times in Benaras and used this technique of facial contortion much to the applause of the audience.

"Shiv, don't be depressed. The good news is that you could make your way through Bollywood by hamming and make a decent living. No problem. Nobody here cares, or even knows the difference. If you are decent looking, have connections, get the right break, and have a decent memory to cram the lines and can ham convincingly, you will get by just fine. The bad news is that this is not acting. If you really want to be an actor and attain mastery in this art form, please don't ham. Actually feel the anger and not just pretend to be angry – get angry! Imagine what it would be like if the person you truly, deeply loved, if you were to return home and find that person in bed with someone else. How would you feel? Hurt? Angry? Disappointed? Furious? Feel like killing them? Feel like throwing a chair through the window? Feel like crying? Just try to imagine the scenario. This is the 'magic if.' *What if* this was to happen to me? Not to my friend, not to my neighbour, but to *me*. How would *your* hurt and anger be channelled? How would *your* pride react? There is a rich mix of emotions that would be stirred within *you*. A true actor will rake up those appropriate emotions within himself at the precise moments when the character he is portraying should be feeling those emotions."

Guruji moved closer to Shiv and looked straight at him.

"Believe me Shiv, if you can put yourself in the shoes of the man who comes home to find his wife in bed with a stranger, then the lines you utter under that imaginary spell will come out just right. You won't need to contort your face or make gestures like Ravana. If deep down you feel like the character should feel, lo and behold, your face will show it, your entire body language will show it. You don't need to put on a mask or gesticulate wildly. If there is anger brewing within you, your voice will automatically be the right tone, volume, timbre, everything – you don't need to artificially raise your voice. If your emotional state mirrors that of the character in the script, your entire performance will come out right. Magically!"

"Guruji, what if I've never been in a similar situation before? What would I do then?" asked Meghna, trying hard to think how she would perform such a scene if she found Raman in bed with another woman. She just couldn't imagine her husband ever cheating on her. It just didn't seem like a possibility.

"Good question. You will never have been in every possible situation imaginable. It is impossible. As an actor, however, you may be called upon to play out any possible scenario. How do you cope? The answer is, try to approximate as close a situation as possible. Let me give you an example. Suppose you have to play the role of a cannibal murderer. How would you do so? You've never murdered anyone, I hope; and neither have you eaten another human being, I hope so too. So how do you play the role of a cannibal murderer?"

There was silence. Meghna was thinking hard.

"So Meghna, in a Bollywood remake of *The Silence of the Lambs*, I cast you in the role of Hannibal Lecter, the cannibal murderer. How will you play it? Should you ham?" teased Guruji.

"Definitely not ham." Meghna was quick to reply. It was below her dignity to even consider hamming.

"So Meghna, how will you feel like a murderer?" Guruji bent forward menacingly at Meghna, "and like a cannibal?" Guruji made a slurping sound with his mouth. "How?"

Meghna was perplexed. She shrugged her shoulders.

"Meghna, have you ever killed a fly, or a mosquito or a cockroach?" inquired Guruji.

"Yes."

"How did you feel when you killed the bug? Can you think back to that experience, and then amplify it a bit? Think how powerful and ruthless you felt as you squashed the poor little insect, smashing its body into a lump of dead mass. Feel it! As actors, we have to draw upon whatever life experiences we have. Try to find something that is close enough, and use that experience. An actor's baggage of life experiences is his portfolio; he will need to constantly dip into it and find material of relevance. Therefore, as actors, we must always be seeking out newer experiences and broadening our horizons."

Meghna nodded. There was a reason Guruji had such a formidable reputation in Bollywood. He was a real guru when it came to acting.

"Now, let's get to the cannibal part. What's your favourite dish?" Guruji continued questioning Meghna.

"Rice and prawn curry." Meghna replied, knowing where this was going.

"Yummy! Now suppose you have not eaten for two days, and then I place a dish of freshly cooked rice and prawn curry, just the way you like it, in front of you. You can smell the succulent, fragrant prawns sitting over the rice, the vapours of this delicious preparation filling your nostrils. You are starving. And now, I let you eat this lovely preparation. How would you pounce upon the plate?"

"Like a cannibal!" Meghna replied, excitedly.

"There you have it! There is, after all, a cannibal inside Dr. Meghna! Who would have known?" Guruji smiled.

The class looked thrilled. As if it had discovered something, made an invention. Guruji noticed a spark in the eyes of many. This is what he lived for. This is the reason he taught acting. The joy of passing on trade secrets to worthy recipients.

"Next time we'll put what we've talked about today into practice. Class over."

Amrit opened his eyes and looked down at the script in his hand. He tried to visualise the scene using the Magic If technique.

Amrit is in college and walking down the corridor. Sonal, whom he has never seen before, also a student in the college, walks in his direction. Amrit keeps walking, looking elsewhere. Sonal, carrying a pile of papers in her hand is looking down and doesn't notice Amrit at first as she passes him. Just when Sonal is about to pass Amrit, two students come running into the corridor from one of the classrooms, and accidentally collide with Sonal, throwing her off balance as she tries desperately to regain her balance and prevent the pile of papers in her hand from falling. At just the right moment, Amrit instinctively grabs hold of Sonal, who was about to fall, and stabilises her, holding her in his arms. There, for the first time, their eyes meet and they instantly fall in love. They keep looking into each other's eyes, not realising that Amrit has her balanced in his arms, in a Clark Gable-Vivien Leigh *Gone With The Wind* type of pose. This romantic pose lasts for what seems like eternity – the two completely smitten. The spell is finally broken when the college bell rings. Amrit, reluctantly, lets go of her and Sonal, embarrassed and blushing, composes herself and turns to walk away. Before Amrit can go far, he feels a tap on his shoulder. He turns around; it is Sonal.

"Excuse me, I think you have something of mine." Sonal says, pointing to the pile of papers in Amrit's hand.

"Oh! I'm sorry! I just…" Amrit hands the papers back, mumbling apologetically.

"It's okay. I think I have all my stuff back now. Thanks." Sonal smiles, still slightly embarrassed.

"Do you?" Amrit says, a bold and telling look in his eyes, as he rolls his right hand over his heart, smiling his handsome smile, those deadly lady-killer dimples on display.

Sonal looks down, embarrassed, then back at Amrit, smiles, turns around and walks away. Amrit stays there, watching her, as she is about to round the corner. Just then, Sonal looks over her shoulder. Amrit is still there, watching her. She smiles at him. Amrit smiles back. Sonal disappears behind the corner.

"I think you left your heart here too, Miss, right here." Amrit says to himself, cupping his hand around his heart and then blowing a kiss into it, and walks off with a spring in his steps, smiling.

Amrit opened his eyes. *Now!* He had to make the scene this way. *Think of Sapna!* Amrit told himself. *When you look into Sonal's eyes, imagine Sapna's eyes.* This is where the rubber meets the road, Amrit knew. The actor within him was up for the challenge. Actors live for stuff like this. Besides, this was a romantic scene. He should be able to crack it!

"Hi! I'm Amrit." Amrit introduced himself to Sabina Khan, who was playing Sonal. Sabina wasn't an especially attractive girl, but had been a veteran of many Jai Jai TV serials, and was a known face on Indian television. She had also played bit roles in some movies. *She is so unattractive.* Amrit couldn't help but notice. He knew he would have to dig deep and stay concentrated to get this scene right. *It's not Sonal, it's Sapna! Amrit, it is Sapna.* As if almost magically, Amrit superimposed Sapna's face on that of his co-actor. His smile widened, a glint automatically appeared in his eyes. *The power of imagination!* Stanislavsky's Magic If was working!

Cut!

The scene worked out great. "Good scene! Good job Amrit." The director cried. Amrit was relieved that his first scene as a professional TV actor had gone fine.

Amrit nodded to the director, who was standing next to the camera. Also standing next to the camera, Amrit noticed, was Chotte Laal, looking on intently. As Amrit walked off the set, Chotte Laal smiled and winked at him.

"*Baagho mein bahaar hai, kaliyon pe nikhaar hai...*" Chotte Laal hummed to Amrit. Amrit beamed back. Chotte

Laal had just recited a line from one of the most memorable romantic songs ever picturised on Rajesh Khanna in a Bollywood movie. True or not, comparison with the greatest romantic hero in the history of Bollywood by a dressman who had served with the legend himself was the greatest confidence boost Amrit could get. Amrit knew he was good. But actors need appreciation. They are always insecure. Right now, Amrit was far, far away from that feeling. Amrit put a hand on Chotte Laal's back as they walked into the studio makeup room.

"*Baba,* let me tell you something about Rajesh Khanna." Chotte Laal took the jeans and t-shirt from Amrit.

Amrit was all ears, as he wiped the last of the makeup from his face using a cotton-wool swab.

"All these guys who go around wearing the 'superstar' badge these days in Bollywood after a movie or two of theirs becomes a hit – none of them knows what a superstar is. The one and only superstar Bollywood has ever had was Rajesh Khanna. My god, what he was! The highs that have been touched by him, nobody else has even come close." Chotte Laal was animated.

"Really!" Amrit was genuinely interested.

"Really! What a man he was! Even at his peak, so humble, so kind hearted. You know, I have sat and had Black Label whiskey with Rajesh Khanna. After shooting, he would make all the unit members sit with him and drink. He never had any airs. He was so warm." Chotte Laal was getting emotional, then chuckled.

"You know, once our unit had gone to Switzerland for a shoot. The customs inspector at the airport stopped us. We were carrying lots of spinach in our baggage. The customs inspector wanted to know what the spinach was for? He wouldn't let us take it. It was against their rules in Switzerland. We had to explain to him that the hero of our movie, Rajesh Khanna, loved spinach. This was for him. He would still not budge. Then we got in touch with the Swiss tourism department, and they had to intervene. They ordered the customs inspector to let it go. They knew who Rajesh Khanna was. They had been begging him to come shoot in Switzerland. You should have seen the face of the customs inspector." Chotte Laal laughed a two-toothed laugh, his whole body shaking, as he reminisced.

"*Baba,* do you know what a superstar means?" Chotte Laal had a look of challenge on his face, as he dared Amrit to answer. Amrit shrugged his shoulders.

"You know, young girls, no more than sixteen or seventeen, used to inscribe 'Rajesh I love you' with knives on their arms, here." Chotte Laal pulled back his shirt sleeve and showed Amrit his forearm. "Here. They used to send him love letters written in their blood. Not just one. Hundreds. I have seen with my own eyes. They would run away from their homes, good homes, to come to Mumbai, just for a glimpse of Rajesh Khanna. They would wait outside his house, follow him to the sets, screaming, 'Rajesh, marry me! Rajesh, marry me!'" Chotte Laal paused, and tapped Amrit on the shoulder, "That, *baba,* is superstar."

Udita Usgaonkar had bedbugs to thank for her meteoric rise to fame. A music company had just recorded an album of raunchy dance numbers, a genre of music that has become extremely popular in nightclubs and bars throughout India, and they were keen to produce an equally raunchy music video to go with the title song of the album. Riding on a wave of sexual renaissance that was sweeping through modern Indian youth culture, the focus was on fusing songs that had Indian lyrics, often suggestive raunchy ones, with modern western beats added by a growing breed of remix DJs. These remixed and fused numbers were hugely popular and sold like hot cakes, ringing in large profits for music companies that churned them out in rapid succession. BMC Records had just produced a remixed album titled *Save Me From the Bedbug* and the title track was a duet by the same name. The song went something like this:

Woman:

Ohhh I am in so much trouble and alone in the house,
The most terrible thing that could happen it just might!
A nasty bedbug has just crawled into my blouse,
And I fear any moment now the rascal will bite!

Ohhh such a tight situation and do what a poor girl can?
Ohhh such a tight situation and do what a poor girl can?

Man:

Don't worry my beloved I am there,
I am a virile man and I will be your keeper,
I will extract the bugger go he might anywhere,
Whether in your blouse or even bloody deeper!

Ohhh don't worry now you have a man!
Ohhh don't worry now you have a man!

Woman:

Ohhh such a tight situation and do what a poor girl can?
All of but sixteen and so dear to all kith and kin,
Let my virginal chastity be feasted on by a strange man,
Or to let the damn bedbug do the damage to my skin!

Ohhh such a tight situation and do what a poor girl can?
Ohhh such a tight situation and do what a poor girl can?

For the music video, BMC Records was looking for a voluptuous girl who would be willing to expose as much skin as could be exposed in the video without getting it banned. When Udita Usgaonkar arrived at the audition wearing her trademark pump-up bra, breasts full on display, the producers at BMC knew Udita was the girl to fit the blouse. The video was shot exceedingly sexily, making Udita look like a cavernous village virgin thoroughly confused between choosing the ills of the bedbug or the lecherous man who appeared with her in the video. The video ended with the man finally getting his way and Udita and him ending up on a haystack in a buffalo shed. The highly suggestive last shot of the video was of the man trampling the bedbug under his feet, and then the blouse worn by Udita in the video causally floating through the air in slow motion like a parachute and falling over the squashed insect's bloody body, with the words "Blood Was Finally Drawn" appearing across the screen.

As soon as the video premiered on television it was a massive hit. All the music channels played it at least once every hour. The blouse worn by Udita in the video became a fashion statement, worn by young girls on college campuses from Delhi to Dalhousie. There was even a major controversy surrounding the video, with some feminist groups demonstrating outside the Parliament in New Delhi claiming the video portrayed Indian women as helpless and diminutive objects of desire and asked for it to be banned. There were counter demonstrations by other groups, claiming that the video portrayed the Indian woman as liberated and armed with choices, finally able to decide what she wanted. The demonstrations cancelled each other out and the video stayed on air for four months

– a record for material of this genre. Udita became known as India's Number One Item Number Girl – the *bedbug girl!* She was flooded with offers to do similar *item numbers;* and most of these offers she accepted.

The phone rang in Mike Patel's first floor office in the Panchratna Building in Mumbai's Opera House Area. The building was home to the offices of members of the Mumbai Diamond Merchants Association. This nondescript and inelegant building, lying across from the Western Railways line and not far from Roxy Cinema, which was playing the latest Bollywood hit, is one of the world's most busy diamond exchanges, with hundreds of millions worth of deals struck on a daily basis. The whole building was abuzz with activity and chatter in Gujarati, the *lingua franca* of the diamond trade in India.

Mike Patel was one of Bollywood's most famous producers. Though Mike's original business was diamond trading, and original name Mansukhbhai Patel, Mike, as he was now called, had always been more charmed by the glitz and glamour of Bollywood than by his family's sprawling jewellery trade. Mike's elder brother was known as the diamond king of India. He had offices in Antwerp, Belgium, Ramat Gan, Israel and in New York City's 47th Street Diamond District, and spent most of his time outside India. Patel junior, however, was more devoted to handling the family's *other* affairs. In addition to being a Bollywood movie producer, Mike was a renowned fixer and pimp. As an influence peddler, Mike Patel would supply Bollywood starlets to the beds of leading men from all walks of life – politicians, bureaucrats, foreign visitors – any and everyone who needed his services. Extremely well networked within Bollywood and the political and industrial establishments of India, Mike was known to be able to produce any girl, no matter how big a star she was. Every cunt, like every diamond, has a price – a jeweller must be able to value it – Mike would boast to friends and associates. Mike was a very useful man for all and sundry. Sex as bribe worked wonders to get a job done. Whether it was to get a government tender for a road project or a hydroelectric dam, or to help reduce the excise duty on a shipment of imported goods, a sexy Bollywood lass sent to the bed of a politician (and, of course, cash transferred to the politician's Swiss bank account), would get the job done in a jiffy. Mike also worked as a conduit for politicians wishing to invest their black money into Bollywood and thereby recycling their ill-gotten wealth. Laundry money is one of the reasons Bollywood is such a prolific producer of films. Black money is cheap money, and many are willing to risk it on risky Bollywood ventures. Mike Patel was point man for many such people wishing to pour money into his films. His last venture, a Rs. 500 million mammoth production starring the biggest Bollywood stars, had sealed Mike's spot as one of Bollywood's biggest producers.

The phone call was from Bandhoo Kumar's secretary. The veteran politician had seen Udita in the now famous *Save Me From the Bedbug* video and had been completely smitten by her. He just had to have her. A *farmaish*, a request was sent to pimp-friend Mike Patel. Mike promptly replied that the job would be done. And so, Mike got to work immediately to deliver the *bedbug girl* to Bandhoo Kumar's bed.

A lot needed to be done. Nothing that Mike had not done before, or could not do. Auditions had to be organised for a 'new' music video, with an unusually high price offered for the female lead. Naturally, word soon got around to Udita, the reigning queen for such videos, who was soon at a hired Mumbai studio waiting her turn to audition for the part. The entire thing was beautifully stage managed, making it look like a genuine audition. Scores of girls were auditioned; and rejected. Udita was told that her audition was the best, and that she was chosen for the music video. The music video was to be shot on location in London, and would require Udita to spend a few weeks filming there. The remuneration offered was five times what Udita was expecting. She was thrilled and immediately signed the contract.

CHAPTER 5

Amrit looked at his wrist watch. He would have to hurry. It was already seven. He was to head to South Mumbai to pick up Sapna at eight, and then get to the lounge bar by 8.30. It was Meghna and Raman's wedding anniversary today, and they had decided to celebrate it at a plush lounge bar on Marine Drive.

At 8.30, when Amrit and Sapna walked in, Raman, Meghna, Bhola, Riz and Shiv Shankar Pandey were already there.

"Happy Anniversary!" Amrit presented Meghna with a gift-wrapped box. "Wow … this is a mini reunion!" Amrit and Sapna exchanged greetings with their former classmates.

"You didn't have to…" Meghna exclaimed, as she took the box.

"Open it! What's in it?" Bhola asked impatiently, putting down a skewer of chicken satay.

"Opening *baba!* Have patience!" Meghna said as she opened the box to reveal a linen tablecloth.

"That's lovely! It's so sweet of you! Thanks!" Meghna and Raman said in unison.

"*Oye* sisterfucker! Tablecloth! You've become domesticated or what? The other day you brought me *mithai!*" Bhola quizzed, and then looked at Sapna with a perplexed look on his face. "What have you done to my friend? Tablecloth? What is next? Pressure cooker? Nappies?"

Bhola cringed when he saw Sapna giving him a nasty, piercing look. "*Oh bhabhi,* I was just joking. Relax *pleajze.*"

"Amrit, Sapna, have you met Raman, my husband?" Meghna introduced Raman.

"Nice to meet you! So, how many years do you complete today?"

"Well, five … but it seems like fifty," Raman said.

"Why? Already fed-up of me?" Meghna poked an elbow into her husband's rib cage.

"No darling … it would take me many, many lifetimes to get fed-up of you!" Raman beamed back.

"How sweet! This is called true love!" Riz announced, popping a pitted olive into his mouth.

"You still in India? I thought you were off to Switzerland to shoot for your launch movie?" Amrit was surprised to see Riz.

"Change of plan. We are shooting the indoor scenes first. The unit leaves for Switzerland next week." Riz clarified.

"Can't believe you are going to be a moviestar soon! I'm so excited for you. You're going to become a celebrity!" Meghna said turning to Riz.

"Don't you dump us when you become a celebrity, okay?" Bhola said, teasingly. "*Saala* will not even recognise us then."

"*Chal* Bihari …you are already dumped." Riz retorted, as he popped another olive into his mouth.

"When Meghna becomes a celebrity, she will *pukka* dump you Raman. Better watch out." Amrit said with a mischievous smile. He knew Meghna was obsessed with becoming a celebrity. It was the burning desire of her life.

"Yes, I will dump him and marry Amrit, who will also become a celebrity!" Meghna replied.

"*Kya* celebrity-celebrity *laga rakha hai!* You know, my grandmother in Bihar used to say, the girl you marry should pass the beggar and leper test." Bhola announced.

"The *what* test?" Sapna asked. Shiv Shankar Pandey straightened from his slouched position on the velvet sofa.

"The beggar and leper test." Bhola explained. "Before marrying a girl, ask yourself the question: would she marry you if you were a beggar and a leper? If the answer to that question is yes, only then marry the girl. Otherwise, don't. Those girls who come for celebrity status, they are not good. Never!"

"Amrit from Amritsar doesn't want to become a celebrity. He wants to become an artist…an art film actor … with a proper *jhola* hanging around his waist." Sapna added.

"Sapna *didi*, tell me, where can I get Amitabh Bachchan-style clothes?" Shiv asked Sapna, as he lit a cigarette.

"Why do you need Amitabh Bachchan-style clothes? And since when have you started smoking? You can't smoke here – this is the non-smoking section. *Saala burbak … kavwa chale hans ki chaal.*" Bhola hit Shiv on the back of his head.

"Sorry *bhai* I did not know! I have just taken up smoking; it is to make my voice heavy, like that of Amitabh Bachchan's." Shiv put out the cigarette. "The clothes I want because I want to get a portfolio of photographs clicked, with me in Amitabh Bachchan clothes. I will then distribute those photos to all the movie producers. I want one photograph in each of Amitabh Bachchan's various garbs – dressed like a coolie from *Coolie*, like a cowboy from *Satte Pe Satta*, like a gangster from *Don*, like a…"

"Shiv Shankar Pandey!" Riz cut him off. "Remember one thing, as long as you have a hole in your arse, you will never become Amitabh Bachchan. So stop trying."

"Try the Harish Sahota store. He makes filmi stuff. You might get Amitabh stuff there." Sapna tried to be helpful.

"Hey guys!" Meghna suddenly erupted, putting down her glass of red wine. "Guess who I saw the other day, being driven in a Hyendai Sonata Gold car? It was Harish Sahota, the most famous Bollywood designer! It was so cool. He was sitting next to the driver in the front of the car, instead of in the rear – not like a businessman or socialite auntyji type, very cool."

"What cool? He is so gay. Everytime I see him on TV, he talks in such a womanlike manner – his tone is so 'oh my god! I love pink! I just love pink chiffon!' Have you seen how he uses his hands?" Bhola did an imitation of Harish Sahota, flapping his hands up and down like a penguin.

"Is he really gay? I don't think he has ever admitted it." Raman chimed in.

"Can't tell for sure. But he does send mixed signals." Amrit was not sure either.

"I don't think he's gay." Sapna added, "I once saw him propose to that tarot card reader woman, she's so hot, what's her name – Ramona!! Yeah, he proposed to her on that TV show, what was it called – *Tea Party With Tapan* – yeah, the talk show hosted by famous Bollywood producer-director Tapan Grover. Maybe he's bi. I don't know. Who cares?"

"Oh my god, Tapan Grover is such a big producer-director. I can't think of anyone who has a better record at the box office. His last movie, *Love Love Everywhere* was such a big hit!" Meghna clapped her hands. Meghna would die to be in Tapan Grover's movies, which always had the biggest stars, the biggest budgets, and were all shot at exotic locales abroad.

"Tapan Grover is another one in the same gay category. Someone told me Tapan Grover and the main male lead in his film had an affair." Bhola said disdainfully.

"I wouldn't be surprised. Maybe Harish Sahota, their costume designer, joined in too and they had a threesome! On the sets of *Love Love Everywhere*! The star, the director and the costume designer – *Love Love Everywhere* between them! Ha!" Sapna speculated.

"You know what upsets me." Amrit suddenly sounded very serious.

"Now what?"

Sapna detected a change in mood.

Amrit continued.

"The way guys like that designer Harish Sahota and producer-director Tapan Grover go on pretending that the realities of India don't exist. That upsets me."

"What do you mean?" asked Meghna.

"Well take Harish Sahota for example. The fellow is so obsessed with clothes and looks. Have you seen him in interviews? There is a certain abstraction from India, its realities, its culture – as if he were designing in London or in New York." Meghna rolled her eyes. Amrit sensed he had made an incomplete point and needed to add more meat to his argument.

"Okay, look at Tapan Grover's movies. Look at the sets, the locations, the clothes. It is so *not* India. It is so not even Mumbai. His characters live in some dreamland that is part New York chic and part English countryside. Everybody wears DKNY and Polo Sport and lives in beautiful manors and loft apartments. The only thing Indian left is the language and the genre. It's almost as if the bastard is ashamed of being Indian."

"Amrit, it's about being aspirational. We all want to look up, not down. All of Bollywood is escapist. Maybe Tapan Grover is escape to the west." Meghna countered.

"I know, I know. I don't expect Tapan Grover to set up his plots in the middle of a Dahisar slum colony in Mumbai with the hero stumbling over dogshit and open sewers while he sings and dances … but Tapan Grover … just totally goes overboard … There is nothing Indian left in his films." Amrit was animated.

"He has no choice. Look at the state of this city, it's so third world – jam packed streets, overflowing drains, rubbish, slums, pollution, people and poverty everywhere." Raman made a valid point.

"Yeah! It's a total shithole. No wonder nobody shoots in Mumbai anymore." Riz agreed.

"What do you mean? The whole of Bollywood shoots in Mumbai. That is why it is called the Bombay Film Industry – Bollywood!" Shiv Shankar Pandey was confused. Had he come to the wrong town?

"Riz doesn't mean indoors, in the studios. He means outdoors." Amrit clarified. "When was the last time you saw a Bollywood song picturised outdoors in Mumbai? In like a street or a park or something?"

There was silence.

"Exactly." Amrit said excitedly. The point was made. "Can't remember, can you? That's because nowadays all outdoor scenes in Bollywood movies are shot abroad. Switzerland, America, Singapore, Seychelles. Not in Mumbai. We're just so ashamed to show the city we live in."

"Old black and white movies were extensively shot on the streets of Mumbai," Raman said.

"Correction, they were shot on the streets of Bombay, not Mumbai. You are talking about 30 or 40 years ago – Bombay, as the city was then called, was still worth showing. It wasn't the overcrowded and polluted Slumbay of today." Amrit interjected.

"Slumbay! That's a good name! Maybe they should rename the city one more time. Bombay to Mumbai to Slumbay! Will be more apt for sure! *Achcha hai.*" Bhola seemed excited at the prospect of yet another name change for Bombay.

"It's indeed a pity. India's best city is a shithole. Even Bollywood acknowledges that. Even films where the stories are based in Mumbai are shot abroad – the streets of Singapore look better than those of Mumbai – by far! I agree with you there." Meghna said, contemplatively.

"Yeah … it's kind of funny, no? A girl and a boy in a Bollywood movie meet at a college in Mumbai, but the college looks more like Cambridge University than any campus in Mumbai, and then they sing a song in a Swiss meadow, get married against the backdrop of an Australian beach, and then settle down in a New York City apartment and audiences are still supposed to believe that the story is Mumbai-based!"

"Amrit *bhaiya*, I would rather see the pretty campus of Cambridge, the unspoilt valleys of Switzerland and a nice beach in Australia over the paan-stained, unkept passageways of Mithibhai College Andheri or the polythene bags strewn Hanging Gardens or the overcrowded and filthy Juhu beach. Anyday!" Shiv said with a flourish of his hands.

"That's escapism, Shiv! Typical Bollywood escapism. But do you realise, we live in this shit-hole, not in the other world shown on the screen. Maybe because we are fed so much of that escapist fare – over eight hundred movies a year and thousands and thousands of hours of television programming – that we are somehow fooled into believing all is well. Just look around. All is not well. How much longer do you think this city is going to cope? Ten years? Twenty years? The infrastructure is already broken." Amrit shook his head.

"One hundred and fifty rupees only!" Shiv pulled out one hundred, and one fifty rupee note from his pocket and held them up for everyone to see. "That's all it takes to repair it! For one hundred and fifty rupees, I can get a three-hour ride in an airconditioned, luxury multiplex cinema – good songs, good locations, pretty damsels, a plot that doesn't tax my mind too much, and a generally feel-good ending! That's what I call a good value-for-money Bollywood flick. The answer to India's infrastructure problems! Just go watch a Bollywood movie." Shiv laughed, exposing his tobacco-stained yellow teeth.

"Why don't you smoke some crack instead, huh?" Amrit was visibly irritated. "That might be a better fix.

And I've heard it's quite cheap – your one hundred and fifty rupees would take you much further than three hours. Just ask one of the druggies you see lying around on the pavements. I bet they think they're living in heaven. You could join them too…"

"Hey … chill Amrit! Why are you getting angry with poor Shiv? He doesn't run this city. Chill!" Sapna tried to calm Amrit down.

Amrit was quiet. He saw Sapna's point. It was not Shiv's fault. Part of the problem was to know where to begin, where to point the first finger. Nobody seemed to run Mumbai. Nobody seemed accountable. It was nobody's city. It just ran itself. Further and further down a spiral of decay, dilapidation and ruin; like a ship slowly sinking in mid-ocean and the captain nowhere to be found.

"It's about economics, guys! It's always about economics!" Riz said coolly as he sipped his Long Island iced tea. "It's not just a coincidence that Tapan Grover's movies rake in serious box office collections abroad – with the NRI audience. He's a great businessman. Think about it. A cinema ticket costs 8 pounds in London, whereas it costs only Rs. 150 in India. Do the math – four Indian cinemagoers equal one cinemagoer in London. Now tell me – isn't Tapan Grover smart showing Amitabh Bachchan as the stern, NRI tycoon climbing off a helicopter onto the lawns of his English countryside estate with half a dozen white servants scuttering around him? It's the ultimate wet dream of every desi in Southall and Queens. It sells faster than onion *bhaji*!"

Amrit looked perturbed and pensive.

"But I still think Tapan Grover is a fucking homo!" Bhola exploded in laughter. After a pause, Amrit broke out in a smile too.

"That he probably is!" Amrit added, the smile widening, the dimples deepening.

"Hey Riz." Bhola called out, as if he was going to make an announcement.

"What is it Bihari?" replied Riz, as everyone listened on intently.

"Tapan Grover will probably make a homo of you too – when you do his film. I've heard butt-sacrifice is a precondition. All his male stars have had to do it. No exceptions; even if you are a star son! He will do you *bhai*. *Marega teri!*" Bhola said, shaking his head.

"Fuck off Bhola. I will never do that. And why are you always picking on me – damn you Bihari – just because I'm a star son. You're just jealous." Riz stormed out of the lounge bar.

"Oh now …look what you've done. Today is my anniversary. At least not today." Meghna protested.

"Let him go, spoilt brat." Bhola shook his head.

"You two just can't ever seem to…" Meghna paused mid sentence. A stocky, moustached, middle-aged man appeared beside the table. It was Vikramaditya, the son of Rajkumar, the leader of the strongest radical political group in western India.

"Hello. I am Vikramaditya, of the Bahubali Party." Vikramaditya demanded attention.

"Hello, how do you do?" Raman spoke, cautiously. Men like Vikramaditya were best kept at an arm's length and Raman knew that.

"*Aee ladki,*" Vikramaditya said, pointing to Sapna, "you're *filmi na?* I saw you in TV ad. Come I buy you drink." Vikramaditya made a kissing sound with his lips, as if he was calling a puppy to him.

"No thank you, I am fine right here." Sapna replied sternly.

"*Aee* too much *bhau* you are eating? Come come ... I will take care. I have money." Vikramaditya made the kissing sound with his lips again.

"*Arre bhaiya*, she said *na* she doesn't want your drink. Go your own way now." Amrit said.

"*Saale bhaduae*, who are you, her pimp?" Vikramaditya was angry at being snubbed.

"Listen sir, we don't want any trouble. Why don't you just leave us alone, please? She's not interested." Meghna tried to intervene.

"You are *filmi* too..." Vikramaditya pointed a finger at Meghna. "You ... some other night ... today ... this one!" Vikramaditya broke into a smile, as he shifed the finger to point at Sapna, and said, "But I am interested."

"Listen Mr. Vikramaditya, you are mistaken. You've come to the wrong place." Raman tried to placate the political scion. "We are just ordinary people having dinner..."

"What wrong place?" Vikramaditya cut him off. "All *filmi* girls are whores. Drop money, and they will part their legs. Simple. Tell me your price." Vikramaditya pointed to Sapna, who was now getting increasingly uncomfortable, and held on to Amrit's arm.

"Listen, leave right now." Amrit ordered Vikramaditya.

"*Aee bhaduae*, English *chhaap*, you are a tough negotiator. *Achcha bataa*, what is she like in bed ... money is no problem ... *chikni hai?*"

Amrit stood up and faced Vikramaditya.

Slap!

Amrit landed a tight slap on Vikramaditya's face.

Commotion broke lose, as four men appeared from nowhere and grabbed Amrit, lifting him off his feet, and before anyone could react, they had hurtled him outside the lounge bar.

"Hey ... what are you doing?" Meghna cried out.

Amrit was thrown on the road, towered over by four of Vikramaditya's men, who were punching and kicking him. One of Vikramaditya's men broke a bottle of beer on Amrit's head, rendering him unconscious. He was about to stab Amrit with the broken beer bottle, when a hand held him.

"Stop! Or your mother will not recognise you once I'm through with you." Seeing what was happening, Bhola had jumped into the fray to his friend's defence.

"Beat up the bastard." Vikramaditya commanded his goons towards Bhola. The first of the four clicked open a Rampuri knife and charged at Bhola, attacking his right arm with it, in an attempt to chop it in half. With lightening speed, Bhola moved his other arm to intercept the goon's wrist, turned it around, and in a slick move, twisted his wrist until the knife dropped from his hand. A quick sweep of the leg from Bhola threw the man off balance, and he fell to the ground with a painful thud. Bhola now took a wrestling stance, his legs parted, he clapped his hands and patted his inner thighs, inviting the other goons to fight him. Two of the goons now moved towards Bhola, one armed with the broken beer bottle and the other with a motorcycle chain. They were cautious in their approach, having just seen a demonstration of Bhola's fighting skills. They had underestimated him. The one with the motorcycle chain attacked first. Like a hawk, Bhola picked up the move from the corner of his eye, and shot out his left arm to intercept the chain, grabbing hold of it, wrapping it around his wrist in a quick rotation of the arm, and then yanking the chain towards him with great force, pulling the goon with it close and then lifted the man off his feet and high above his head. Bhola held the man aloft in a Herculean pose, and then threw him like he was chucking a bag of potatoes. The man landed a few feet away, and broke a few bones as he fell awkwardly on the raised pavement. Almost instantly, Bhola swung a full 360 degrees, launching into a spin kick, and landed an accurate blow on the face of the other attacker with the broken bottle, who fell to the ground in a heap.

The fourth goon now charged at Bhola. Bhola butted his head into the charging man's torso, in a blow so powerful the man collapsed too.

Meghna and Raman rushed to Amrit, who was regaining consciousness.

"Are you okay?" Raman asked, examining the spot on Amrit's head where he was hit.

"Yeah! Just a little sore..." Amrit's expression suggested he was in pain, as he stood up.

"No bleeding, thank god. You'll be fine. Just put some ice on it." Raman prescribed.

"I'll take him to my aunt's flat. It's not far from here, in Colaba." Sapna fished out the motorcycle's keys from Amrit's pocket.

"You sure you can handle it? I mean, can you drive a motorcycle?" Meghna asked.

"Absolutely. Just help him on to the motorcycle." Sapna directed Meghna, Raman and Shiv as they placed Amrit on the pillion seat of the motorcycle, placing his arms around Sapna's waist, and the two rode off on the RX100.

A large tiger's head stared at Amrit and Sapna as the door opened. Sapna's aunt's Colaba flat was a Rajasthani antiques emporium on the inside. Besides stuffed animal carcasses, which were all victims of the Rathore family's proud hunting history – tiger heads, cheetah skins, birds and antelopes of various kinds, and even a pair of elephant tusks – the walls of the flat were covered with all sorts of Rajasthani tid bits.

"Wow! I feel like I am in a museum. Are those guns real?" Amrit pointed to the pair of antique muzzle loader guns strung on the wall.

"Yes they are. How do you think they killed all this wildlife? The Rathore family is big into hunting." Sapna said as she led Amrit through the corridor into the living room.

"Sit."

Distracted by this new environment, Amrit had almost forgotten all his pain, as he sunk into a camel-skin sofa.

"Here." Sapna handed Amrit a bag of ice. "Put this on your head. I'll go make you some tea."

"Thanks." Amrit put the bag of ice to the spot on his head where he was hit by the bottle. His eyes scanned the walls around, this time, viewing a selection of antique swords and daggers of various shapes and sizes.

"Where is your aunt?" Amrit called out to Sapna with a sudden sense of panic.

"She's gone to Goa for the weekend." Sapna shouted back from the kitchen.

Amrit sunk back comfortably into the sofa. He picked up a photo frame that was lying on the adjacent gunmetal coffee table. There were old, black and white family photographs of men and women dressed up in fine

Rajasthani clothes – the men wearing turbans and dangling swords from their sides – the women in sarees worn the traditional way with the *pallu* wrapped around the head – and the children seated in the front. There were photographs of men on elephants, with guns, returning from a tiger hunt. Amrit wondered if the dead tiger in that photograph was the same one whose stuffed head now hung in this flat.

"Tea." Sapna placed the cup on the coffee table.

"Sapna, are you a real princess or something?" Amrit asked.

"Yes of course! You better learn to treat me special, *oye* Amrit from Amritsar. You're lucky – I generally don't hang out with commoners like you." Sapna made a coy face at Amrit.

"Will your dad kill me and hang my head on the wall – like one of these animals – if he found out about, you know, you and me?" Amrit sipped the tea.

"Absolutely not. He would just chop you up and feed you to the tigers. You are not even worthy of these walls." Sapna teased.

"*Achcha!* I picked a fight for you there, and now I'm not even worthy of your wall." Amrit protested.

"*Gulugulu...*" Sapna came up and grabbed Amrit's cheeks in her hands, "How quickly you get angry, my dear commoner boyfriend."

"Where are you in these photographs…. Show me. I can't tell. There are, like, two dozen people in that photo." Amrit pointed to the old black and white photographs.

Ting Tong! The doorbell rang.

"Who could that be?" Amrit was worried Sapna's aunt might be back from Goa. He did not want to end up like one of the creatures on the wall.

"Relax. It must be Bhola. He called me earlier and took the flat's address; he said he'd come to see how you were doing. I'll show you the photos later. I have an old album."

It indeed was Bhola.

"Amrit ... how are you *bhai?* How is your head?" Bhola came up and took a look at Amrit's head.

"I'm fine now *yaar.* You were the hero tonight. You saved my life!" Amrit smiled.

"What are you saying ... how dare those bastards touch my brother Amrit. Bhola might not be a hi-fi man, but he knows what friendship is. They touched my friend, and they paid for it. *Saale harami!*" Bhola sounded like he still wanted to beat those goons some more.

"Bhola would you like some tea?" Sapna asked.

"No *bhabhi* ... no thanks." Bhola replied.

"Why do you call her that?" Amrit protested. "I'm not married to her!"

"*Oh ho* ... don't put too much tension on your head Amrit *bhai* ... relax ... we are only in private over here, there is nobody else. Whatever you may say, in reality, you are my brother, and Sapna is my *bhabhi.*" Bhola came up and hugged Amrit. Sapna blushed. Bhola may not have been very polished, but she knew he meant well. He was warm and genuine.

"Okay, now I will leave. I just wanted to see that you were okay." Bhola got up to leave.

"Sit Bhola, what's the hurry?" Sapna suggested.

"No *bhabhi*, I have to drive all the way back to Versova. It's late."

"By the way, when is your aunty coming back from Goa?" Bhola asked, as Sapna walked him to the door.

"In three days. How do you know she's in Goa?" Sapna was surprised.

"A little *bard* told me. Good night." Bhola smiled as he shut the door. Unknown to Sapna, he had shut this door many times before – for Sapna's aunt was a regular client of Bhola's – and Bhola had secretly been to this Colaba flat many times before. In fact, the leather sofa in Bhola's apartment had been a gift from none other than the royal Rajasthani lady, who had offered Bhola one lakh rupees to be her male consort in Goa this weekend. It was a 'no-husbands' pleasure trip organised by a group of socialite women from South Mumbai. "Not enough money!" Bhola had said, when he turned down Sapna's aunt's offer. The actual reason, of course, was that Bhola had many of his clients on that same pleasure trip, and did not want to pick one lady over the others and jeopardise future business. Instead, he decided not to go with any of the numerous ladies who had offered to pay him for the trip.

"Is that your mother?" Amrit pointed to the lady in the old black and white photograph standing next to Sapna's father.

"No. That's my father's friend, aunty Pooja."

"And that one. That lady with your dad?" Amrit pointed to another photo of a lady who had her arms affectionately wrapped around Sapna's dad.

"No, that's not my mom either. That's Lovleen aunty. My father had a lot of female, what shall I call them, companions. He had a glad eye. My mother ... she became an alcoholic too, like most in my family. My parents were always fighting. Amrit, I never told you, but my mother died of alcoholism."

"I am sorry to hear that." Amrit said as he straightened up against the bed's ornate headpiece.

"It's my dad's fault. He drove her to that state. My mother died a broken woman. She couldn't take it," Sapna explained.

"Why did your father do that – I mean, all the drinking, the womanising?"

"Amrit, royal men are brought up in a certain way. Like kings. They are groomed for the high life … polo, gambling, philandering … and then, after the Indian government abolished royalty and put an end to privy purses and all the benefits that the royals had enjoyed, from then on all hell broke loose. The family could not accept the fact that they were no longer royals – just ordinary folks – they still carried on living the way they used to. And then when the money started running out, they couldn't take it. My father took to the bottle. And gambling. Then when the debts mounted, he started selling off the family estates … till finally, there was nothing left to sell. And then he started drinking even more heavily and gambling and womanising even more. My parents would have bitter fights. It was all a downward spiral from there on." Sapna looked sad as she turned the pages of the photo album.

"You must have had a pretty tragic upbringing, then." Amrit put his arm around Sapna.

"No, I had my *ayah* – Achla amma – I'll show you her photo." Sapna quickly turned to a photograph of a gentle-looking woman. "And I had my best friends in the world. I'll show you their photo too."

"That's a TV!" Amrit looked at the photo Sapna was pointing out.

"No, it's not just a TV silly, it's a TV and a VCR. They were my best friends." Sapna took the photograph out of the album and held it to her chest fondly. "I grew up with them."

"I don't understand." Amrit was confused.

"Amrit, my parents were never around. I spent all my time in front of the TV and the VCR. I watched endless movies, Bollywood movies, day and night, with Achla amma by my side. Oh how much fun we had! We watched all the masala movies…. I wouldn't miss a single new release. Bollywood became my surrogate family. That became my life, my alternate existence." Sapna recalled with curious joy.

"Is that why you wanted to come to Bollywood? Is that why you like the mindless masala films?" Amrit thought out aloud.

"Perhaps. They may be mindless for you, Amrit, but to me, all that emotion, family drama, music, characters, situations … everything that you call masala … became my family. Bollywood saved me, emotionally." Sapna had become sad.

"But now I don't need a TV and VCR, or even Bollywood … I have you!" Sapna suddenly cheered up as she hugged Amrit.

"Amrit, I wanted to ask your permission for something," said Sapna as she looked into Amrit's eyes, her hands wrapped around his neck.

"Permission? For what?" Amrit sounded amused, as he petted Sapna's head.

"I got offered that movie role … you know, the audition you had taken me to in Bandra. I got a call from the producer today. They want to sign me on as the second lead in their movie. Shooting begins next week." Sapna's eyes were searching Amrit's face for reaction.

Amrit burst out laughing.

"*Permission!* You don't need my permission! Of course you should do the movie. That's fantastic!" Amrit sounded excited.

"Why did you need to ask me for permission?" Amrit teased.

"Well … I have to…" Sapna continued, shyly, "I just have to. You know … you are…"

"Okay, I grant thee permission!" Amrit said jokingly, pretending to be king.

"I'm serious Amrit. Are you sure you want me to do this? I won't if you tell me not to." Sapna looked straight at Amrit, meaning every word she said.

"And then we can move down to Bangalore. I will take up the nine to five computer job, you can stay at home and cook and clean, and we will live happily ever after … like in the masala movies!" Amrit burst out laughing.

"Amrit!" Sapna beat his chest with her fists. "Be serious. This has to do with our lives."

"Okay okay. Serious." Amrit quietened down. "I do want you to pursue your movie career. Go for it!"

Sapna continued looking into his eyes, hoping he would change his mind. She was prepared to drop everything and move with him to Bangalore if he so much as only hinted at it. The greatest joy in the world for her would be to be with her Amrit.

"What do you want in life Sapna?" Amrit asked as he turned over and looked up at the ceiling. Sapna did not reply. Amrit turned his neck and looked directly at Sapna, and repeated the question.

"Above all, I want security Amrit. I come from a family that is really messed up. They are all living in the past, in an imaginary era that is now long gone. It's a dysfunctional family. I can't go back to Jaipur. That place suffocates me. It's so pathetic. I came to Mumbai to run away from it all. I like Bollywood because it gives me a new reality, even if it is imaginary."

"You are deeper than I thought! I thought you were just a pretty dumb girl … or a dumb pretty girl!" Amrit said jokingly.

Sapna hit him with a pillow.

"Why don't you find a nice man and settle down with him? That will give you security." Sapna hit him with the pillow again.

"Okay okay *baba* relax. I was just kidding." Amrit embraced her tightly. She pinched him on the stomach.

"Ouch! What was that for?"

"Just." Sapna had a distant look in her eyes.

"Women are so difficult to understand. They never say what they mean, and they never mean what they say." Amrit shook his head.

"Maybe you are just too dumb. You don't get it. No sex for you tonight. Good night." Sapna switched off the lights.

CHAPTER 6

Amrit's next shoot for *Saas Ka Sindoor* was at an outdoor location in Film City, Powai. Today, he was to shoot a major scene, he had been informed on the phone by the scheduler from Jai Jai Productions. What might that scene be, Amrit wondered, as he stepped into the vanity van? Asleep on the divan was Romesh Paul, the reigning star of television, and the main protagonist of *Saas Ka Sindoor*.

When shoots are outdoors, that is, away from studios, the producer usually provides the vanity vans for the actors. The vans, usually specially made bus-like vehicles, meant for actors to get ready and have their makeup done in, are invaluable for one great reason – they are airconditioned! In the typically hot and sapping humidity of Mumbai, a type of weather condition that seems to be ever-prevalent, the airconditioned haven of the vanity van becomes a magnet for all and sundry on the sets. Actors, of course, are the supposed primary beneficiaries of the comfort that the vanity van provides. Actors, like fresh vegetables in a refrigerator, need to be protected from the wilting Mumbai heat, and like dressed up dolls, they sit in the airconditioned vanity vans, like eggs on a refrigerator shelf, till their shot is ready. Waits can run into hours; often an actor would be called to the sets at 7:30 am and will be called for his first shot at, say, 9:30 pm. Veteran actors can be seen catching some shut-eye, prostrate on the meagre divans provided in the vans. This is sometimes the only way they get their sleep. Crucial actors in daily soap operas get home for barely three-four hours, usually in the small hours of the morning, some not at all for twenty-four hours at a stretch. These fortunate unfortunates have to eat, sleep, shower, shave – everything – on the sets itself, with the vanity van serving as their mobile home away from home.

Usually, shooting the actual scene would only take a fraction of the total time. It is all the prep time that goes into getting the scene ready that causes the long waits. The director would usually describe the shot to the cameraman, and tell him where to place the camera, define its movements for the scene. The cameraman would then begin lighting the scene, a process that could go on for hours, as the cameraman would tweak the various lights, from all angles and of all intensities, using his light meter or even the palm of his hand, to get the lighting just right. Lighting is crucial. And a good cameraman will take as long as it takes to make sure all unnecessary shadows are removed, the intensity is right, each actor gets the right light, etcetera etcetera. This etcetera etcetera tinkering can go on for hours, adding to a lot of dead time on the sets. Seasoned actors like Romesh Paul would take naps during this dead time. New ones, like Amrit, would sit there agonising about their lines, thinking up various ways of saying them, long after they are ready with the lines.

As soon as actors arrive on the set, they go around hunting for the script for the day's shoot. It is never that they come prepared and ready knowing what scene(s) they'll be performing that day. Bollywood is not organised. In the world of Bollywood, especially in television, everything is last minute. Sometimes, whole units are ready and waiting, director, cameraman, lightmen, actors, everybody – waiting for the script to arrive from the producer's office. And then, like a much expected messiah, some nondescript office boy would arrive and pull out sweat-moistened papers from under his shirt – scripts for the day's shoot – often untidily scribbled words in romanised Hindi, on loose A4 sheets of paper, hurriedly photocopied for there to be atleast two copies – one for the director and one for the actors. Sometimes, there would be only one copy, the original, to be shared between the director and all the actors.

To outsiders, as well as to newcomers who have just joined the Bollywood caravan, this functioning might appear more akin to a chaotic mela set in the oppressive boiler-room like heat of Mumbai's weather, with long and trying hours rather than anything glamorous and glitzy they might have otherwise expected. Forget glamour and glitz, Bollywood sometimes lacks even the basic amenities and working standards. These are soap sweatshops, a nonstop cycle of shoot-print-edit-broadcast-repeat. Miraculously, it works. The juggernaut continues. Nearly one thousand movies and hundreds of thousands of hours of television programming are churned out ever year by Bollywood. With the same surety as the rising of the sun and the moon, soaps continue to be beamed into millions of television sets across India and in the diaspora abroad, on time, every time.

Amrit tip-toed into the vanity van as inconspicuously as he could. He did not want to wake up Romesh Paul.

Just being in the same space as Romesh Paul, the great star, gave Amrit goosebumps. Amrit was handed a script by Shweta, the Assistant Director, or AD, and asked to go sit in the vanity van and prepare. Amrit poured over the script, careful not to make a sound even while turning the pages.

"What time is it?" Amrit heard a sleepy voice. It was Romesh Paul. He was waking up.

"It's about 4:30, Mr. Paul." Amrit said politely.

"Mr. Paul! Good damn sisterfucker! I haven't heard that in a while!" Romesh Paul smiled, as he rubbed his eyes and pulled himself up from the divan.

"You're the new boy. I can tell you're new to Mumbai. Hi! What's your name?" Romesh now looked up at Amrit, still drowsy from sleep.

"Hello sir! I'm Amrit. It is a real honour to be working with you. I'm a big fan of yours." Amrit was beaming.

"Hmmm…" Romesh looked at the script in Amrit's hand.

"What's the scene?" Romesh inquired. Amrit handed him the script.

"Interesting scene." Romesh announced, after reading it. "I hope you've got balls, young man! This scene requires balls."

Amrit smiled, nervously.

"I want to tell you one thing." Romesh got up and started making his way to the toilet.

"If you are a good actor, which I assume you are, given that you have been selected for this role, ignore everything the AD says. They are just kids on a fad. Just nod your head to them in agreement when they sit with you and go through the scene, but in front of the camera, do what *you* feel is right." Romesh instructed Amrit and then disappeared into the toilet.

Almost exactly on cue, the door of the vanity van opened and Shweta entered. She wore a brown khadi kurta over a pair of blue jeans, had large beads dangling from her earlobes and had her hair cut short in a boy cut. She was the junior most of the five ADs on set today for *Saas Ka Sindoor*, and had been assigned the task of making sure the actors were ready with their lines. As Shweta sat down on the divan, she looked at the script, and then at Amrit.

"Where is Romeshji?" Shweta asked.

Just then the toilet door opened and Romesh Paul emerged, water splashed over his face.

"I am here, darling!" Romesh came and sat down besides Shweta, smiling.

"Right. This scene is that Romeshji you are trying to bribe, you…" Shweta pointed at Amrit, not knowing his name, as he was a newcomer.

"And you…" again pointing at Amrit, Shweta continued, "will say no to the offer of bribe made by Romeshji. That's all there is to this scene. Make sure you memorise your lines and say them without change. Vinta doesn't like actors changing lines."

Amrit was pained to see the AD, who, if she hadn't made a deliberate effort to look ultra-arty, was mildly attractive, had deconstructed the scene in such a cut and dry manner. To Amrit's mind this was a multi-layered complex scene – and he had already worked out the various nuances and feelings each word, each pause would evoke. Then Amrit noticed Romeshji nodding fully in agreement with Shweta. *Romeshji is right! Shweta is totally out of her depths here.* Amrit felt best to follow Romesh Paul's advice and nod his head in agreement as well. He'll do the scene the way he wants to, the way he feels it ought to be done. Amrit nodded his head in agreement too.

Satisfied that the actors were on the same page as her, Shweta left the van. Romesh eyed her ass through the kurta that dangled over her jeans as she walked down the steps, opened the vanity van's door, and stepped out. Then, he turned to Amrit, with a naughty look in his eyes.

"She has a nice ass, no?"

Amrit smiled, trying to be neutral.

"You should try and get into that ass. Looks nice and juicy!" Romesh continued, wiping his face with a towel.

Amrit was now embarrassed. He tried to change the direction of this conversation.

"It is a real pleasure and honour to be working with you, Romeshji. You are such a big star, I can't believe I'm working with you."

"Hmmm…" Romesh sounded disappointed at the change of topic. He wanted to stay with Shweta's ass.

"Where are you from Romeshji?" How did you get into acting?" Amrit was genuinely curious.

"Hmm…" Romesh stood up, took a long yawn, stretched his arms and then sat down at the makeup table.

"I used to be a FMCG salesman. In Kolkata. Then I got posted to Mumbai. Gave up my job. People said I was handsome, I should try for Bollywood. So, I tried and I got here." Romesh was examining his jawline in the mirror, noticing the beginnings of a double chin, mentally thinking back to the days when undoubtedly he must have been a very handsome young man.

"You know…" Romesh tried to recall Amrit's name from memory.

"Amrit." Amrit helped out.

"You know Amrit, when I was in Kolkata, I was such a dasher. I screwed so, so many women. God! I have fucked wives of marwari businessmen in their very homes!" Romesh was reminiscing, examining the grey in his hair.

"Really? The husbands didn't find out? And why did the wives do that, cheat on their husbands?" Amrit asked.

"Amrit, marwari men are very *dheela,* very limp. Their wives are always on the lookout for strong, robust men. *What* women!" Romesh kissed the air. "The things they would do to please a man. They set new standards in oral sex."

"You mean they were very good at giving head?" Amrit asked.

"Not just head, my friend, they would not stop just there. They would bloody dryclean me completely!" There was a glint of the old times in Romesh's eyes.

Amrit felt embarrassed at the explicit nature of this conversation. Moreover, he now wanted to concentrate on the script and in preparing for the scene. Staying here in the vanity van with Romesh Paul, though entertaining, would be a total distraction from the important work of preparation. So, Amrit decided to leave the vanity van and prepare outside.

"Wow! Romeshji, you have such an interesting past. I will sit with you and hear all your stories someday. It is a real opportunity to be working with you, sir." With that, Amrit excused himself and left the vanity van.

Monica was the reigning bitch queen of *Saas Ka Sindoor.* Thirty-two years old, married to a Mumbai businessman and mother of a six-year-old boy, Monica had once bumped into Vinta at a party. Vinta had offered

Monica a role right on the spot. Monica had no acting background, and had never planned on a Bollywood foray; but Vinta had assured her that her lack of experience would not be a problem. Thus, Monica debuted on *Saas Ka Sindoor*, using her real-life name on-screen too. She played Romesh's on-screen second wife, and was the evil sister-in-law of the household. Her trademark was a 'snake-styled' bindi that was affixed on her forehead whenever she appeared on screen, and an evil-sounding signature tune, which would play everytime her character made an on-screen appearance. Monica's character, with its snake-bindi and evil background score had become a huge success. Her sweet-on-the-outside but evil inside sister-in-law character had become a pivot of the show, adding oodles of melodrama with great effect. Everyone in India seems to know or have an evil sister-in-law in the family. The more evil and melodramatic the punches that Monica delivered on screen, the more she was relished by the audiences. Indian audiences just loved to hate a bitch like her. More moolah rolled in for Vinta.

In real life, however, Monica was the gentlest of beings. She came to the sets of *Saas Ka Sindoor* dressed in a plain salwar kameez, her six-year-old son in tow. Noticing Amrit, leaning against the vanity van, pouring over the script in deep concentration, she said a congenial "hi" to him.

"Hi! I'm Amrit. A big fan of yours, Monicaji!" Amrit had replied back.

"Call me Monica. Here, have some." Monica offered Amrit a candy bar from a little box she carried for her son.

"Thanks." Amrit took one.

"Welcome to *Saas Ka Sindoor*," she smiled.

Amrit instantly liked her. She was kind and gentle.

She had made an effort to make the new cast member of *Saas Ka Sindoor* feel at home. Amrit appreciated that.

Monica disappeared into the vanity van. Amrit returned to his script, going over each word, working out the meanings and nuances he would want to convey. Going through a dozen possibilities. Rehearsing fifty times. Fine tuning his performance in his head.

When Monica came out of the vanity van, she was wearing a heavy silk saree, her hair was done elaborately with a large wig in place, the so-popular deadly snake-bindi in place on her forehead. She had walked into the vanity van the simple and kind-hearted person who had just offered Amrit a candy bar, and had emerged a completely different person – the evil sister-in-law. *Wow! The power of makeup!* Amrit stared at her, with his mouth open.

"Oh god! The expression on your face Amrit! You look aghast! It's still *me!*" Amrit was reassured to hear her kind voice. It *was* still her! Amrit smiled back warmly. He liked Monica. From the script Amrit could tell that he had no scenes with Monica today, but he hoped he would get to shoot with her sometime. She seemed like an instinctively good actor, who, without any training, was completely at home in front of the camera and comfortable with her co-actors. Good actors always look forward to acting with other good actors, and Amrit was no exception to that innate urge. "Magic can happen when good actors share a stage," Guruji had once said in class. Amrit hoped to create some of that magic with Monica some day.

Today, however, he was to go up against no less a stalwart than Romesh Paul, the most formidable actor on Indian television. For years, Romesh had ruled *Saas Ka Sindoor*. Today, Amrit had a major scene with him – a scene of great confrontation. Amrit wanted it to go well. He turned his eyes back to the script.

The scene to be shot involved Romesh Paul, the father of the girl whom Amrit had fallen in love with in college, and Amrit. Romesh, who plays the rich and arrogant businessman Mr. Singhania in *Saas Ka Sindoor*, finds Amrit unsuitable for his daughter. The scene begins in Romesh's luxurious drawing room, where the two are standing. Romesh and Amrit were both ready with their costumes on, their faces made up, well rehearsed with their lines. The lights were focussed on them, the camera was rolling, everything was in place, and then the director called.

Action!

Romesh: "Sit down, young man."

Amrit sat down on the plush leather sofa. Romesh moved to the bar, pouring scotch from a crystal decanter into a cut-glass tumbler.

"Scotch?" Romesh offered Amrit.

"No thank you, sir. I don't drink." Amrit responded.

"Hmmm ... don't be shy. Scotch helps lubricate men's minds. Have some. I insist. It's eighteen years old, like my daughter." Romesh placed a glass of scotch before Amrit, and took a seat across from him. After taking a sip from his glass, Romesh continued. Amrit didn't touch his glass.

"Sonal is my only child. I have raised her in great luxury." Romesh gestured with his hands to the richly appointed surroundings.

"Everything she ever wanted, she got. Silly girl!" Romesh chuckled, putting his glass down.

"But some things are not worth having." Romesh said, icily, looking straight at Amrit, a sly smirk appearing across his lips.

"Look, young man. Let me be straight with you. You look like a handsome fellow, and have done a great job of getting my daughter trapped. I will give you ten lakh rupees to break off your relationship with my daughter and forget about her."

Amrit stood up, rage swelling inside him.

"Why? Is it less? Okay, twenty lakhs."

Amrit's eyes were now bloodshot. He looked straight at Romesh, and then when he was just about to turn around to leave, Romesh commanded, "Wait."

Amrit stopped. Romesh could tell his offer would not be taken. He switched gears, rising from the leather couch, walking up to Amrit, placing an arm around the young man's shoulder.

"My daughter is young; she is immature." Romesh was now speaking in a low, fatherly tone.

"You are a fellow she is infatuated with. That's all. Infatuation. You have hit a jackpot here, you know that – hooked a super rich girl." Romesh chuckled again. "Twenty lakhs is not bad for the effort, is it? It's the easiest money you'll ever have made? Take it." Romesh was now talking like the shrewd businessman he was, trying to cut a deal.

"Excuse me sir," Amrit replied, in a voice that was refined, deliberately concealing a storm of anger that was welling inside him.

"You are a very honourable man. Today, when you called me to your house, I thought I was going to meet the father of the girl I love, the girl I want to marry." Amrit paused.

"I may be poor, sir, but I too have my honour; and I am certainly not for sale. My love for your daughter is true, as I'm convinced her's for me is too. If I knew you had called me to your house to insult me, I would never have come." Amrit's each word was pregnant with emotion, his eyes expressive, as he tried to plead with his future father in law. This scene was shaping up well – and both Romesh and Amrit knew it. There was an energy in the area around the scene, like an electromagnetic field, which actors can detect. Every single person around was watching with rapt attention – the technicians, the lightmen, the cameramen, even the spot boys. They had dropped whatever else they were doing, and watched, thoroughly absorbed in the action, as the scene unfurled before them. The confrontation was building up well, and all were eager to see how it went.

"Don't be a fool, young man … I know your type … road-side romeos." Romesh thundered, raising his voice in an arrogant fury, his tone unabashedly aggressive and threatening, as he raised a finger in Amrit's direction.

"I can have you eliminated in a second if I want," Romesh made a slashing gesture across Amrit's throat with his raised finger, anger in his eyes.

Rage was building up inside Amrit's chest, as he breathed heavily. As he stood there, even his silence resonated tension, a tension that gripped every member of the unit who was now watching.

"Mr. Singhania I do not fear death." Amrit finally broke his silence, his tone heavy but still checked, still respectful, his words spoken deliberately. "But till the moment that I am alive, I will continue to love Sonal." Amrit stood there like a fearless tiger, eyeball to eyeball with the tycoon whose daughter he wanted to marry.

After a long and pregnant pause, Amrit spoke again.

"You are the father of the girl I want to marry, and you are elder to me in age. The way I was brought up, I was taught to respect my elders. As an elder, and as Sonal's father, I have the deepest respect for you. But make no mistake, my respect should not be seen as fear. For I fear no one and nothing in this world. You may threaten me or you may try to bribe me, but I will only stop seeing Sonal on one condition."

"What?" Romesh desperately blurted out, feeling defeated.

Amrit paused. The delay adding to the gravity, as he saw discomfort grow on Romesh's face. Finally, Amrit spoke.

"I will never see Sonal again if she says that her love for me is not true, and if this is *her* wish. I give you my word on that." Amrit said sternly.

Romesh brightened, mentally working out possibilities of how he would try to engineer such an outcome.

"And one more thing sir," Amrit broke Romesh's chain of thoughts. "If Sonal says that she loves me, and wants to spend the rest of her life with me – if that is her wish – then I also give you my word that till I breathe, I will let no force in the universe let her be separated from me." Amrit bowed down and touched Romesh's feet in an act of seeking blessings, and before Romesh could react, Amrit was erect again, facing his future father in law. "And bless me so." With these final words Amrit clasped his palms together in a *namaskar*, had one final poignant look into Romesh's eyes, turned around, and strutted off, his head held high.

Cut! The director called.

As soon as 'cut' was announced by the director, there was a storm of spontaneous clapping from around the set. Amrit turned towards the audience from where the clapping had come. It was difficult for him to see against all the bright lights that were pointed straight at the scene, but he noticed that all the figures seemed to be huddled around the camera and the monitor, clapping away. The director, the lightmen, the cameraman's assistants, the spot boys, all and sundry – were clapping – including Chotte Laal, who was clapping vigorously, his two incisors dangling as he beamed at Amrit. Amrit smiled back. He felt a big relief. Romesh came up to him and put a hand on his shoulder. He was smiling too. "Good scene," Romesh said and then he put forth a hand, which Amrit promptly shook. The clapping intensified.

Wow! Amrit couldn't believe it. The first scene he had done with the great Romesh Paul, the king of Bollywood soaps, had met with applause from the entire unit. Amrit was just relieved to have been able to stand up to the formidable Romesh. This scene had gone really well. Amrit felt a deep sense of satisfaction, as he scanned all the appreciative faces. This is the moment actors live for. It is their moment of highest glory. It is what sustains them. It is what makes it all so worthwhile. A true actor would work for nothing and just this.

Amrit was at the red light at the Andheri flyover, waiting for the signal to turn green so that he could get on to the Western Express Highway, that would take him straight to Meghdoot Studios for the Govardhan Bollywood Talent Hunt. This was a real opportunity, a chance to get at par with all the insiders. If he cracked this talent hunt, it would land him a lead role in Govardhan Motion Pictures' next movie, an unparalleled launch pad. The competition would be tough, Amrit knew. Every actor worth his salt would be there, to take a shot at this god-sent opportunity for strugglers. Govardhan Motion Pictures had invited entries from all over India. Of the thousands of entries, only a hundred were shortlisted for the final auditions. Amrit had been one of them. The best male and best female new talent, as adjudged through the auditions, would be launched as the lead pair in a Bollywood movie produced by Govardhan Motion Pictures. The Govardhan Bollywood Talent Hunt was a chance not to be missed.

Amrit was running late. A glance to his wrist showed it was 3 pm already. Amrit's slot was at 4 pm. He wanted to get there by 3:30, so that he would have at least half an hour to revise the lines one more time before the audition. The light turned green. Amrit turned the accelerator and the RX100 flew off the block, leading the pack of traffic that flowed onto the Western Express Highway. Just as Amrit was about to turn the corner and merge with the traffic on the highway, he noticed a police van parked on the side and a police officer waving him to stop. *Shit! I don't have time for this.*

Amrit kept the engine of the RX100 running, as he waited for the police officer to walk up to him. Amrit was impatient. He wanted to be back on the road and making his way to the audition. The man walking up to him was an inspector, about five feet eight, and dressed in a well-ironed Mumbai police khaki uniform. He wore stylish Ray Ban sunglasses, with silver tinted lenses – the kind worn by the cop in the *Terminator* movie – whom he had an uncanny resemblance to as he walked up to Amrit.

"*Kai re,* you are in a big rush?" Amrit could see his face reflected in the Ray Ban's silver lenses as inspector

Gaitunde, as the nameplate on his chest read, came up before him.

"Going for an appointment, sir. Running rather late though." Amrit blurted, fast.

"Appointment? In Mumbai? You've come from Punjab for the appointment, *huh*! On the bike?" Gaitunde quipped. Amrit's motorcycle, which he had brought down with him from Amritsar, had a Punjab registered number plate.

Amrit was in no mood for jokes. The clock was ticking.

"What is the problem, sir? What have I done wrong that you have pulled me over? The light was green when I crossed." Amrit said in his defence.

Inspector Gaitunde didn't seem happy with Amrit's impatience. He wanted to take his time here.

"Green, *huh*." Gaitunde looked at the Punjab registered number plate on the RX100. "You are from Punjab, *huh*. Everything looks green to you, *huh* – like the green fields, *huh*. Licence. Registration."

Amrit pulled out his license from his wallet and handed it over to the cop. He then fished out the registration papers from his backpack and handed them to Gaitunde.

"Here."

Gaitunde looked up at Amrit. He didn't like the way Amrit had said "here." Here was a man who thought he was king – and this was his kingdom – the streets of Mumbai. And suddenly this kid from Punjab, a distant green-ness he had heard of and seen only in Yash Chopra movies, was telling him "here!"

"*Kai re*, Punjab number plate on your bike, why?" Gaitunde switched to English. Maybe he wanted to talk law now.

"So?" Amrit replied curtly, glancing at his watch.

"What is your business in Mumbai, Maharashtra?"

"I am an actor, going for an audition." Amrit replied, rather sheepish to admit that he was an actor. Amrit was always slightly embarrassed to admit that he was an actor. He was not famous yet – and so, really could not claim being anything more than an actor who was working his way up. When you tell people you are an actor, they expect to take a closer look at you and realise they are speaking to a Raj Kapoor or a Marlon Brando. Anything less than that is a fake – a wannabe – and invited a smirk most likely.

Gaitunde smirked. "Hero, *huh*?"

Sisterfucker, give me my papers and let me go. Amrit wished he could say this to Gaitunde. But he just let his face show it instead.

"This is Mumbai, my Mumbai – *mee Mumbaikar* – you understand hero? You non-Maharashtrian, why you come here? This city is already overcrowded. Punjab number plate … go back to Punjab."

"So what if it is a Punjab number plate. Is Punjab not in India? Or, for that matter, isn't Mumbai a part of India? Am I not free to go and live anywhere within the territory of the Republic of India, as per a right granted to me by the Constitution of India?" Amrit snapped back. He had been told Mumbai was a xenophobic city. Now was absolutely the worst time for him to have to deal with xenophobia.

"Pollution certificate." Gaitunde demanded. He wanted to play hardball now. He was not going to eat shit served by this twenty-something lad from Punjab on his home turf. Amrit knew he was in a bind now. His Achilles heel – no pollution certificate for his bike – had somehow been grabbed by Gaitunde. Amrit had forgotten to get the bike's pollution test done and renew its pollution certificate – and Gaitunde, almost instinctively, as experienced cops usually are, put his finger on the one area where Amrit *was* actually in breach of the law.

Amrit knew he now had to make an about turn and not play debating society championships with Gaitunde. Gaitunde held the ace. Amrit had to win him over so that he would let him go. Time was running out. This was now serious.

"Sir, why are we arguing? You are like my father, like my uncle. Think of me as a nephew who has come from the north to visit you in your great city of Mumbai. I respect you a lot, and am sorry if I have said anything wrong."

"Pollution." The demand for the pollution certificate was repeated in a slightly, but perceptibly, softer tone.

"I must have left it at home, *uncle*." Amrit was off his bike now and had quickly pulled out a hundred rupee note from his jeans pocket and held it hidden in his left fist.

"Sir, I know you want to help your little nephew. And with god's grace, he will achieve what he has come to achieve, and with your blessings, when he becomes a star, he will not forget you, and what all you have done for him, in days when he was totally unknown and there was nobody there to help him…"

Somewhere in that impromptu speech, Amrit slapped his left wrist on inspector Gaitunde's palm and released the hundred rupee note, and then folded the inspector's fingers around the note. Gaitunde had looked down at that moment, and through those silver glares, noticed what had happened. The inspector took the hundred rupee note and put it in his trouser pocket.

Amrit knew he could go now. He got back on his bike, kicked it to life and waved at Gaitunde, smiling.

"*Jai* Maharashtra!" Gaitunde waved back at Amrit and signalled him to go.

"Punjab! Wait a minute!" Amrit turned his head worriedly to Gaitunde's call. *Now what?* He really didn't have time for any more altercations with the law.

Gaitunde pulled out a polythene pack from his shirt pocket containing a white powder. Packed carefully in double polythene zip-lock bags was pure white powdered cocaine.

"You spend time with Bollywood people? Here, if you want, I can supply you some coke." Gaitunde offered Amrit the packet.

"It is pure hundred per cent cocaine. Model-types love this *stuff*. You want this *stuff re*?"

Amrit stared at the packet, and then at the silver Ray Bans. *Inspector Gaitunde is a drug dealer too!* Amrit couldn't believe it.

"No, thank you *uncle*." Amrit turned his head and readied to take off.

"If you ever need, come find me here. I am on duty everyday at this crossing." Gaitunde's words were drained out by the RX100's engine sound.

"Vijay" was the name most repeated for characters played by Amitabh Bachchan in his movies. Inspector Vijay, Son Vijay, Playboy Vijay, Don Vijay … the word "Vijay" spelled victory for each of these movies at the box office. Perhaps wanting to repeat that same type of commercial success, Vijayendra Kumar Srivastava, when choosing an on-screen name for his new job as "Video Jockey," or "VJ," at a popular music television channel, decided to pick "VJ Vijay." Video Jockey Vijay a.k.a Vijayendra Kumar Srivastava hailed from Chennai, though his accent might fool you into thinking he was from California.

"Yo dude! How're they hangin'?" he screamed out to the crowd that had gathered as the audience for the Govardhan Bollywood Talent Hunt, with both his arms raised in a sort of eagle spread, with the shoulders shrugged, head tilted to one side, inverted mike in hand close to his lips. Like a hip-hop rapper on stage at a rock concert, VJ Vijay jumped from one end of the stage to the other, waving to the crowd with his hand made out in a "yo!" fashion – thumb, index finger and pinkie pointing out and the other fingers wrapped in.

"Who's the cool daddy?" VJ Vijay repeatedly asked the audience.

"VJ Vijay!" he announced, and then made the audience repeat it again and again.

"Who's the cool daddy?"

"VJ Vijay!" the crowd responded. As the host of Govardhan Bollywood Talent Hunt, VJ Vijay's job included getting the audience all charged for the auditions. Excerpts from this talent hunt were to be broadcast on VJ Vijay's music channel.

VJ Vijay was serious about being 'cool.' His job depended on it. He worked for a 'cool' channel, a music TV channel that was supposed to define the youth, and hence, had to be cool. And nowadays, cool almost always meant American cool. There was no other kind. In fact, some of the shows on VJ Vijay's music channel had it as their theme to contrast between what was *cool* (thoroughly American) and what was *uncool* (Indian, *ghaaty*, villagy). The bosses at the music channel wanted a brown Indian face that could be painted American-cool and sold to the teeming brown masses of the subcontinent. VJ Vijay was to be that concoction.

"Our next contestant is Amrit! Laaadies and gentleman, welcome Amrit. You're on dude!" VJ Vijay signalled to the usher in the wings who signalled to Amrit that it was his turn on the stage. Fifty boys and fifty girls had been finalised for the Govardhan Bollywood Talent Hunt, based on photographs that they had sent in. Amrit had received an email notifying him that he had been selected for the contest, and had been sent a script that he had to come prepared with to deliver at the talent hunt. Amrit had held his breath as he opened the email attachment to reveal what the script was. He had been thoroughly relieved to see that it was a romantic scene where he is professing his love for a girl, and not a sad scene where he would be required to shed tears. Romance was his strong point, and Amrit intended to really exploit the piece of good fortune that had come his way in the form of that romantic scene. Now, up on the stage, Amrit rolled out the lines as he had practised them ferociously over the last two days, each word delivered with the precision of a master. Amrit would have to pull out all the stops if he had to crack this one. The best acting talent from all over India was there at the contest today, the winner assured a launch in a Bollywood movie produced by Govardhan Motion Pictures. The judges for the Govardhan Bollywood Talent Hunt included a famous actress from the past, a film director, a film journalist and an executive from Govardhan Motion Pictures. Through the glare of the lights focussed on him, Amrit could make out the judges seated in the front row, as they carefully watched every nuance of his performance, as he enacted the scene solo on the stage, imagining a partner. Of course, in Amrit's mind, the imaginary partner was Sapna. Just as he switched into actor mode, opening up his mind's eye to actually *believe* that he was speaking to Sapna, everything fell in place. His body language, the play of words, the look in his eyes, the dimples flashing as he cruised over the playful words in the script, and then turning serious, as he mouthed the passionate portions – everything happened automatically, just as Guruji had said it would.

"Wow! This man can act!" VJ Vijay strolled back on stage leading the audience in a round of applause as Amrit finished his lines with a flourish. Amrit smiled, bowing to the judges and the audience, soaking in the applause.

"Now … can he also dance?" VJ Vijay challenged. The audition also required Amrit to perform a Bollywood dance number. Song and dance are an integral part of all Bollywood movies. Anyone serious about a career in Bollywood had to be proficient in dancing, Bollywood style dancing. With singing, an actor could get away because all songs in Bollywood films are sung by background singers, with the actor merely lip syncing along. There is no such substitution formula when it comes to dancing. The actor and actress have to dance. Maybe one day, computer technology would advance enough to have expert dancers proxy for the actors, and the actor's face added later on using computer graphics technology. Until then, actors had to do the dancing. If you didn't know how to dance, you could kiss your Bollywood career goodbye. The song on which Amrit would have to dance had deliberately been kept a mystery, perhaps a technique used by the judges to see how good and spontaneous a dancer each candidate was. As the music drifted out of the large speakers placed backstage, Amrit automatically began to sway to the music, his thoughts drifting back to the first dance class at the Academy.

"Boys and girls," began Muhammad Akbar, "today is your first dance lesson with me at the Anil Taneja Academy. Today, I will not teach you any steps or movements. I just want to see you dance."

Muhammad Akbar was the best dance master in Bollywood. He had trained the best of the best.

"First, I want to ask you, who is the best dancer in the world?" Muhammad asked the class.

There were blank looks. Then, suddenly, Shiv Shankar Pandey spoke up, "Amitabh Bachchan."

Everybody laughed.

"Silence. No, it's not Amitabh Bachchan." Muhammad said.

"Anybody else?"

"Prabhudeva?" Meghna guessed.

"No. Closer than Amitabh Bachchan though. But it is not Prabhudeva." Muhammad smiled.

Nobody seemed to know.

"Everytime you dance, think of him. He is the best dancer in the universe – Shiva. Nataraj." Muhammad clasped his hands in a sign of reverence.

"*Anandtandava* – Shiva's dance of bliss – unites two aspects: inner tranquillity and outside activity. As a dancer, you must strive for that ultimate. On the inside, be tranquil – still – and on the outside, active. It is a paradox, but a connection is possible between the two. Today, I want you to dance keeping that in mind. I am not going to give you any steps. I will play the music. Listen to the music. And do what the music tells you to do. Remember, tranquillity inside, activity outside. I want you to open up and express yourselves via dance. I will play a song, and I want you to dance to the music. Let your body pick up the beat and be moved by it. Forget about steps and choreography. Just move with the music. Okay."

"You, Prabhudeva" Muhammad pointed to Meghna. "And you, Amitabh Bachchan," he pointed to Shiv Shankar Pandey. "You two come here, in the centre. Hold hands. The rest of you, sit down and watch."

Muhammad placed Meghna and Shiv standing facing each other, holding hands. "Now, you two, I will be playing a song. I want you to dance to it. Keep in mind two things. Dance to the music. Listen." Muhammad cupped his hand around his ear, to emphasise '*Listen.*' "Ears are a very important part of dancing. And second thing, dance with your partner. This is not a solo dance. You are dancing with a partner. So be in sync. Express yourselves via dance. I want to see passion. Okay, ready, start."

Muhammad hit the PLAY button and sat down next to the boombox at the front of the class. Dance music pumped out of the speakers. Shiv immediately took off as soon as the music started – freeing his hands from Meghna's grip, and started twirling around in a circle, doing a bhojpuri one-legged hop dance. Meghna was shocked as she tried to match Shiv's odd dance, which was totally out of sync with the music. On seeing Shiv break into this most unusual dance, the whole class erupted into laughter. The laughter had an encouraging effect on Shiv, for he began dancing even more vigorously, and totally out of sync with the music and his partner, pumping his hands in the air and gyrating his body as if he were receiving electric shocks. Meghna looked on with horror, trying desperately to coordinate her moves with

Shiv's – torn between trying to follow Shiv's out of sync steps or do her own thing. The class members, seated, were enjoying the show, and cheered Shiv on, who, encouraged beyond belief, now shifted from wild-beast style bhojpuri dancing and started going through his whole repertoire of Amitabh Bachchan inspired steps. Steps from his famous holi numbers, party numbers, running-around-trees numbers – all of Amitabh Bachchan's popular steps were on view now. Shiv had gone totally berserk and was now oblivious to the music, cheered on by the laughter and whistling of the crowd, which was enjoying watching Shiv make a complete buffoon of himself. Before Shiv could transition to a Bachchan-style bhangra step, Muhammad hit the STOP button on the boombox.

"Hey! Do you have ears?" Muhammad scolded Shiv. "What did I tell you? Listen to the music." Muhammad again cupped his hand around his ear. "And be in sync with your partner. You did neither. I said passion, not Bachchan." The class erupted in laughter. Shiv's obsession with Bachchan was now a running joke in the class.

"Quiet. Both of you sit down." Muhammad trained his eyes on the seated students now, trying to pick another pair. "You," said Muhammad, pointing to Amrit. "And you," he said, pointing to Sapna.

"Okay now you two try. Remember, the two things I said. Listen to the music." Muhammad cupped his hand around his ear. "And be in sync with you partner. Dance with passion."

Amrit stood there facing Sapna. Sapna took a stylish step forward as Muhammad hit the PLAY button and came closer to Amrit. A spell came over Amrit; in the presence of such beauty and grace, he got inspired. Eyes still locked with Sapna's, Amrit instinctively placed an arm on her back and dipped her; she responding to his touch like a well-trained mare. The song's tempo began to pick up, and so did Amrit and Sapna's steps. They were so marvellously in step and graceful in tandem. The song quickened in beat. Amrit swung Sapna around and spun her around like a ballerina. He dipped forward, holding Sapna in a passionate hold and lowered her to the ground, his powerful arms bearing her delicate weight and she followed, trusting him completely not to let her fall, and in sync with the tempo he pulled her up at the last moment, always maintaining eye contact. Slowly, their dance began to take a life of its own, a most beautiful and graceful dance. There was silence in the class; a strange spell had been cast over everyone, as they watched, completely absorbed in this exquisite dance which looked rehearsed and choreographed, whereas in reality it was totally spontaneous.

Eyes still locked on to each other, Amrit pulled Sapna up into the air and then twirled her around his back, turning around in tandem to hold both her hands, fully in sync with the music. As the music came to an end, Sapna and Amrit ended with a graceful twist and were still looking at each other. The class was spellbound. They had just seen a magnificent performance, totally spontaneous and unrehearsed. Meghna broke the silence by clapping her hands, "Wow!" There was a round of applause, true adoration. Muhammad Akbar clapped too.

There was roaring applause as Amrit finished his dance and walked off the stage, making way for the next contestant called upon by VJ Vijay. Amrit knew he had nailed it – both the acting bit and the dancing bit. *Yes!* Amrit punched the air as he descended the stage steps. Actors know when they have done a good job, and Amrit knew he had done well here. Of course, with this kind of competition, he wondered if his best was good enough to win the Govardhan Bollywood Talent Hunt and land him that coveted leading role in a Govardhan Motion Pictures movie.

Amrit was one of the last contestants, so he decided to hang around to watch the remaining contestants perform, and see how they did. The one to perform after him was a popular male model from the fashion world, but he seemed rather wooden to Amrit, especially when he danced. After that came a pretty girl who had appeared in several TV serials, who seemed spontaneous and delivered her lines well, and also did a good job with the dance portion of the audition. Her body movements were especially rythmic and well rounded, making Amrit wonder if she had been trained in Bharatnatyam. Amrit felt she had a chance, and wondered what it would be like to work with her.

The contest now over, Amrit headed to the men's room. He wanted to wash his face. It had been a nervous last few hours. First, with Inspector Gaitunde, and then, the charged performance on stage. He wanted to cool down.

In the men's room, Amrit was surprised to find VJ Vijay.

"Hey dude, you were cool!" VJ Vijay greeted Amrit.

"Thanks, VJ Vijay." Amrit turned the tap on, and dabbed his face with some cool water, and then looked up at VJ Vijay in the bathroom mirror.

"So, what does it really mean to be *cool*?"

"Dude, cool just *is,* maa'n! You know what it's, it's cooool ... like kinda from the gut ... it just *is* maa'n...'know vat I mean?" VJ Vijay did the yo-thing with his hands. "Peace bro!"

"So, is Amitabh Bachchan *cool*?" Amrit asked, as he soaped his hands, still not sure what VJ Vijay's VJ gibberish meant.

"Oh yeah, loads maa'n! Loads! He's the big cool…with a capital B." VJ Vijay did a little dance and then came to a stop, doing another *yo* with his hands.

"But Amitabh doesn't do the *yo;* he talks straight, walks straight, fights straight…. How about Mahatma Gandhi … is he *cool*?" Amrit asked.

"Hey dude don't get o'all political and o'all maa'n … chill maa'n …don't bust my nuts fellow … here … pull on a reefer 'n chil with the homies…" VJ Vijay passed Amrit a joint which he had pulled out of his pocket. Amrit politely refused. VJ Vijay lit the marijuana cigarette and took a deep drag from it. Then, he patted Amrit's back, and with a glazed look in his eyes, blurted out words mixed with pot smoke,

"It's all good maa'n … all good … you're cool."

"Thanks. So, when do we get the results?" Amrit asked, drying his face and hands with a paper towel.

"Soon … maa'n … soooon…" The marijuana made its way into VJ Vijay's body, visibly relaxing him, hampering his speech, as he slumped down along the bathroom wall, crossing his legs to sit down on the floor in a sloppy yogic posture, pulling deep on the joint several times. In a few seconds VJ Vijay was spaced out, his eyes barely staying open, his body a loose mangle of arms and legs.

Amrit nodded a goodbye to VJ Vijay, which remained unacknowledged, and walked out of the bathroom, still unsure what 'cool' really meant. Of the three – VJ Vijay, Amitabh Bachchan and Mahatma Gandhi – Amrit certainly didn't know who fit the definition best.

CHAPTER 7

Sapna was on a beach in Mauritius. She was shooting the climax of her movie, which was a supernatural thriller. It was a one-hero, two-heroine project. Tamanna Kapoor was the other heroine in the movie. Tamanna was playing a ghost who had fallen in love with Sapna's husband. She had lured him to a beach in order to make love to him. If she succeeded, as per a boon provided to her by the gods, she would get reincarnated into Sapna's body, and thereafter lead a happy life with her man, exorcising Sapna's soul from her body and turning it into a wandering ghost. Sapna had dreamt of this happening and had come to the beach to disrupt Tamanna's plan. So, the sequence involved Sapna, Tamanna and Sapna's husband. Sapna's husband was being played by the veteran actor Mahendra, who couldn't make it to the shoot due to chest pains. Poor Mahendra, who had turned sixty-six this year, was still playing twenty-five-year-old characters on screen, having just got a facelift from a renowned plastic surgeon in New York. Now, it appeared, he would also need a heart bypass, and would be out of action for a few months. The producers of the movie had decided to go ahead with the half-finished movie anyway, planning to shoot Mahendra's bits later on a Mumbai beach. It might look a little jarring, but the producer didn't want to abandon the project after having sunk in so much money already. Besides, the director had assured the producer that by using some clever editing and shot-taking techniques, he would be able to manage so that the end product would look just fine.

The scene to be shot was that Tamanna, or rather Tamanna's ghost, dressed in a rather skimpy white nightgown, would be singing a love ballad for Mahendra on the beach, with the aim of having sex with him and achieving her salvation. Sapna, on the other hand, would be hiding behind rocks and watching the whole thing, trying to figure out how to keep her husband from Tamanna's seductive ways, who would be walking along with Tamanna on the beach, gradually falling into her trap as the song progressed. Sapna would let the song finish, and only then stop Tamanna.

Tamanna Kapoor was infamous in Bollywood for being bitchy. She was very difficult to work with. She threw tantrums. And she was especially concerned and worried about being overshadowed by other actresses. Since this was a two-heroine project, it was important for Tamanna that she looked better than Sapna. Now, for most people, that would translate into doing your best. But not for Tamanna. Tamanna had to actively make sure that Sapna was let down. She had to take an interest in what Sapna was wearing, what her makeup was like, what her lines were in a particular scene, etcetera, etcetera.

When Tamanna found out that Sapna was going to wear a bikini in the song sequence about to be shot, a chill ran down her spine. *Oh lord! She will steal the show! She will look better than me. People will say she is better. No way!*

Tamanna immediately summoned the director of the movie.

Tamanna: "Why is Sapna wearing a bikini?"

Director: "Tamannaji, because she has come for swimming, that's why."

Tamanna: "Then why am I also not wearing a bikini?"
Director: "Because you are dignified. You are trying to seduce. You must look classy."

Tamanna: "Well if *I* have to seduce, then shouldn't *I* be the one wearing the bikini?"

Director: "Madam, the art director wants it this way. Trust me you will look most amazing in the scene. I will shoot you brilliantly!"

Tamanna: "No. I think I should also wear a bikini. Or Sapna should also wear what I am wearing."

Director: "Madam please don't change. Shot is almost ready."

Tamanna: "Change it or I'm calling packup."

Director: "Okay ... okay ... I will adjust. You don't worry Madam."

Packup was a nuclear threat; a trump card used by stars to blackmail when they wanted their way. The bigger the star, the bigger the danger of him or her calling *packup* and walking away from the sets, leaving the director and producer twiddling their thumbs, precious time and money wasted.

There was a lot of commotion following Tamanna's threat. The director made an urgent phone call on his mobile to the art director, who was in Mumbai. Then, after some hectic words on the phone, the director hung up, and went over to the producer and had a heated exchange with him. The producer now called the art director on his phone. There was a heated exchange between the art director and the producer. Then, the director got on the phone again with the art director. Finally, the director, the producer and the art director all agreed on something. The director now walked up to where Tamanna was seated, this time, with Sapna.

Director: "Tamannaji, everything is worked out. Sapnaji is also going to wear a white nightgown. No bikinis. Is that okay?"

Tamanna: "You are changing the dresses? Oh, well. You're the director. You know best. Let's shoot. Is the shot ready?"

Director: "Yes, Madam. Excellent! Excellent! Please come!"

Sapna had no idea what had just happened. The bitchy Tamanna had robbed her the chance of wearing a bikini on screen and letting her show off her lovely body and get one up on Tamanna. Petty as it was, it was important for people like Tamanna. Bollywood actresses' reputations are everything for them. Once they are stars, they are not actors. Tantrums, not the necessities of the script and the character, determine what they wear, what they say. In due course, Sapna would learn too.

After the day's shoot, Sapna decided to go to the beach for a walk. Even though she had been shooting outdoors all day long at the beach, she still longed to be by the sea. She strolled down the white sandy beach of the Hilton Mauritius Resort & Spa, looking at the sun coming down across the vast Indian Ocean. An evening breeze was blowing through her jet black tresses, as she pushed a few strands back from her eyes. She had just taken off her makeup with an astringent and the breeze felt cool on her freshly cleansed face. Her thoughts went back to the beach at Madh Island, and to that magical night with Amrit. Sapna dialled Amrit's number on her mobile phone.

"Hi Amrit!" Sapna's excited voice came over the phone.

"Hi Sapna." Amrit sounded preoccupied.

"Are you busy?" Sapna asked.

"No no. Tell me, what's up?" Amrit tried to sound upbeat.

"Nothing. Nothing really. I was just thinking of you … was really missing you, so I thought I'd call." Sapna kicked a little pebble playfully with her toe.

"How's work going in Mauritius?" Amrit asked.

"Okay." Sapna didn't sound too happy.

"Why? Are you not happy?" Amrit quizzed.

"I could be more happy by being with you. You know that, don't you, Amrit?" Sapna was beginning to sound very sentimental.

There was silence. Sapna continued.

"Amrit, have you ever thought of settling down? Maybe move to Bangalore, take up that computer job, start a family…"

There was silence again from Amrit's side.

"I miss you, Amrit." Sapna's voice sounded heavy.

"Sapna, look, we've talked about this before. I know you want me to quit all this and move to Bangalore; we both get married, settle down there. But I *can't* right now. I need to stay the course. I can't…can't get married now." Amrit sounded irritated.

"Why not? Do you not love me?" Sapna said in a low, insecure voice.

"This is ridiculous, Sapna. You're always trying to corner me. Look, I need space. I need to concentrate on my career right now. Besides, married actors are not as popular in Bollywood, you know that. We've got to do what's good for our careers right now."

A cool breeze blew in from the Indian Ocean and made Sapna shiver. She felt cold.

"Listen, Sapna, I've to go now. Have to rush for an audition. It's for a main lead in a primetime show! Will talk later. Okay bye." Amrit hung up the phone.

Sapna wrapped her arms around her body and continued walking down the beach, thinking of Amrit. *What has overcome him? He seems to have become so distant, so insensitive to my feelings. Maybe he doesn't love me at all. Maybe we shouldn't have...*

A bird like chirp from her Nokia mobile broke her thoughts.

"Hello." Sapna was hoping Amrit would call back!

"Well hello Sapna! This is Zaeed Zakaria! How are you?"

"Who? How did you get my number?"

"Zaeed Zakaria ... Zakaria Industries ... I got your number through a friend ... I hope I'm not impinging upon your privacy?" Zaeed said in a crisp Oxford accent.

"No." Sapna realised who he was. Zaeed Zakaria. Heir to one of India's oldest and largest business empires; and Mumbai's most eligible bachelor.

"Well good! You know Sapna I've been trying to get in touch with you for a while. I am a huge fan of yours...but you probably have millions already, so I thought I'd wait for them to make their calls first."

Sapna giggled. Zaeed heard her giggle.

"You must be looking absolutely smashing right now. I know how you look smiling. I've seen you in that toothpaste commercial."

Sapna giggled a little more, this time a little more cautiously to not be audible.

"Listen Sapna, I don't know if this is in order. I happen to be in Mauritius – on business – and heard you're on the island too. I know this place that serves fantastic seafood ... and it's not caloric, trust me. Could I have the pleasure of having you dine with me tonight?"

Sapna didn't know what to say. This was Zaeed Zakaria. Any woman of marriageable age in India would die for such an offer from one of the country's most eligible bachelors. Mothers would go on pilgrimages to the Himalayas for their daughters to receive such a phone call. And here she was, undecided, keeping the billionaire on hold.

"Yes."

"Brilliant. I'll pick you up at 8 from the Hilton lobby. See ya!"

Amrit now looked forward to every scene he had with Romesh Paul. They had developed a great on-screen chemistry, and Amrit wanted more of that magic. Romesh Paul today, however, was down with a terrible case of influenza. He had been running high fever, as he sat at the makeup table, having base powder rubbed on his face.

"The under eyes; make sure you fill in the under eyes," Romesh instructed the makeup man. Main stars of long-running Bollywood soaps almost all sported dark circles under their eyes. Constant eighteen plus hour shifts, for seven days a week, often for months without a break, did bring on the dark circles. Romesh had been the main lead actor in *Saas Ka Sindoor* for the third year running now. The longer an actor stayed in this line of work, the deeper and darker the furrows under the actor's eyes became. The makeup artists were experts at filling them up — a bit of skin coloured makeup base, and then some powder, and voila! Sleepy, puffy under eyes were turned into a bright, just-woken up glare.

But today Romesh was especially run down, and that's why he was asking for extra help under his eyes. He had been shooting non-stop for eighteen hours. Vinta had cast him in another Jai Jai soap, another daily, and that now meant Romesh was pulling two back to back shifts as he tried to juggle the two roles. He had just arrived at the sets of *Saas Ka Sindoor* for a twelve-hour shift, after a full eighteen-hour schedule at the previous show. Usually, he could handle these back-to-backs, but with his influenza and fever, running nose and sore throat, plus the body breaking pains that accompany influenza, Romesh was at break point. He could barely stay awake, and even tea and coffee seemed not to work any more. He looked really run down.

"The show must go on!" quipped Amrit, smiling and trying to raise Romesh's morale.

"Young man, the show *will* go on." Romesh replied. The makeup man was now filling his under eyes. Romesh shut his eyes. He knew what he was talking about. Almost three years ago, when *Saas Ka Sindoor* had become a big national hit, and Romesh was the star of every dinnertime TV audience in India, he had once had to shoot for twenty-four hours, non-stop. Partly high on instant success, the bloatedness of the head that comes from having people point at you when you walk on the streets or recognise you when you enter a shopping mall, as the star from *Saas Ka Sindoor*, Romesh had let out a tirade at the executive producer of the show who had pushed Romesh to the limit.

"This is ridiculous. I am an artist, not a machine. I have been shooting non-stop for eighteen hours now. I am just blurting out my lines, barely awake. And you want me to do another six hours? Do you realise that I am also running high fever? Is this a bloody sweatshop or what? I don't get paid enough for this nonsense."

Romesh's words were repeated verbatim to Vinta in a matter of minutes by one of her on-set informants. Nandini, Vinta's second in command, was on the sets shortly thereafter, and sat Romesh down alone in the makeup room, and handed him a modified script.

"Read it." Nandini had curtly said as she thrust the script under a confused Romesh Paul's nose.

Romesh picked up the paper and read it. The script had changed. It showed that Romesh's character would be involved in a serious car accident. The accident would be so bad that his face would be badly scarred. He would then undergo plastic surgery and get a new face. Romesh was sleepy but not that sleepy to miss what this change in the script implied. *He was going to be replaced by another actor! Shit!* Accidents followed by plastic surgery were Vinta's pet ploy to change actors who had become too big for their boots. She would simply draft another actor to play the character played by Romesh, and it would all look justified in the show because of the accident-plastic surgery plot twist.

"Accident? Why?" Romesh quizzed Nandini, pretending not to know what was going on here.

"Romesh, Vinta wants to replace you."

"Why?"

"I don't know." Nandini shrugged her shoulders, playing her own game of pretence.

A shiver ran down Romesh's spine and all the sleepiness vanished in a second. He made quick mental calculations. Whatever Romesh Paul was today, was all due to his role in *Saas Ka Sindoor*. If tomorrow, he was replaced by another actor, the world would soon forget him. In television, out of sight was out of mind. He had just bought a new one bedroom flat, and a small car, all on a bank loan. Without the regular Jai Jai pay cheques, he would surely default on the mortgage payments for his flat and his car – he would lose them! He would lose everything! Oh no!

It was the end of the world for him. What had he done? The television ratings for *Saas Ka Sindoor* were healthy, surely it wasn't his acting. Oh! It must be what he just blurted out to the executive producer a little while ago. Oh no! That had got relayed to Vinta. *I see; this was because of that outburst. God!* He had to mend fences here, and quickly.

"Look Nandini, I am sorry if I said something wrong. I didn't mean to. I was just very tired and sick and you know…"

"Call Vinta." Nandini cut him short and thrust her cellphone in his face. "Tell her this." Nandini pressed a speed-dial button.

"Yes," came the cool and calculating voice of Vinta from the other end.

"Vintaji, Romesh Paul here. I am really sorry if I offended you. I didn't mean to. I was just very tired, running fever, have been shooting non-stop you see…"

"Listen motherfucker." Vinta cut Romesh off impatiently. "Always remember one thing. You are *nothing*. Absolutely nothing. Not even worth the drop of stray semen your mother conceived you from, you understand? I make and break actors. Actors are my slaves. You are just a slave. When I say shoot now, you shoot now. Do you get me?" Vinta paused for breath.

"There are thousands who line up outside my office every day begging for work. You are lucky. So just thank goddess Kaali and work. Or else I will discard you like a fly that has dropped into a cup of milk and chuck you out. Understood?"

There was shocked silence from Romesh.

"Understood, you sisterfucker?" Vinta yelled.

"Yes. Yes. Understood Vintaji. Understood." Romesh replied, his hands trembling as he held the cellphone.

"Good. Remember, this is your final warning. Give the phone to Nandini."

Nandini took the phone, keeping her eyes on Romesh, and replied "okay" a couple of times, and then hung up. Putting the cellphone away, Nandini took the script from Romesh's hand. Romesh was still shaking. Nandini tore up the script and announced, "No accident. We shoot as per the original script," eyes still on Romesh, as she enjoyed the tormented look on the poor actor's face.

Relieved that he was still part of the show, and that his life had not come to ruin, Romesh let out a deep gasp. From that day on, he had stayed a noble serf in the service of Queen Vinta, just the way she wanted it, just as every surviving actor at Jai Jai Productions did.

Today, even with searing temperature and sleep deprivation, Romesh did not complain.

"Romeshji, you are such a professional and dedicated actor. It's truly inspiring. Even in this condition, with high fever, no rest, you choose to shoot. Amazing." Amrit remarked, truly impressed with what seemed like voluntary dedication.

Romesh let out a chuckle as he opened his eyes and looked at his face in the mirror. The makeup artist was putting on the final touches to his face. *What does this boy know, still wet behind the ears!* Romesh chuckled a little more, and then, looking through the mirror at Amrit, said, "The show *will* go on!"

Puneet Arora had been part of the cast of *Saas Ka Sindoor* for a year now. A native of Delhi, he had moved to Mumbai four years ago. After three years of struggle, and unemployment, he had finally managed to land a role in *Saas Ka Sindoor*. Amrit and Puneet had found that they had a common love for tandoori chicken, a north Indian delicacy hard to find in a predominantly vegetarian Mumbai. Over many late night tandoori chickens at painstakingly discovered roadside stalls, Puneet and Amrit had forged a bond that was now beyond their culinary common interest. Puneet played a distant cousin of Romesh Paul's in *Saas Ka Sindoor*, and though Amrit and he were yet to appear on screen together, Amrit always liked hanging out with Puneet whenever he was on the sets. It reminded him of home.

"Hey Amrit, don't tell anyone, but you've got to watch out for Vinta." Puneet chomped down on a chicken leg, grilled red in the tandoor and garnished with spices and lemon juice. "She is absolutely crazy man. I shouldn't be saying this, if one of her spies hears this, they will throw me out of Jai Jai."

"Relax *yaar*, don't worry. There are no spies here." Amrit said, pointing to the wide empty road where the tandoori stall was located. Amrit and Puneet had driven down to this roadside stall, which was a few kilometres away from the shoot, on Amrit's RX100. The tandoori chicken was tasty; the drive had been worth it.

"I won't tell anyone. Why are you so scared anyway?" Amrit bit on a breast piece.

"No dude, you don't know. Vinta is like Hitler. And you know how hard it is to find work. There are thousands who want your spot. Vinta knows that. That's why she behaves like this. *Saali kutiya*. Do you know what happened once?"

"What?" Amrit mumbled.

"Vinta once slapped a director on the sets."

"No! *Kya keh raha hai?*"

"Yes! God promise. She slapped the director of the serial. While the shoot was going on; in front of everyone." Puneet looked up from the chicken leg he was munching on.

"But ... why?" Amrit asked, squeezing some lemon juice on his piece of chicken.

"You won't believe it. Because the director changed a word in the script. He felt a word was not appropriate, it was taking away from the meaning of the scene, so he replaced it with another word. Vinta happened to be watching from the sides, must have slipped in quietly. She just went up to the director, without even saying hi or anything, straightaway gave him a tight slap on the face. In front of the whole cast and the crew. *Slap!*"

"No way! That's terrible." Amrit spat out a piece of chicken bone.

"Yes. The poor chap was in tears. I mean, this director was no kid, he was a veteran from the National School of Drama, an old timer with grey hair and a grey beard. He had directed serials for the last 15 years. The man knows more about drama than the whole of Vinta's *khandaan* put together. Poor chap." Puneet chewed slowly.

"So, what did *he* do?" Amrit threw the eaten bones away, feeling angry on behalf of the director.

"What *could* he do?" Puneet said with a show of resignation, "He washed his face and returned to complete the scene, with the script unchanged."

"What?!! He carried on! I can't believe it." Amrit was flabbergasted.

"Amrit, my friend, he has a family to feed. He's not like you, who can write software programmes as a freelancer and make money; or quit anytime and go and join that software company in Hyderabad. We people have families and responsibilities."

"In Bangalore." Amrit corrected Puneet.

"Yes, whatever, Bangalore. It's tough here man. We are all replaceable. Jobs are scarce. I was jobless for three years. I have seen the ugly side of the struggle. *Kuttae ki zindagi hai.*"

Amrit felt uneasy. He also felt enraged. The scene playing out in his head. The old director, standing there, holding his grey beard, embarrassed, tears in his eyes, having to swallow his pride.

"Puneet, this Mumbai is a strange town *yaar*. This kind of a thing can only happen in Mumbai." Amrit handed a hundred rupee note to the roadside food-stall operator.

"What do you mean?" Puneet asked.

"You're from the north, from Delhi. You know what I mean. Do you think Vinta could have got away with such a thing in Delhi? Slapping a grown man, in front of everyone, like this, dishonouring him. If she had as much as *tried* to slap a man in Delhi, he would have tracked her down later and stuck a bamboo up her ass! Bitch!" Amrit's blood began to boil. The tandoori chicken had instigated his north-Indian tendencies.

"See that's the problem with north India. Too hot blooded. That's why it is so unsafe out there. So much crime and violence." Puneet bit on the last of the chicken.

"You want to know something about crime? You know why this goon business thrives in Mumbai?" Amrit asked.

"Why?"

"Because Mumbai culture is very *bindaas*. You know these goons failed miserably in north India. They said they would collect *hafta* from all shopkeepers and street hawkers on the streets of Delhi.... They had to give up, you know why?"

"Why?"

"Because even a bloody nondescript street hawker in Delhi selling vegetables is willing to stand up to these goons. When the goons went asking for *hafta*, these hawkers rolled up their sleeves and stood up to fight the goons. Each one of them, individually, stood up to the *goondas* and told them on their face, 'you sisterfucker, if you have drunk your mother's milk, you come and confront me. I am not going to give you a single paisa as *hafta*. I'll cut off your balls and give those to you if you want.'"

"Really?" Puneet threw the final chicken bone away.

"Yes. The goons had to give up."

"Man! People in north India have too much free time on their hands. Always looking for a fight. People in Mumbai are too busy, too business oriented, too *bindaas*. A vegetable hawker here would say, 'okay, let me pay the *hafta* and avoid the confrontation. Let me compromise. I'll make it back in a few hours of business.' But no, the guys back home in the north will say, 'Let business go to hell, let's pick a fight. C'mon! Let's fight.'" Puneet hopped on his toes like a boxer, his hands held in fists over his face.

"Stop it!" Amrit said, "At least people there live with their heads held high." Amrit was still feeling enraged about the director who was publicly slapped by Vinta.

"What head held high my friend?" Puneet straightened up. "Women can't get out of their homes after dark in north India. It's too unsafe for them. What head held high? It is a shame. Here, in Mumbai, women can safely roam the streets even at two in the morning. Look! Look!" Puneet pointed to a group of girls walking across the street. "This ... this is head held high! Look at your watch. Would you find women on the roads at this time in Delhi or in Amritsar? No chance."

"You've been in Mumbai too long, Puneet! But you are right, Mumbai is more cosmopolitan. Credit given where credit is due." Amrit shook his head in agreement.

"*Chalo*, let's go. Dinner break is over. Not bad tandoori chicken – for Mumbai, that is!" Amrit smiled, as he brought the RX100 to life. "I still have one scene left for the night. The AD must be looking for me. Hurry up Puneet."

As Amrit was about to turn on the ringer of his phone, he noticed three missed calls on his mobile phone from an unknown number. During shoots, Amrit generally put his phone on silent mode. All the three missed calls were from the same number. Amrit looked at his watch; it was 11:30 at night. He had just finished his last scene for the day for *Saas Ka Sindoor*. He debated whether he should return the call. In any other normal field of occupation, 11:30 pm would be considered beyond office hours, but not in Bollywood, which was most active in the dark hours. Suddenly, Amrit's phone lit up; though still on silent mode, Amrit could see the number that was calling him. It was the same number as the one from which he had got those missed calls!

"Hello," Amrit said, excitedly.

To a struggling Bollywood actor, his mobile phone is *the* beacon of hope. The greatest fantasy of a Bollywood struggler is to receive that golden telephone call from a big producer wanting to sign him for his next big movie. So all calls, even missed ones, are taken very seriously. Missed calls from unknown numbers especially so – they add to the mystery and to the excitement – could they be from Yash Chopra or Subhash Ghai, or one of the other big movie producers in Bollywood?

"Am I speaking with Amrit?" a polished, delicate voice came over the speaker.

"Yes, this is Amrit." Excitement was evident in Amrit's voice.

"Amrit hi, this is Rajeev Chatterjee. I got your pictures and wanted to talk to you about casting in Tapan Grover's next movie."

Amrit's heart started beating faster. *Was this the golden call?*

"Yes." Amrit tried to sound very matter-of-fact.

"I wanted to meet you about that."

"Yeah, sure. Would love too." Amrit's mind was racing. He didn't want to sound too eager, yet he didn't want to pass on the chance to be cast in a Tapan Grover movie. There was one problem. He had a 7:30 am shift the next morning for *Saas Ka Sindoor*, which would probably run into the night again…

"When?" Amrit finally blurted out.

"Can you come now?" Rajeev Chatterjee asked.

Amrit looked at his watch again.

"Ahh … isn't it kind of late now? Would you prefer that I come sometime tomorrow…?"

"No. Right now is fine. It is urgent. I have to finalise tonight itself and Tapan is screen testing tomorrow."

Amrit was excited, and in two minds. The late night timing sounded odd. But then Bollywood was odd in its ways of functioning. Could he afford to let go of this potential opportunity?

"Okay. I've just gotten out of a shoot in Andheri East. Where are you located?"

"My office is in Versova. Take down the address."

Amrit scribbled the address and driving instructions on his pad.

"It'll take me twenty minutes to get there."

"See you." Rajeev hung up.

Amrit got on his RX100 and took off towards Versova. The night was cool and the sea breeze felt nice on his face, as he gunned the motor of the bike to full throttle. The excitement of possibility made even the dogs chomping on the wayside rubbish look happy. Even the homeless people asleep on the road divider that came into focus in the headlight of the RX100 looked so content and blissful, their heads resting against makeshift cobblestone pillows, their eyes shut in soothing calm. Hope is a great elevator and the hope of a big-banner movie break had suddenly elevated Amrit's spirits to a new high as he zipped through the relatively empty night streets of Mumbai.

Rajeev Chatterjee's office was on the first floor of a two-storied house in Versova's mixed slum area. Amrit had long given up judging Mumbai offices by what they looked like from the outside. Even the most nondescript and run down quarters housed big name producers. As Amrit walked up the stairs, he could hear the wooden planks creaking. It was an old house, perhaps an illegal construction – maybe part of the notorious Mumbai land-grab mafia land. Who cared? Even if Amrit was called to the centre of Dharavi slums to audition for a major role, he would do it.

Amrit knocked gently on the door, trying to be as quiet as possible so as not to disturb the neighbours.

"Coming," came a soft voice from inside.

Rajeev Chatterjee was a lightly built man, about five feet three inches tall, with a peculiar stub moustache, and short cropped hair. He was wearing a lilac coloured linen kurta, its buttons opened till mid-chest, revealing a thick gold chain. Amrit thought Rajeev reminded him of a thin Russian male ballerina he had once seen performing in a TV programme.

"Hi!" Rajeev greeted with a broad smile and invited Amrit to come in. He looked happy to see Amrit.

Once inside, Amrit couldn't imagine the transformation. Rajeev's office was a fifteen feet by fifteen feet psychedelic haven, like something out of the 1960s flower-power era. The furniture was minimalist – two bright red leather bean bags on the floor, next to which was a mattress laid out on the ground, covered in pink bedsheets, with matching pink cushions. There was a lava lamp next to the mattress. The lighting in the room was subdued, like that in a chic lounge bar, coming mostly from two red coloured huge heart-shaped aromatic candles that were placed on matching red pedestal stands. In the corner, on the floor, was a Bose Wave music system, playing techno-trance music on low volume. A bundle of incense sticks bellowed smoke from a corner of the room, giving the room a disco-like smoky feel, and a heavily sweet, musky odour. The walls too, were painted in a light shade of red, giving the room a warm reddish glow.

For a moment Amrit felt he had come to the wrong address; but then he spotted two of his portfolio photographs scattered carelessly on the mattress. Obviously, Rajeev had just been studying them carefully and was expecting Amrit. *So many missed calls, so much urgency.* Amrit's mind was ticking. *This guy seems serious to get me. But why?* He wondered what the role was about. He hoped it was the main lead, and not some sidey, character role. Amrit brushed aside negative thoughts and tried to stay positive. Maybe this is how Bollywood works. *This is how new stars are discovered! Maybe Rajeev had seen the next Bollywood star in me!* Amrit took a deep, sweet-smelling breath, feeling upbeat and trying to control his excitement.

"Please. Please have a seat." Rajeev pointed Amrit in the general direction of the bean bags and the mattress. "Anywhere."

Amrit settled down on a bean bag. He would have preferred a chair, because the bean bag hardly provided any support. Amrit sunk in awkwardly, the centre of gravity of his body falling backwards, as he planted his feet on the ground and tried to stay balanced, using his knees to anchor his body. Amrit felt like he was dangling from the side of a hammock. Rajeev came and settled down on the mattress besides Amrit, sitting cross legged, and took the photographs on the mattress in his hands and began flipping through them like through a deck of cards.

"You are a very handsome man." Rajeev eyed the photos. "From Punjab ... Punjabi men are handsome, strong men."

"Thank you." Amrit replied, shifting his weight forward and trying to sit up straight.

"So, you're working for Jai Jai Productions right now." Rajeev continued.

"Yes. In fact, I was just leaving the set after a shoot for Jai Jai when you called. Sorry I missed your calls; I usually keep my phone on silent mode during the shoots."

"No problem." Rajeev said out loud in a singsong way, as he put the photographs away and tapped Amrit's protruding left knee. Amrit felt slightly uncomfortable by the way in which Rajeev had touched him.

"You must be very tired. After a long day's work. Would you like something to drink?" Rajeev asked sweetly.

"Oh no. Thank you. Very kind of you." Amrit replied. He was eager to hear more about the Tapan Grover movie and the role.

"Oh come on. Don't be shy. Would you like something *hard?* Like vodka or whiskey?" Rajeev's emphasis on the word "hard" made Amrit feel uneasy. There was something terribly fishy about this guy.

Then, as if detecting Amrit's discomfort, Rajeev straightened himself up, looked at Amrit and said in a professional tone.

"You know Amrit, I am *very, very* close to Tapan Grover. He trusts me to do the casting for him. I have casted for all his movies."

Amrit nodded.

"And not just Tapan, for others too. I am a very influential casting agent. Just today I finalised a troupe of

Russian dancers. Those girls were so gorgeous. They are for a song and dance sequence in an upcoming David Dhawan film."

Rajeev paused, expecting Amrit to say something.

"Good. That is very good, Mr. Chatterjee." Amrit said, almost feeling obliged to say something.

"Call me Rajeev." The hand patted Amrit's left knee again, and this time stayed there for a few seconds.

Amrit's mind was racing. He was not at ease. Something told him there was something not right. *Aah! This Rajeev fellow is a homosexual! He's called me here for one purpose. Shit!* The truth suddenly dawned on Amrit. *What if he is as influential as he says he is?* Amrit didn't want to annoy Tapan Grover's casting agent. But he certainly did not want to offer his bum to this faggot, or have anything to do with his. Amrit was on full alert now. Thinking of a way to manoeuvre through this treacherous situation.

"You know Amrit, I get a lot of people who want a break in films, who are doing television serials, like you. They tell me, 'Rajeev, we are tired of working for Jai Jai, get us into the movies now, please.' So many." Rajeev said with a gentle, effeminate wave of his arm, which made Amrit think back to the Russian ballerina he had seen on TV.

"Tapan Grover is looking for a fresh face for an exciting role. My influence with Tapan is like a bottle of a very expensive perfume; I have to be very judicious where and how to use it. And for whom." Rajeev paused again, looking at Amrit with an expectant look in his eyes.

This time Amrit did not respond. Silence persisted.

"I will be straight with you, Amrit. What can you offer me so that I get you the role? I can give it to so many boys." Rajeev squinted his eyes, his mouth remained open.

"I'll give you more than your usual cut – ten per cent more." Amrit was hoping to drag this conversation to a financial track, hoping that Rajeev would bite the commercial carrot Amrit was dangling before him.

"No. No. Money isn't everything." Rajeev had now planted his hand on Amrit's knee again. This time, permanently. Amrit's body stiffened, conscious of an awkward touch by an awkward man. Rajeev now started massaging Amrit's thigh, moving up from the knee.

Bastard gay! He is exploiting struggling actors, in this sex-den of an office. Amrit felt the urge to land a strong punch on Rajeev's nose; that would certainly have altered the geography of his face for all times to come. Instead, he took deep, cleansing breaths, controlling his anger.

"If you entertain me, I promise I will get you the role. Promise." Rajeev's hand was now moving further up Amrit's thigh, as he tried to heave his twig of a body towards Amrit.

In a flash Amrit stood up, a movement so quick it frightened Rajeev Chatterjee.

"You've got the wrong man, Mr. Chatterjee. I am an actor. The day you need an actor, call me." Amrit turned and left, racing down the steps. He was angry. Angry for saying what he said. Angry for not saying more. Angry for not breaking Rajeev Chatterjee's jaw. Angry for being humiliated like this. Angry for finding himself in such a helpless situation. Angry for not having any connections in Bollywood. Angry that this is how the system worked. Just angry.

He kicked the RX100 to life, which also growled angrily, and the two sped off into the night.

CHAPTER 8

Udita and Mike Patel sat next to each other on the Picadilly Line tube. They had just landed at London's Heathrow Airport some time ago, and were now on their way to central London. This was the first time Udita Usgaonkar had ever been outside India. Hailing from a lower middle class family, Udita felt her dream was coming true. She was in London for a shoot! Wow! She had become a star! Her father, a lower level clerk in the Indian Railways, was at first reluctant to let her daughter travel abroad alone. Dressing up sexily was one thing, but leaving home for a month and that too totally alone was another matter. *What would people think? How will I get her married tomorrow?* All these questions had cropped up in his mind. But Mike Patel had gone to their humble one bedroom first floor flat in the Panchvati Lower Income Housing Society in Virar, and over a cup of very sweet tea, convinced Udita's father that her daughter was now a star and that it was perfectly normal for stars to travel abroad on work.

"Look at Aishwarya," said Mike to Udita's father as he lowered the cheap white porcelain cup from his lips, "she is already working in Hollywood. Our Indian girls are doing wonders these days. Udita has the same potential. You must not stop her from achieving her destiny, and from doing the country proud. Besides uncle, I am there *na*, like your son. No need to worry." Udita's father, a simple man, believing the smooth talking Mike Patel, had reluctantly given his consent.

The train stopped at Hammersmith, and looking at the tube map drawn on the carriage wall, Mike pointed out to Udita in the most brotherly fashion that they had one more stop to go before they reached Earl's Court, where they would get off. Mike knew that these first few days in London were crucial. He would have to win Udita's confidence, and then, very carefully, like a master craftsman, deliver her to Bandhoo Kumar's bed. Udita, meanwhile, felt she was living a dream. At Earl's Court, Mike and Udita got out of the train, took the lift to the top floor, and exited the station. Mike guided Udita through the streets of Kensington to the hotel where they were to stay. Udita noticed how different London was from India. "Wow! It is so pretty, so clean."

"Yes it is. Get used to it Udita. As a Bollywood star, you will be spending a lot of time in foreign countries. Get used to it!" Mike Patel smiled.

Udita was brimming with emotion. She had finally made it! Or so she thought. All Bollywood movies had large portions shot outside India, and the stars spent large chunks of their time away from the heat and dust and noise and pollution and chaos of India. Would she also become one of them? Just the thought of it gave Udita goosebumps. *Wow! I would get to see the world. Such a beautiful world! So unlike my native Mumbai. So pretty! So nice!*

For the next two days Mike Patel's only aim was to make sure Udita had the time of her life in London. Udita was told the rest of the cast and crew for the shoot had been delayed in Mumbai and would be arriving after two days, so they had two days to take in the sights and sounds of London. On day one, Mike took Udita to all the major tourist attractions. Buckingham Palace, The Big Ben, the Houses of Parliament, Madame Tussauds Wax Museum. After a fine three-course lunch at an Italian restaurant, he took Udita on an afternoon boat cruise on the river Thames. In the evening, he took her to watch a West End musical. "This is just like our Bollywood movies!" Udita had commented with excitement after watching the show – "with all the dancing and the singing!" Tomorrow, I will take you shopping, said Mike, as he bid Udita goodnight at the entrance of her hotel room. Mike's room was just adjacent to her's. The next morning, after a full English breakfast, Mike hailed a black cab and took Udita to Oxford Street. He handed her a wad of currency notes while in the taxi. "Five thousand pounds. Buy whatever you want. A heroine must be well dressed." With the money in hand, which Udita took reluctantly, she bought herself new dresses from Selfridges, lingerie from Marks & Spencer, bags and shoes from Morgan, perfumes from SuperDrug, eyeliners, mascaras, and all sorts of lotions and potions from The Body Shop…by the evening, she had blown the money. Udita was really on a high now, just the way Mike had planned. For a lower middle class girl from Virar, this was too much to digest too soon. She absolutely loved it! The addiction that money and its effects bring can be dangerous.

"Tonight, we'll dine at a very special place. The Ritz Carlton Hotel. It is truly exquisite. Look really nice. It's where the Queen of England dines." Announced Mike to

Udita. Udita nodded. Mikeji was such a nice man, she thought. She had total faith in him now. He had picked her out of a thousand girls at audition for the music video. He had convinced her father to let her come to London. And now, he had shown her the most wonderful time in London and had been so kind. She couldn't thank him enough. He was going to make her a star!

As they walked to their table at The Ritz Restaurant, Udita carried off her newly bought black lace backless Armani dress with ease. The white-gloved server led them to a corner table Mike had reserved. "This way sir, madam."

On a higher floor in the same impressive building of The Ritz Carlton Hotel, Bandhoo Kumar sat in Room 415 sipping Johnny Walker Blue Label Whiskey and smoking a Cohiba cigar, and looking out of the window at the traffic milling around Hyde Park corner. He was dressed in his trademark white kurta and *dhoti*. Politicians in India had to always *look* like the common man. Even when they were in London. They all wore the common man's clothes – handspun cotton clothes as prescribed by Mahatma Gandhi during the freedom struggle against British imperial rule in India. Gandhi and his ideals were long gone from the political landscape of India, but the white cotton clothes had stayed on as remnants of that long-forgotten era. For now, handspun cotton clothes, albeit bought from expensive designer shops in Delhi and made to look authentically rustic, are all that India's politicians have in common with the people they represented. Everything else about them is thoroughly uncommon. Behind closed doors, these politicians lived lives of great luxury, with every conceivable amenity available on the planet at their disposal. They were all corrupt; and had millions stashed away in anonymous bank accounts. To win an election in India, a politician needs millions; and once in power, the thing topmost in the politician's mind is to quickly recover that investment and make a fortune many times that amount. Paralysed by corrupt money and crime, politics in India has become a hideous cesspool in which only creatures such as Bandhoo Kumar thrived. And Bandhoo Kumar did epitomise the modern Indian politician – astute, two-faced and ruthless in seeking and using power.

About five feet tall, Bandhoo Kumar looked older than he was. Fat and balding, a lifestyle of excesses had taken a toll on his physique. Excessive eating, drinking, smoking, and all the tension and uncomfortable travel that came with being the leader of one of India's major political parties, and no exercise, had left him pudgy and grossly unattractive. That, of course, didn't matter, because Bandhoo Kumar didn't have to be attractive – he paid for sex – that is, when he didn't have it with his wife. Bandhoo Kumar was married, and to the outside world he was happily married, with two grown daughters who were also married and had children of their own. Not only did Bandhoo Kumar pay for sex, but he also paid for getting ready for sex. Suffering from erectile dysfunction, Bandhoo Kumar had turned impotent years ago. In order to get a worthwhile erection, he had to use a strong cocktail of drugs such as viagra and cialis. Where he lacked in potency he made up for in appetite – Bandhoo Kumar had a voracious appetite for sex and had bedded many a Bollywood starlets – all with the help of chemicals, of course. Today, as he sat on the sofa of his hotel room, he glanced at the two tablets of viagra lying in a little dish on his bedside table, and he hoped, that Mike Patel would be able to deliver tonight as promised.

Seated across the room from Bandhoo Kumar, dressed in an elegant Canali suit, and smoking a Monte Cristo cigar was the soft-spoken, extremely well groomed, middle-aged Hans Dietermund.

"More whiskey, Hans?" Bandhoo Kumar offered, as he poured himself another peg.

"Oh no, no, thank you sir." Hans replied in a heavily accented tone, placing a hand over his tumbler. Hans and Bandhoo Kumar had sipped whiskey many a times over the last twenty years. Hans had reason to be especially indebted to Bandhoo Kumar, for in the last two decades of their association, Bandhoo Kumar was directly responsible for Hans' meteoric rise at the Zurich Generale Private Bank. When the two men had first met, at a conference to alleviate poverty in the Third World at Buenos Aires, Argentina, Hans was an Assistant Manager in the private banking division of the giant Swiss bank that was a sponsor of the conference. Bandhoo Kumar was then a junior minister of state in the Ministry of Rural Development, Government of India. With the rise of Bandhoo Kumar's political graph, and the corresponding humongous increase in the ill-gotten wealth that comes with rise in a political position in India, Hans and his Swiss bank had also gained; for Bandhoo had funnelled all his thousands of millions of rupees in bribes, commissions and kickbacks to his numbered account maintained with Hans at Zurich Generale. With this kind of money flowing in, Hans' career graph at the bank grew by leaps and bounds, and he became a star banker, the youngest Managing Director in the three hundred-year history of the private bank. Both men shared a symbiotic bond of trust. Bandhoo knew his money was safe and anonymous with Hans; and Hans was only too happy for him and his bank to be serving as bankers to one of India's most prolifically corrupt politicians.

"There was a wire of three hundred million euros that came in this week into your account," Hans announced as he ashed his cigar. "What would you like me to do with it? The usual?"

"The usual," came Bandhoo Kumar's matter of fact reply. Hans nodded his head. He never asked where the money came from. He had a general idea. Bandhoo Kumar "usually" liked the money to be split three ways — one third invested in US Treasury Bonds, another one third put into gold, and the remaining third into a diversified multi-currency global mutual fund.

"Very well. I shall have it arranged through our brokers." Hans added, always professional, always obedient.

"How is business, Hans?" Bandhoo Kumar asked casually.

"Okay, can't complain. A lot of the Arab money that left after September 11 is now back. People realise Switzerland will always be a safe haven, no matter what happens. We don't buckle even to American pressure. They've tried. They've not even been able to trace the Nazi money, and it's been decades since World War II!" Hans chuckled, taking a final puff on his cigar and then putting it out in the ashtray. He was a fine Swiss banker, the kind Bandhoo Kumar loved. Always discreet, always dependable. No matter where his dirty money came from, Bandhoo knew that once it was with Hans, it immediately became clean and respectable, like Hans' fine suit.

"If I may now take your leave, sir." Hans rose, straightening his expensively tailored jacket.

"Thank you." Bandhoo Kumar rose too, and shook Hans' hand, and then walked him to the door.

Bandhoo Kumar was now alone in his room. He blew out a large cloud of cigar smoke, and pressed the TV remote to switch to the DVD channel. He pressed the PLAY button with his thick thumb. The DVD he had brought with him from India took some time to load. Finally, the menu selection came up, and he selected Item No. 3 *Save Me From The Bedbug*. The screen came alive. *This girl looks so hot!* mused Bandhoo Kumar. *Tonight, I'll be her bedbug!* And he let out a funny chuckle, followed by a bout of cough, which he just about managed to douse with sips of whiskey from his glass, leaving his face red and his chest heaving. Bandhoo Kumar's asthma and heart disease played up whenever he smoked or got excited, and in spite of doctors' advice, he didn't mend his debauched ways. "I will continue to serve the people of India till my last breath," he had often announced proudly at election rallies, much to the applause of illiterate destitute masses who barely knew his real ways.

"Udita," said Mike Patel as he took a sip of the expensive chardonnay, "this lifestyle of a star – the money, the foreign trips, fine dining, shopping – do you know how many girls would do *anything* for this? I get hundreds of girls every day who come to my office begging for just a chance. You know, you are really lucky."

"Thanks Mikeji. I am very thankful to you. And I will work with full diligence and do my best. I won't let you down," replied Udita, sincerely and really meaning each word. She was ready to work hard to earn her spot among the stars.

"No problem. It is a very, very competitive place – this Bollywood – and you should not forget that. Girls would do *anything*, absolutely *anything*, to get what you have. Never forget that. You too can go very far, you know. It all depends on you, *how far do you want to go?*" said Mike, as he dug into his foie gras.

"Do you have the fire, the ambition, the drive, to really make it, *no matter what?*" asked Mike.

"Of course I do, Mikeji. I want to be a star too."

"These … these music videos you do … these are no big deal."

Udita looked up, downing her chardonnay obligingly. It was important for a star to drink wine, Mike had insisted.

"If you really want to be in the big league, you need to do movies. Films. Big banner productions. As the heroine. You need to have burning ambition inside you for that – a real go-getter attitude. Do you want to be a heroine?"

"Yes," said Udita, already tipsy. Alcohol was new to her system, and it didn't take much to get her high.

"Then you need to impress the right people." Mike suggested, leaning forward, as if conveying a major secret to Udita.

"You are lucky. I can introduce you to just the right person. That is, if you are interested…" teased Mike, all part of a well worked out strategy he had used many times before.

"Of course, yes!" exclaimed Udita, taking another gulp from her refilled glass.

"Have you heard of Bandhoo Kumar? The politician. He also sits on the board of Govardhan Motion Pictures –

Bollywood's largest film production company. He is extremely influential. If he so decides, you could be signed up as the heroine for the next Govardhan movie."

"Really?" Udita said drowsily. Then after a pause, she added, "How?"

Mike didn't respond. After an agonising silence, Udita asked again, impatiently,

"How? Mikeji, how?"

"I don't think you can do it," declared Mike, in a sceptical tone, eyeing her dismissively.

"No, sir, I can. I can! Just tell me how to," insisted Udita. She didn't want the dream to end.

"Udita, you will have to be open about yourself, about your body, like a true actress should be. Have no inhibitions. Bandhoo Kumar will want to *test* whether you are open, whether you have the right stuff. He may want to even sleep with you. Just to see if you are trained well enough as an actress and truly comfortable with your body." Mike rattled off, making it sound all very academic and legitimate. "And if you pass the *test*, he will sign you on to become a heroine. You could be the next big star. Believe me, all the Bollywood heroines have had to pass the *test*."

"What?" Udita said, confused. Her head was spinning. Had she heard correctly? Something to do with an acting test? Sleeping with Bandhoo Kumar? Comfort with body? The wine had got to her.

"It's no big deal. Once you pass the test, you will be famous – a heroine – known all over the world as a Bollywood diva. How proud your parents will be? Everybody will recognise and respect you. What a life you will lead, like these last two days! Wow!" Mike continued his spiel.

Udita's head was dizzy. They all do it. An acting test? Sleeping? Sex? Comfort with body? Stardom? Heroine. The lifestyle! The shopping! The Ritz!

"Don't think too much. Chances like this don't come always. You are lucky Bandhoo Kumarji is here tonight, and I can introduce you to him. This is your *only* chance to become a heroine. Don't forget, there are thousands who would jump at this chance. Don't lose your chance to become a Bollywood star!" Mike drilled on. He had the bird in his sights; he just needed to take aim and fire.

"But…" Udita mumbled on, not being able to think clearly.

"If you miss tonight's chance, that's the end of your career, your dreams. Finished." Mike dropped his heavy silver fork into his plate and stood up, startling the people at the neighbouring table. Mike was a master pimp.

Udita began to shiver.

Softening up, Mike now said, sitting down, "Come on, let me take you to him. Don't you trust Mikeji? This is in *your* best interests. For *your* career. *You* could be the next big thing. I can see your potential. Please." He implored her.

Udita finally succumbed to Mike's tactics and uttered a meek "Okay." Her head was still spinning from all the alcohol, and she kept thinking, but not very clearly.

"Good." With this, Mike rose, and Udita followed him. She felt she was in a trance. Things were happening so fast. She loved being in London; this was the best time she had ever had in her life. If this is how stars lived, she certainly didn't want it to end. She too wanted to be a Bollywood heroine. But sex…what would her father say if he found out? But then this was normal in Bollywood.

She had read in gossip magazines too. Producers *test* their heroines before casting them. How did it matter? A small price to pay for stardom? For this lifestyle…

"Here we are." Udita and Mike were at a door that read Room 415.

"Think of it as an audition. You are a professional. You did the audition for me so well, and look you are here in London today. Do this audition well too, and you will be a star. *Pukka!* Make him happy. Good luck! Or, sorry, as they say in the acting profession, break a leg!" With this, Mike knocked on the door thrice.

Bandhoo Kumar's face greeted them.

"Come *beti* … come sit here." Bandhoo Kumar welcomed Udita into the room. Mike left from the door itself.

"Mike has been saying so many good things about you. I just saw your performance too," said Bandhoo Kumar, pointing to the TV screen, which was still playing Udita's *Save Me From The Bedbug* music video.

"How wonderfully you dance! *Wah! Wah!* What tremendous talent you have! You are gem of our country!" The politician said, making superlative gestures with his hands.

"Mike tells me that you want to become a Bollywood heroine. I say why not! You have it in you. Don't you? Come just do a little dance and show me, like you did in that song, *Save Me From the Bedbug*." Bandhoo gestured to a vacant space in front of the TV, as the spot where he wanted Udita to dance.

Udita, heavily intoxicated with wine and the high life of the last two days, got up and stood at the spot, and automatically started gyrating to the music from the TV.

Bandhoo Kumar started clapping along, cheering her on. Then, he took out a few hundred pound notes from his pocket, stood up on his toes, twirled the notes around Udita's head, and stuffed them into Udita's exposed cleavage, letting his hands linger over her breasts. Udita, drunk and dazed, and knowing what those currency notes could buy on Oxford Street, let Bandhoo Kumar do as he pleased. Encouraged, Bandhoo Kumar started dancing alongside Udita, clapping and singing along with the song. Udita, bemused at watching this round, balding man of her grandfather's age in a white kurta and *dhoti* behaving in this manner, let out a laugh. Bandhoo Kumar laughed along too, taking a final swig from his whiskey glass, and then placing the glass over his head, he did a little dance. "Look, I can dance too!" he said, the whiskey glass balanced on his head, clearly enjoying himself. Udita laughed more. Suddenly, Bandhoo Kumar started coughing and went back to the comfort of his sofa. He was totally out of shape and even this slight physical exertion had left him breathless. Udita noticed Bandhoo Kumar's plight and went up to him, and sat down besides him. "Are you okay? Do you want some water?"

"No, no *beti*, I will be fine," said Bandhoo, already feeling much better after catching his breath.

"Come sit on my lap." Bandhoo patted a spot on his thighs.

Udita hesitated. Bandhoo pulled out another wad of hundred pound notes. Udita went and sat on his lap. Bandhoo Kumar stuffed those hundred pound notes into her cleavage. This time, however, he planted his hand firmly, massaging Udita's breasts. Instinctively, Udita pulled Bandhoo's hands away. Years of conditioning in Indian values don't go away easily. Udita might have dressed and looked western, but deep down she was still the lower middle class girl from Virar whose parents expected to marry her away into a similar family. Every girl in India is conditioned to guard her chastity with her life – to be kept intact till her wedding night – as the ultimate wedding gift for her husband.

Bandhoo Kumar removed Udita's hand and looked straight at her.

"Don't you want to become a heroine? I am about to get you signed up for a movie. Don't annoy me and ruin your career, your life, everything." The last line he said very sternly, and firmly planted his hand back on her breast and squeezed, looking straight into Udita's eyes as he did so. Intimidated, Udita didn't resist. She let Bandhoo play with her boobs. After some time of fondling her breasts, Bandhoo began to undo her dress. Udita instinctively wanted to stop him, but then checked herself.

"*Beti*, just pass me those pills lying on the bedside table." Udita brought Bandhoo his viagra, which he popped.

Now, he lay Udita on the bed, her breasts exposed and in full view. He lowered himself onto the bed and began to suck on her nipples. Udita let out a moan. Bandhoo Kumar continued. He began to undress Udita completely. Soon, she lay naked on the bed.

"What a beautiful body. You will become a star. A big star," Bandhoo said.

Udita lay there, unprotesting, and now beginning to feel more relaxed. The wine had dulled her senses, making her slightly sleepy.

Bandhoo felt something grow in his *dhoti*. The viagra was kicking in. He pulled out his *dhoti* and revealed his member. Udita saw it. It was soft and tiny, reminding her of the sausage in her plate of English breakfast from the morning. Bandhoo Kumar's body was utterly ugly. A huge stomach dwarfed all his other features. His tiny penis was gradually beginning to take life. Feeling ready, Bandhoo now entered Udita, who began heaving. It wasn't the penetration that was bothering her, it was the weight of Bandhoo Kumar's heavy and rounded frame on her. She felt nauseated, as Bandhoo Kumar loaded atop her like a heavy caterpillar on a thin twig. As he began to move, he kissed Udita on the lips, making a squeaking noise with his mouth. Udita felt a disgusting onion-garlic taste, from the food Bandhoo had eaten earlier in the evening. Suddenly Bandhoo let out a long drawn fart, and then an expression of pleasure spread out over his face, which was only inches away from Udita's. Fart-smell spread all over the room, and nauseated Udita further. It was all over. Bandhoo Kumar had come. And farted. Releasing gastric pressure as well as seminal pressure, all in one go. And now, exhausted and sweating, he lay on his back, breathing heavily. Udita was happy to have him off her; his weight had almost squashed her. *This was it*! In barely twenty seconds, Bandhoo Kumar had come, and was now lying on the bed next to her, falling asleep.

"Good night. Shut the door when you go." Is all he said, turned around, and started snoring.

Udita sheepishly picked up her clothes, dressed, and got ready to leave. Now that the *test* was over, she wanted to talk about the movie role Mike had promised. But as she saw Bandhoo Kumar passed out there on the bed, lying on his back, naked, snoring, with his gigantic hairy stomach rising and falling with each breath he took, and his penis shrunk back to walnut size, she felt a little embarrassed, and decided to leave. She had just lost her virginity to a fat old man her grandfather's age with erectile dysfunction. Worse, she had done so not out of love or within the sanctity of a married relationship, as perhaps her father would have wanted her to, but as a recruit to the oldest profession in the world.

"Amrit! It's VJ Vijay from Govardhan Bollywood Talent Hunt." Amrit gripped his cellphone tighter. *It was VJ Vijay! The results of the Govardhan Talent Hunt!* Amrit's heart began to race.

"Dude! I told you you were cool, maa'n! I have some really cool news for you! You've won! You won the Govardhan Bollywood Talent Hunt and were judged the best in the male actor category. Congratulations dude!" VJ Vijay sounded excited. Amrit felt a rush of adrenaline. He couldn't say anything.

"You're gonna be cast as the hero in a Bollywood flick to be made by Govardhan Motion Pictures. You'll be launched dude! You'll be a star!" VJ Vijay rattled off.

"Thanks. I am very grateful. Thanks." Amrit finally spoke, regaining composure.

"Cool, dude! We'll be getting back to you shortly with the details. Go out, have a drink, celebrate! Peace bro!" VJ Vijay hung up.

Amrit was elated. *Yes!* He punched the air in excitement. *Yes!* Amrit could see his Bollywood dreams finally taking shape. This Govardhan break would put him in orbit. Amrit couldn't stay still. Excitement was tingling in his body. He went to the kitchen and put some water to boil for tea. A broad smile came across his face as his mind began fantasising about all the possibilities, the future, a Bollywood career, stardom. *No, I shouldn't jump the gun* – Amrit tried to remind himself. He picked up the newspaper lying on the kitchen shelf and tried to distract himself. He wished he could start shooting for the movie tomorrow! Amrit turned to the Page 3 gossip columns of the newspaper.

"What!" Amrit said out aloud, as he looked at the newspaper headline staring at him.

'Upcoming Bollywood Actress Sapna is Zaeed Zakaria's Latest Girl!'

Amrit read further:

Zaeed Zakaria, heir to the vast Zakaria business empire that traverses interests in shipping, petrochemicals, hotels & resorts and airlines, and upcoming Bollywood actress Sapna, were spotted together in a posh Johannesburg restaurant. Zaeed, who is often seen driving his red Ferrari when in Mumbai, turns thirty-four this year, is Mumbai's most eligible bachelor, can now add Sapna to his long list of glamorous girlfriends! The Eton and Oxford educated billionaire seems just as passionate about his new lady love as he is about his business ventures.

"What the fuck…" Amrit couldn't believe his eyes. "My Sapna! With Zakaria! How could she?" Zaeed was renowned for changing girlfriends like underwear. Amrit continued reading.

On Sapna's birthday, while she was in South Africa shooting, Zaeed had flown there, and had got himself packed in a large cardboard carton and got the package delivered outside Sapna's hotel room door. Sapna was shocked to see such a large box outside her door. She had got the hotel concierge to open it for her, and, when the box opened – voila! There came out prince charming Zaeed Zakaria himself – with a "Surprise! Happy Birthday Sapna!" sign dangling from his neck.

The gossip columnist further reported that Sapna was most thrilled at this display of affection and had immediately hugged Zaeed. Both were not seen to emerge from Sapna's hotel room till the next morning.

Amrit was appalled. *Sapna! What's wrong with you?* How could she have fallen for such antics? *Bloody circus or what! What's the big deal in putting yourself in a box and doing all this theatrics?* Amrit decided to call Sapna.

"Hi Sapna! It's Amrit!" Amrit sounded rushed.

"Oh hi Amrit. How are you?" Sapna responded.

"Good. Thanks. Hey, happy belated birthday."

There was silence.

"So," continued Amrit, "I read in the papers. You and Zaeed Zakaria…"

There was another long silence.

"Are you seeing him, Sapna?" Amrit finally spoke.

"Look, Amrit. I really care a lot about Zaeed. Did you know he packed himself into a box and had himself delivered to me on my birthday!" The excitement in Sapna's tone infuriated Amrit.

"So?" Amrit said in a disinterested tone.

"So?" Sapna said angrily, "So could you ever do that for me?"

"I wouldn't want to do that. Bloody *naatak*, antics of a rich playboy." Amrit bit his lip.

"Amrit, I don't want to talk to you. You are so insensitive. That is your problem…"

"Sapna, I don't like you getting close to Zakaria." Amrit cut her off.

"Listen Amrit. Relationships are a lot about timing. There was a time I was very, very excited about you. Right now, I need to explore my feelings for Zaeed. You need to recognise that. I want to know if there is something there…" Sapna said.

What? What the hell is Sapna saying? Amrit was flabbergasted. There was a long silence.

"Are you sleeping with him?" Amrit asked.

Sapna went silent.

"I want you to stop meeting Zaeed Zakaria." Amrit's voice was sterner, and his tone raised. "Have you heard me, Sapna. I want you to stop."

"Goodbye Amrit. If you don't want to be sensitive and understanding, I don't want to talk to you." Sapna hung up the phone.

Amrit swung his arm and tossed the cellphone against the wall. The instrument smashed to bits on hitting the wall. Amrit was angry. And in tears. *Bloody Zaeed Zakaria and all his money. Bloody Sapna…all she is looking at is money…bloody whole world.* Amrit held his head in his hands. He had lost Sapna. He was powerless. Amrit felt cheap; inadequate. In front of Zaeed Zakaria's billions, he was nothing.

The doorbell rang. Amrit quickly washed his face and combed his hair to look presentable.

"Oh hi Puneet!" Amrit smiled as he opened the door to his co-actor from *Saas Ka Sindoor*. "Come in."

Puneet took his Ray Bans off as he entered Amrit's flat and sat down on the sofa in the living room.

"I hope I have not come at a bad time?" Puneet asked, eyeing Amrit carefully.

"Of course not! I'm glad you came. Do you want something to drink?" Amrit offered.

"No. Thanks. I actually came to ask for a favour." Puneet said, rather sheepishly.

"Amrit could you lend me five thousand rupees, please?"

Amrit was surprised. *Why?* Puneet Arora was one of the most popular actors on TV – *he* was running short of money? Just look at him—he was dressed in Diesel jeans, Armani jacket, Ray Bans … *he* needs money?

Puneet, as if guessing Amrit's thoughts, explained.

"I am running very short of money. You know that actors don't get paid that well in television. And payments are received after many months." Puneet looked embarrassed.

"But you dress so well? You drive a nice car!" Amrit asked. "I mean, I can help you, but…"

"Well, one has to keep up the appearances. You have to look like a star always – look rich and happening. The car is on a loan. The clothes – well – I overspend on them using my credit cards. I have a wife and a kid to support. Truly speaking, in an expensive city like Mumbai, I just lead a hand-to-mouth existence." Puneet looked sad.

"This expensive façade I need to put up totally drains all my earnings. And I don't have any family money to fall back on. I am not a second generation filmi chap, you know! Just a daily wage earner." Puneet looked down as he spoke.

Amrit was amazed. If *this* was the condition of Puneet Arora, what might be the plight of lesser known artists?

What could be in store for them? For every successful Puneet Arora, there were thousands of unsuccessful actors.

Could Puneet be conning him? The thought crossed Amrit's mind. No! He knew Puneet well enough. He had too much self-respect. He trusted Amrit and therefore had spread his hand before him. Puneet was too self-respecting otherwise. He knew Amrit would keep it to himself.

"My credit cards are all maxed out. I am due a few cheques next month. As soon as I make the mandatory credit card payments, I will return the money. Thanks man!" Puneet took the wad of notes handed to him by Amrit.

"No problem, take your time." Amrit said, sympathetically.

"God bless you." Puneet left.

Now, all alone, Amrit's thoughts went back to Sapna. Suddenly, his whole world seemed to have turned upside down. He couldn't believe what had happened. *This was his Sapna! She was doing this? Bloody Zaeed Zakaria.* Amrit wanted to beat the billionaire heir to a pulp.

To rid himself of all the negative thoughts that were erupting in his head, Amrit decided to go for a walk. He also needed to buy a replacement for his smashed mobile phone. Without his phone working, a struggling actor is cut off from the world. Who knows who might be trying to get in touch with him?

Amrit strolled off to Lokhandwala market. There, he picked up a brand new Nokia mobile phone, and dropped his old sim card into it. As Amrit walked back, his new mobile phone began to ring. It was the first call he had received on his newly bought instrument.

"Hey Amrit, how're they hangin'! It's VJ Vijay again, from Govardhan Talent Hunt. You cool bro?" VJ Vijay said in his cool way.

"Hi VJ Vijay. I am doing fine, thanks. How are you?" Amrit tried to focus on the call.

"Not too bad, not too bad. I have some not so cool news dude. There's been a mixup bro. Sorry man, the Govardhan movie thingy ain't happenin'. I mean it is happenin', just that they're taking Riz Khan, Sandy Khan's son, for the movie instead. Don't get me wrong man, you were the best, talent-wise, all the judges agreed. The judges had chosen you; you were the winner of the talent hunt. They thought you were the coolest, dude!"

"So? Why is the role going to Riz then?" Amrit stopped walking, suddenly worried.

"Chill dude, not my fault bro. What to do, it is a directive that just came from the top, from a dude no less than the Chairman of Govardhan Motion Pictures. He wants Riz to be cast in the main lead. We have to listen to him bro. He says take Riz; we've got to take Riz."

"Hmmm…" Amrit was seething.

"Dude, off the record, it's Riz's father, Sandy Khan man. He's damn close to the Chairman, you know that, don't you? Sandy Khan even agreed to act in the movie for free if Riz was chosen. Sorry dude. Better luck next time." VJ Vijay hung up.

Amrit looked down at his newly bought Nokia instrument. He had an urge to smash it too. Sense prevailed, as he realised he was running low on cash. He had just destroyed one instrument and brought a brand new one; he had given Puneet Arora a loan, and had not done a software project in two weeks. He couldn't afford to continue to vent his anger on mobile phones. For a moment, Amrit wished this was some bad joke. He wished the phone would ring again and VJ Vijay would tell him that he was playing a prank and that since Amrit had won the Govardhan Bollywood Talent Hunt he would be cast in the Govardhan Motion Pictures' movie as promised. But he knew it wasn't. He had heard from others too that Sandy Khan had made a standing offer to all producers in Bollywood. Anybody who would sign Riz for their movie would get the services of Sandy Khan, for free. It was an irresistible 'buy one, get one free' offer, given that even at his age Sandy Khan's popularity among audiences could match that of any younger Bollywood star. Sandy Khan was still one of the highest paid actors in Bollywood. Getting him for free was just too juicy an offer to pass off. Producers had lined up at Sandy Khan's residence in droves, with scripts tailor-made to fit the father and son combination. They knew Riz was the weak link, but with Sandy Khan thrown in for free, the economics worked out just fine. The ploy worked fabulously, with Sandy Khan and Riz lined up to feature together in half a dozen Bollywood capers. Of course, efforts were made to keep these arrangements secret. Only the insiders knew what was actually going on. PR gurus and spin doctors were hired to tell the rest of the world that it was just a coincidence that both father and son were to appear in so many movies together. Tag lines would announce: "The combination works really well!," "The script demanded it," "Casting Riz had nothing to do with his father," "Riz is going to be bigger than his father." Such and many more fabricated soundbites would appear regularly in the media.

Those in the know, including Amrit, knew what was going on here. Baby Riz was getting a kangaroo ride into Bollywood in papa Sandy Khan's pouch. Riz would be thrust down the audiences' throat so many times, chased down by his much loved and respected father, that he would finally one day become palatable to the audiences.

"Ten or fifteen?" Amrit speculated aloud. "How many flops would it take before Riz would make it?" As soon as Amrit got back home, he switched on his laptop and logged on to the Internet. He decided to take on a few software projects. He was running low on money, and it would also help take his mind off Sapna.

CHAPTER 9

Zaeed Makes Sapna Sapnaa!
The Page 3 headline in the newspaper grabbed Amrit's attention. Amrit had just woken up late in the afternoon, after a full night of software programming. He put down his cup of tea and quickly turned to the text of the article.

That Zaeed Zakaria is a devotee of numerology is well known. Now, he has got his arm-candy, the rising Bollywood starlet Sapna, also introduced to numerology. Zaeed Zakaria and his obsession with numerology go back almost a year. Zaeed, was actually christened "Zayed," at birth. After losing a drunken bet with a friend, the then Zayed had agreed to visit Manju Navani, the most prominent numerologist in Mumbai. The lost bet required Zayed to take up the numerologically-correct name prescribed by Manju Navani and use it for a month. Manju had prescribed Zayed to replace the "y" in his first name by "e." Since Zayed was born in May, the fifth month of the year, Manju had calculated that the letter "e," being the fifth letter in the alphabet, would bring increased fortune and luck to the billionaire-heir. Since Zayed had lost the bet, he had to go with the changed name for a month — and became Zaeed! That month turned out to be so lucky for Zaeed and for Zakaria Industries — the government granted them permission to launch a private airline, the company stock rose by twenty per cent – that Zaeed had decided to make the "y" to "e" change permanent. Since then, Zaeed had been a devout follower of the science of numerology and of Manju Navani.

It is learnt that last week Zaeed dragged his lady love Sapna to Manju Navani, and the numerologist has added an extra "a" to Sapna's name, now making her "Sapnaa." We hope the change brings as much luck to the pretty damsel as it has to her richy-rich beau!

Amrit rolled up the paper and threw it into the dustbin. *Fucking Sapna! Or Sapnaaaa! She's become such a slut!* The thought of Sapna with Zaeed made Amrit angry. He wished he could be in a one-on-one fist fight with Zaeed – just the two of them, nothing else – none of Zaeed Zakaria's billions to prop him up – just a man-to-man duel. When his temper cooled, Amrit realised it wasn't Zaeed Zakaria who was really at fault. *It is Sapna. She is the one who is going to him!* Amrit felt disgusted. *My Sapna!* She had changed so much. She didn't care for him any more. Yet, he couldn't seem to get Sapna out of his mind. He shut his eyes. Rubbed his stubble. All he could think of was Sapna. Her eyes. Her smile. It lifted his spirits. Then came the thought of Zaeed Zakaria, and anger was not far away. He couldn't seem to get rid of the anger.

Amrit opened his eyes and looked at his watch. He had a 7 pm call time for his shoot for *Saas Ka Sindoor*. He should be making a move soon to get to the sets on time. Mumbai traffic was notoriously slow. Amrit jumped into the shower, shaved, put on a fresh pair of jeans and a t-shirt, and combed his hair. Work, Amrit hoped, would take his mind off Sapna. *Focus on your work and let her go,*

Amrit tried to tell himself, as he picked up the RX100's keys and walked out of the flat.

"*Dada,* respected elder brother, can you do me a favour? I'd like a strong cup of tea please."

"Sure sir."

Dada threw some water from a bottle and milk from a polythene pouch into the pan, turned up the heat on his kerosene stove, the pressure of the flame making a hissing sound, and then threw in a couple of teaspoons of tea leaves and sugar from the open tin cans on his makeshift on-set tea stall. Amrit's eyes focussed on the blue-yellow flame, as it hissed ferociously out of the burner, immediately bringing the liquid in the pan to a simmer. Amrit's mental state was similar to the flame. Anger and ferociousness. Unlike the flame, Amrit did not have an outlet to direct all that pent up heat within him. He stood there eyeing the flame, and felt an impulse to put his hand over it.

"Tea." *Dada* proclaimed as he poured the hot brew out of the pan and through a bright green cheap plastic sieve, the kind that are sold on the pavements outside railway stations, and into a transparent plastic cup. *Dada* let the cup fill fully, which was more than what he usually did. Most cups left *Dada* half-filled, or rather 'cut' in half, and so the name 'cutting-tea,' for the half-filled cups of tea that are served on all Bollywood sets. Even in his current disturbed state of mind, Amrit looked like a hero. He stood out, and everyone immediately mentally marked him as someone who would go far. In serving him a full cup of tea, *Dada* was, in his own humble way, acknowledging Amrit's superior status. The little people of Bollywood would often do this. Especially if the recipient of their preferential treatment was a kind and gentle-hearted person like Amrit was, who would always be deferential and polite even to the minions. His kindness and politeness did not go unnoticed – it only endeared him further to the little people, for whom, a kind "please" or a "thank you" from a hero or potential hero was the sunshine in their otherwise drab existence.

"Thank you *Dada!* Nothing smells as good as your freshly brewed tea!" Amrit made eye contact with *Dada* as he took the cup. *Dada* smiled, his eyes slightly moist.

Back in the vanity van, Amrit sat down on the divan, and placed the cup of tea on the makeup table. Vapours from the tea filled the airconditioned and closed-off environs of the vanity van with a characteristic sweet-tea smell. Amrit sat with his head in his hands. It was 10:30 pm, and he was waiting for his shot to be over so that he could get away. Anywhere. Far away. Maybe near the ocean. The thought of night and sea brought Sapna's memories back to mind. With it, came the corresponding anger. It had started to become a pattern now. Something would trigger Sapna's memory, a pleasant memory, and then would come the realisation of what she was up to now, of Zaeed Zakaria, and that would bring anger and rage, and send his mind spinning. Amrit wished he could be freed of this constant cycle of memory and anger. Wish he could just wipe the slate of memory clean. Wish he could just…

There was a knock on the vanity van's door.

"Come in." Amrit said.

The door opened and Nandini walked in. *Nandini! At this hour! Was everything okay?* Tales of Nandini's brutality had reached Amrit's ears too. Closeness to Vinta had made Nandini a figure to be feared and appeased. Wherever Nandini went, actors went silent and greeted her with deference. She was powerful, an extension of the Queen Bee herself.

"Hi Nandini!" Amrit tried to force a smile.

"Hi!" Nandini beamed back. There was something uncharacteristically casual and happy about Nandini today. She came and sat down next to Amrit on the divan.

"The TRPs for the last few weeks are out. You are a big hit! The scenes in which you have featured have recorded the highest viewership ratings. Especially that confrontation scene with Romesh Paul. That hit a TRP of 15.2! Beat all previous records."

Amrit smiled, genuinely. *Wow!* He knew that scene with Romesh Paul had gone off well. *But a TRP of 15.2! Wow!*

"Amrit, you are a good actor. Truly exceptional. Vinta is going to really expand your role. Maybe even cast you in another Jai Jai show." Nandini looked straight at him.

Amrit looked back into her eyes. She was actually an attractive girl. She had a sharp nose, high cheekbones, clear, smooth skin and a general cuteness about her. Her eyes. Her eyes reminded him of someone. Sapna ... her eyes were quite similar to Sapna's...

Nandini moved forward and kissed Amrit on the lips, thrusting her tongue deep into his mouth. Amrit was startled for a moment, still thinking of Sapna's eyes, and then he felt the warmth of Nandini's tongue in his mouth, and the clasp of her arms around his back. Amrit let go and kissed her back, wrapping his arms around her back, and the two were tightly embraced together now. Amrit felt Nandini's large breasts press hard against his chest; he could feel her nipples firming as they rubbed against him. It turned him on. He held her tighter, digging her breasts deeper into his chest.

Just then there was a tap on the door, and the two instinctively separated. Nandini quickly ran to the bathroom. Amrit picked up the script lying next to him.

The door opened and it was the AD.

"Amrit. We are doing the other scene first; we'll be doing your scene after an hour. Sorry man. But if you want you can go to sleep. I'll come wake you before your scene. Sorry man. Okay bye." The AD rushed off.

Nandini reappeared from the bathroom. She had splashed her face with water and tied her hair back. Amrit noticed her nipples were still erect, poking out of her black t-shirt.

"You wanna go for a walk? I know a quiet spot," Nandini suggested.

Amrit nodded his head, still looking at the erect nipples.

They slipped out of the vanity van and turned towards a forested patch just behind Sankraman Studios, Nandini leading the way. Crickets and other insects could be heard in the night as they walked deeper into darkness. There was a distant din of the generator vans, which grew fainter with every step into the woods. It was pitch dark now and Nandini took Amrit's hand to make sure he didn't get lost as she led him forward. Amrit was still in a daze, almost sleepwalking. Then, suddenly, Nandini stopped and faced Amrit, who, not realising that Nandini had stopped, banged into her. He felt her fleshy breasts ram into his chest and he was instantly turned on. Nandini grabbed him and started kissing him on the neck. Amrit instinctively put his arms around her and bit her neck. Nandini now kissed him on the lips again; warmth filling Amrit's mouth and throat. The two kissed in sustained passion. Amrit felt the urge and slipped his hand on Nandini's breasts and squeezed them gently. They were large and fleshy. Nandini gave out a moan. She then lifted her t-shirt off and helped Amrit's hand on her breast. The feel of warm flesh felt strangely soothing, and Amrit squeezed the breasts again. Nandini then took Amrit's hands off her breasts and took a step back. Amrit was perplexed, as he could barely see in the darkness. Then, he could notice that Nandini was pulling down her panties from her skirt. She came closer again and laid a hand on Amrit's belt buckle, opened it, and undid his pants. Dropping to her knees, Nandini took Amrit's erect penis in her mouth.

"Hmmm ... nice ... I like it," she muttered.

"Fuck me doggy style. Fuck me Amrit." Nandini turned around and went down on her fours, her ass facing Amrit, her skirt raised, as she guided Amrit to take her from behind. Amrit complied, going down on his knees, and rammed his erect penis into Nandini's moist pussy.

"Yes ... fuck me ... fuck me hard." Nandini dictated, as Amrit began to pound her.

"Yes ... harder ... harder..." Nandini cried.

Amrit increased the tempo further. He could barely see around him, in the pitch darkness. He closed his eyes. Suddenly, the thought of Sapna came ... and then came the thought of her in bed with Zaeed Zakaria. Amrit increased the tempo further. Infuriated, he turned his fury into vigorous motion of his hips. Anger was channelled into kinetic energy. He was pumping Nandini really hard now, like a machine that had gone out of control.

"Yes ... oh my god ... you are tearing me apart ... yes..." Nandini's words and her panting only incited Amrit further, who had spread his arms apart, in a crucifixion pose, as he continued to tear Nandini wide in this strange primitive animalistic coupling on this dark, forested spot.

"Udita. It's Mike Patel."

"Mikeji, I have been trying to contact you for so many days…"

"I am so sorry," Mike butt in, "I have been so busy running around trying to get you the lead heroine's role in Govardhan Motion Pictures' next production."

Udita felt a tinge of excitement and her irritation at Mike Patel for having pulled the disappearing act on her lessened.

"There is one final obstacle. Everything has been arranged. The script is ready. The shooting should begin in two weeks. The director, music director, supporting cast, all has been finalised. You are the frontrunner for the heroine's role. Bandhoo Kumarji has really made a very strong case for you to the Chairman of Govardhan Motion Pictures. But there is one more hurdle … final hurdle…"

"What?" Udita's voice betrayed an irritation at this new hurdle.

"The Chairman of Govardhan Motion Pictures, you know, he is a very good man, not like other big personalities in the industry. He is very faithful to his wife." Mike added.

"What is the problem? Why am I not finalised for the role?" Udita was growing impatient.

"I am explaining. Have patience Uditaji. You must talk with patience. Tomorrow you will be a big heroine, you will be giving many TV and magazine interviews, you must be patient. Of course, if that tomorrow comes…"

Mike was deliberately being elusive.

"I am sorry, Mikeji." Udita tried to project a calm and collected side. "What is the problem now? What do you mean by *if*? You had promised me that after Bandhoo Kumar ... I mean ... that everything was final now." Udita was a little embarrassed at the reference to her romp with Bandhoo Kumar in London.

"I know. I know. Bandhoo Kumarji is the one who has brought you this far. Now final obstacle is the Chairman of Govardhan. Don't get me wrong. He is very loyal to his wife."

"Please tell me what I have to do." Udita was now trying hard to control her impatience but not succeeding.

"This ... Chairman ... he likes to watch. He likes to watch, not do."

Mike was silent again. Then he continued after a pause.

"He likes to watch sex. Live. Like cricket match. He wants to see you having sex live. Just watch. Not do."

"What?" Udita exclaimed.

"Relax, Uditaji. All heroines of Govardhan Motion Pictures movies have done it. And it won't be with ugly old man. With a good looking and fit male model. Chairman wants to watch sexy couple."

"I am not doing this. You said Bandhoo Kumar was the *only* time I would have to..." Udita sounded emphatic.

"*Bus.* This is final time. I promise. Just think you are doing it with your boyfriend. For enjoyment. The boy will be a model. Very hot. Just once. And then you will be a heroine. He will sign you on there and then. I promise. It's tomorrow night, arrangements made at Taj Hotel. You have come so far. Please don't ruin your future. You can be the next big thing in Bollywood..."

Udita was silent. Her mind was working. She had already gone far enough. Farther than she would have liked to. Should she trust Mike Patel again? What if he was just using her? But then, maybe this is how things in Bollywood worked. The film magazines had said so too. If the other heroines could do it, why not her?

"Who is the male model?" Udita asked.

Mike was relieved to hear the question. It meant Udita was already halfway there.

"Bhola, the ramp model. Most magnificent body. Very sexy and hot. Women are crazy for him. You will really enjoy. He is also from the acting academy." Mike continued, speaking like a salesman.

"He has agreed?" Udita asked.

"Oh yes! He will also get a role in Govardhan. Who will turn down a golden chance like this, tell me Uditaji? You must consider yourself lucky that you are almost there. Finalised." Mike continued his pitch.

"And one more thing…" Mike added before he hung up. "There are some lines you'll have to speak, dialogues. I will give them to you before the scene. Bye."

Udita was not happy with the lines she was given when she met Mike Patel in the lobby of the Taj Hotel the next day.

"Mikeji, but these are a prostitute's lines. See how dirty they are!" Udita objected.

"No, no, Uditaji," Mike protested, "You are just *playing* a prostitute, *acting*. Like Rekha in the movie *Umrao Jaan*. This is what acting is about. You are playing a character. The heroine of the movie is a prostitute. The Chairman wants to see how natural you look in the role. Do it well. Remember, this is your big chance.

You can be the next mega-heroine. Don't blow your chances."

The presidential suite of the Taj Hotel was divided into two halves. In one, the bedroom, there was a king size richly carved gold bed, with gold coloured silk sheets. The other half was a large sitting area that looked into the bedroom, furnished with gold coloured majestic leather sofas. The sofas had been set to face the bedroom, the large bed being on display like a marionette stage. Bandhoo Kumar sat on one sofa, next to the elegant looking Saville Row suited Chairman of Govardhan Motion Pictures. Unknown to Udita and Bhola, who lay on the golden bed, stark naked, was the fact that there were two miniature video cameras hidden in Bandhoo Kumar's sofa, focussed straight on the bed.

"Start start," Bandhoo Kumar announced, as if he were a referee at a sporting event.

Udita knew she was now supposed to say her lines – the lines Mike Patel had given her. She looked at the Chairman, who looked very serious, and spoke in her best enactment of a prostitute:

> *"What is wrong with debauchery? After all, if something feels so good, what's wrong with it? I believe in fornication – it gives me pleasure, money – two of my basic needs are met. To hell with society. I am not answerable to anyone. I like it and I am going to continue to do it."*

Lines spurted out, Udita lay there, in an awkward, shy naked silence. In spite of her attempt at cultivating a bold, sexy image, she was still the lower middle class girl from Virar, still not completely uninhibited, as, say, a full-fledged prostitute would be. Wine had helped get her through her encounter with Bandhoo Kumar, but today Udita was totally sober. Bhola, more accustomed to such situations, and perhaps just the fact that he was male, decided to make the first move. He placed a hand on Udita's breasts and began to squeeze them. Instinctively, she tried to pull away. Bhola moved closer and took one of her nipples in his mouth and sucked hard for a few minutes. Udita shut her eyes. She felt a tingle between her legs. Bhola was fully erect now. The Chairman of Govardhan cleared his throat, as he watched the bodybuilder get into position over Udita, and slide his penis into her. Bhola's perfectly sculpted abdominal six pack muscles flexed like the pistons of an engine, as he began to settle into a gentle, in-out rhythm. Udita moaned as Bhola slowly quickened his pace.

Bandhoo Kumar looked at the Chairman, who was now looking on intently, craning his neck to catch the action on the bed, like a man at a zoo observing chimpanzees in a cage – a fully concentrated, serious look on his face. Bandhoo Kumar discreetly looked down at the cavity in his sofa where the miniature video camera was hidden. It was there and pointed in the right direction.

The doorbell rang a few times in Amrit's flat.

"Who the hell is that?" Nandini asked, as she pulled the bedsheet over her face.

"I don't know. Maybe the watchman or someone." Amrit rubbed his eyes as he looked at the clock on his bedside table. His head felt heavy. It was 11.30 at night. They could not have been asleep long.

"I'll go see." Amrit rubbed his eyes as he stumbled his way to the main door and opened it.

Sapna!

There she was, standing across the doorstep, wearing an elegant black gown, holding a bouquet of flowers in her hands. Sapna eyed Amrit carefully. He was in his underpants and nothing else, his hair ruffled, with red lipstick marks all over his chest and face.

"Come back here darling!" Nandini called from the bedroom.

Amrit tried to pretend he didn't hear anything. But Sapna *had* heard Nandini's call. She froze.

Sapna was the second unexpected visitor Amrit had opened the door for this evening. For today was Amrit's birthday, and a few hours ago, Nandini had landed at his flat, carrying a bottle of champagne and a tandoori chicken. She had walked right in and hugged Amrit, giving him a peck on the cheeks and had wished him a loud "Happy Birthday!" After downing the champagne and devouring the chicken, both had tumbled into bed.

Amrit could notice the soft expression in Sapna's eyes giving way to sternness. All the champagne in Amrit's veins evaporated, as he stood there, facing Sapna, exposed. Sapna was supremely composed, as she handed over the bouquet of flowers to Amrit and said, "Happy Birthday, Amrit." Almost instantly, she turned around, and made her way down the stairs, even before Amrit could realise what had happened. He stood there, staring at the bouquet of flowers in his hand – they were red roses – Amrit's favourites.

Shit! Amrit shook his head. *Shit!*

"Nandini, listen, we need to talk," Amrit said, scratching his head, as he entered the bedroom. He turned the lights on.

"Okay." Nandini looked up squinting, eyeing the bouquet of red roses in Amrit's hand.

"I think this thing ... between us ... that started that night ... I think it's not going anywhere, and ... look, I'm really sorry ... but I didn't want to get entangled with you like this ... it was just that one thing led to another and now..." Amrit was still scratching his head, his thoughts were with Sapna and how she must be feeling seeing him there, in his boxer shorts, with Nandini. He wished he had not got involved with Nandini in the first place.

"So, what are you saying?" Nandini blurted out angrily.

"Look, Nandini ... you are a very nice girl ... but this thing ... we jumped into this without thinking, without talking ... just got carried away ... it's my fault ... I was just so ... look I'm really sorry, but I think we need to put an end to this ... this ... it was a mistake ... a big mistake." Amrit mumbled.

"I see." Nandini was not happy. "Fine." She got up in a flash, put on her clothes, gathered her belongings, and on her way out of the flat, stopped for a moment and stared at Amrit's face, and then left.

Amrit looked around for his mobile phone. It took him a while to find it, in the pocket of his trousers lying on the floor. He dialled Sapna's number. There was no response. He dialled again. Again there was no response. *Shit! Sapna is not taking my calls. Shit!*

CHAPTER 10

Amrit was in two minds. He stared at the cellphone in his hand. Sapna's number was on display. Should he call her? Should he not? The whole morning had been spent in this state of indecision.

"Hello." Sapna answered.

"Sapna. Hi. It's Amrit." He had finally called. She had finally picked up!

There was a long silence. Amrit didn't know what to say. All of a sudden, he wasn't even sure why he had called Sapna.

"Hi." Sapna said in a low, stern tone.

"Look Sapna … I … I wanted to talk to you … about last night … I…" Amrit's said, trying hard to be coherent. What he really wanted to say was that he loved her so much and wished for her to be with him right at this very moment and for the rest of his life. That he really missed her so much. That he was sorry for last night. That he wished he could turn back the clock to where Sapna had suggested he drop everything and move to Bangalore. That he loved her so so much. That he wished he could hold her right now; that he could look into her magical eyes! That he wished things could be like before between them.

"Amrit … I really don't want to know. I really don't want to talk." Sapna said.

"Sapna! Do you…" Amrit stopped mid-sentence as he heard a faint but distinct voice, a man's voice, in the background. *Who's Sapna with? Zaeed Zakaria! Sapna is with Zaeed Zakaria!* Amrit's mind began to race. *Why is Sapna with Zaeed Zakaria?* Blood began to boil in Amrit's veins. He went silent. The sweet feelings of love from just a moment ago gave way to jealous rage.

"I said I don't want to talk to you." Sapna declared.

Amrit did not speak. His tongue froze. Warmth began to swell in his eyes. He let the phone hang loosely from his hand. Sapna's voice mixed with Zaeed's repeated "Who's it?" came through the phone's speaker. Amrit couldn't bear to hear Zaeed Zakaria's voice in the background. Amrit disconnected the call. All sorts of thoughts came to his mind. Amrit swallowed. He went to the bathroom and splashed some water on his face. Looking at himself in the mirror, Amrit could feel the anger on his red face. He turned to the plastic bucket that was lying on the bathroom floor, and punched hard at it letting out a loud yell. *Yaaah!* The bucket cracked open where Amrit's fist hit the plastic. Amrit took a few deep breaths. There was nothing he could do except boil.

Amrit decided to jog to Olympus gym for his workout. There was too much pent up energy inside him. Jogging, followed by a vigorous workout, he hoped, would provide an outlet for all the anger that was bottled-up inside him. He needed to get Sapna out of his mind. She was no longer his, his rational mind tried to tell him. *Let her go, Amrit, let her go.*

As Amrit jogged over the Oshiwara bridge, he saw a huge new poster announcing the upcoming release of the latest Bollywood blockbuster. There, standing prominently, was Sapna; his Sapna. She had a glint of mischievousness in her eyes – and was looking right down at him. Amrit stopped jogging and stood there staring at the poster. A smile broke on his face. He was smiling back at those mischievous hazel eyes. God he still loved her!

Maybe she looks down upon me now, as if I were inferior to her. She's a star, and I am a nobody. In the caste system of Bollywood, Sapna was on a higher pedestal now. Out of reach. Could a star-non-star marriage work? Could Sapna-Amrit work? What would people say? Oh, look, that's Sapna, the star ... who's she with ... oh, that Amrit guy ... yeah, we saw him on television ... he's lucky to have Sapna. Oh look, here comes Amrit, Sapna's husband. Would Amrit be able to live with such taunts? Always being Sapna's husband for the rest of his life. Besides, Sapna was anyway with Zaeed Zakaria, this was all wishful thinking. He was a better catch for her. It did not matter now that no man ever born loved Sapna as much as he did. It was his fault; he had let her go. He had taken her for granted. Now, he was repenting. It was too late.

"*Bam bhole!* Life without love is very dull. Life after having found love and then losing it is agonising."

Who said that?

Amrit looked around to see who had uttered those words. *There!* Standing with a brass *lota* in one hand and a *chimta* in another, wearing a flowing saffron robe, was a *sadhu*, looking directly at Amrit.

"Free yourself of the agony." The wandering ascetic now spoke to Amrit. "It has been said, 'if you love something, set it free. If it flies away, it was never yours;

but if it comes back, it is yours for life.' This one has flown away. It never was yours. If she is not willing to give up *everything* to be with you, then she doesn't *truly* love you. For if she truly loved you, she would give it all up *just* to be with you. And if it wasn't true love, then, what is it, young man, that you are fretting about losing? Cheer up! *Bam bhole!*"

The swami walked off, clapping his *chimta* a few times as he descended Oshiwara bridge. Amrit's gaze followed the sadhu as he turned the corner of the street, disappearing from view. India is indeed a magical place, Amrit thought. You're walking on the streets with your thoughts in your mind, and suddenly a random swami out of nowhere speaks to you, and seems to know about your most intimate thoughts. Maybe that's why all those foreign tourists keep flowing into India on their spiritual quests. Maybe it's not just all bullshit after all. The swami's words kept repeating themselves in Amrit's head. Did Sapna really, truly love him? If she did, would she not give up everything – her star status, everything that she had achieved – to be with Amrit, now! To be the wife of an ordinary man, when the whole country swooned over her. Was that too much to ask? Or, was that the true test of love? Was the swami right in suggesting that Sapna never truly, deeply loved him? If that was indeed the case, then why was he in such a sullen state, fretting over what? He could still not stop thinking of Sapna, no matter how hard he tried. He just couldn't seem to push her out of his mind. Amrit picked up pace and sprinted off in the direction of Olympus gym. He wanted to tire himself so much that his mind would drop all thoughts about Sapna.

Amrit decided to surf television channels to catch up with the latest in Bollywood. Also, he wanted to keep his mind from wandering to thoughts of Sapna. *That's Meghna!* Amrit stopped at a channel where Meghna was being featured. Meghna had landed a key role in *Mmmangalsutra,* a popular TV soap, and the feature was discussing Meghna's role in the serial and also speculating that Meghna might be appearing in a movie shortly. *Wow! That's great!* Amrit decided to call and congratulate Meghna.

"Hi Meghna! I saw you on TV. Well done! Excellent news about your upcoming movie."

"Well, the movie didn't work out. The serial is going well though, thanks." Meghna sounded disappointed.

"Why? What happened? I thought you were finalised for the movie? At least that's what the TV report said?" Amrit switched his mobile phone to the other ear.

"Well, Amrit, what can I say, I am kind of angry about this. Yes, I was finalised for the movie; we were even going to start shooting. Then, at the last minute, the producer got a call from the president of the censor board. He wanted his niece to be cast in the movie. So, I got bumped off. They cast her instead."

"That just sucks!" Amrit said in disgust.

"Yeah! The producer felt bad too. He was really apologetic to me. Said that he couldn't really afford to alienate the president of the censor board. His hands were tied."

"Well, at least you got some publicity. At least people know you are movie material." Amrit tried to sound upbeat.

"Publicity can be bought, Amrit. Talking of which, why haven't I seen any write-ups about you on Page 3? Have you not got a PR agent?"

"No."

"Amrit! For god's sake you are in a major television serial – *Saas Ka Sindoor* – you should blow your trumpet a bit about it. That way more people will hear about you. More people will give you work. That's how you'll move up the Bollywood ladder. Look, I'll give you the number of this PR agent, his name is Anurag Mehta, he does a good job. He's got links with journalists in all newspapers and magazines. He will hook you up and keep you in the news. Remember, out of sight is out of mind."

"Hmmm…" Amrit mumbled.

"Look, he's not that expensive too. Just fifteen or twenty thousand a month. It's an important investment for your career. Amrit, you've got to play the game right. Don't be a Raja Harishchandra and just do your work and go back home. These things are just as important, in fact maybe even more important."

"But Meghna, if I'm good and act well, I will automatically be noticed. People will write newspaper columns about me if they find my work outstanding. I mean, it seems kind of fake to buy my own publicity." Amrit was clearly not at ease with the whole PR game played in Bollywood.

"If I were not married I'd give you a hug and a kiss on your lips. You are such an innocent puppy Amrit. What are you doing in Bollywood? Look – time to get real. You're a damn good actor, no question about that. But there are hundreds of damn good actors in Mumbai – most of them starving. You want to get ahead, you learn to think with your head, not your heart. You think the articles you read in Page 3 are inspired by good acting? Rubbish. It is all fabricated PR. Guys like Anurag Mehta *get* those pieces published. How on earth do you think a bloody Page 3 journalist would know what food so and so likes or what underwear so and so wears. It's all spin – it's all supplied. C'mon Amrit, don't be so naïve; sometimes, you scare me!"

"Okay, sms me the number. I'll think about it. Thanks." Amrit said and hung up.

Amrit picked up a copy of the morning newspaper – and went straight for the coloured Page 3 supplement. To the rest of the world Page 3 was the place to find the latest gossip and masala about the world of Bollywood and the high-life; but to Bollywood insiders, Page 3 was the trade page. Actors, directors, producers, socialites – anybody seeking publicity – would retain PR agents to get coverage on Page 3. The PR agencies, through links with editors and correspondents, could steer the Page 3 cameras to shine on their clients. For actors, Page 3 was a target vehicle to portray the 'right' image to their target audience and potential employers. A hot actor – one who got a lot of Page 3 coverage – would be coveted by production houses. Buzz was supposed to be good for actors' careers, and actors would go to great lengths to get the right buzz generated about them. Even the small television stars had cultivated PR agents who, for a fee, would provide them regular coverage on Page 3 on one pretext or another.

Amrit's eyes went to a blurb about his friend and colleague Puneet Arora.

Puneet Arora gets puppy dog!

Actor Puneet Arora has just got a beautiful black labrador puppy whom he just can't seem to get enough of. When our Page 3 team met Puneet in his Malad flat, the puppy, whom Puneet has named Tommy, was sitting on his lap, licking his face. When asked why he had chosen a black labrador, Puneet replied: "I love labradors, they are so friendly. I had one growing up. I chose the colour black because I am a devotee of goddess Kaali Mata, and black is her colour." When Puneet gets home from a long day's shoot, he says Tommy helps him relax. With Puneet's role in Saas Ka Sindoor probably going to end soon, Tommy will probably get to see a lot of his master!

Accompanying the piece was a photo of Puneet with Tommy licking his face.

Amrit dialled Puneet's mobile phone to congratulate him.

"Bastard Anurag Mehta! I paid him Rs. 3,000 for that blurb – and look what he did – he gave it such a negative twist. Did you read the last line – makes me appear like an out of work actor. I only told him I was looking for more work – why did he have to write that my role in *Saas Ka Sindoor* was going to end. Bastard." Puneet fumed on the phone.

"Relax. I am sure people will take it in the right light. Besides, as you once told me, any publicity is good publicity." Amrit tried to assuage him.

"That's true. But he had promised me a bigger write-up and more prominently placed on the page. This was just in one corner ... three thousand rupees for *this*!" Puneet mumbled.

"Puneet, did you really pick a black labrador pup because you are a follower of Kaali Mata?" Amrit inquired. Puneet had never mentioned his devotion to the cult of Kaali.

"No man! That is just bullshit I said to appease Vinta. You know she is a big devotee of Kaali Mata, don't you? And her favourite colour is black. Well, I am hoping she will read this piece and maybe extend my role in *Saas Ka Sindoor* or give me another role." Puneet clarified.

Amrit's phone beeped in the background suggesting that there was another call waiting.

"Puneet, I have a call waiting. Gotta go. Will chat later." With this Amrit switched to the call that was on wait.

Amrit sat with his head held in his hands. The call had been from the casting director at Jai Jai Productions, informing him that his character in *Saas Ka Sindoor* was ending – "the character is being sent abroad, to America, therefore the track is ending. Your services will no longer be needed." Amrit had not asked further. He knew what the real reason behind his untimely departure from *Saas Ka Sindoor* was Nandini. This was Nandini's revenge. Revenge for Amrit so unceremoniously dumping her that night. Being Vinta's right hand woman, she would have spun some yarn to get Amrit's character ended. Since Amrit was such a good actor, and well behaved too, Nandini could not have him replaced on grounds of incompetence or misbehaviour. She had to put an end of his character if she wanted to spite Amrit. That's exactly what she did. Vinta never refused Nandini, and must have agreed to the change in plot. Amrit had almost expected it. *Never mind, Amrit. There will be more. You did what was right.* Amrit reassured himself, as he ran his fingers through his hair.

Amrit decided he needed to get some fresh direction in his life. He needed to get himself out of the rut he had got into. He needed to renew his resolve. Reload his guns and jump back into the struggle. So what if he was no longer in *Saas Ka Sindoor*. There were so many other serials. He would try at other television production houses. Launch another strike. Re-circulate his photographs. Audition like crazy. He would not think of Sapna any more and just concentrate on his work. But before he started on his journey with renewed vigour, he wanted to get some inspiration. He knew where he could get that kind of inspiration. He looked at his watch. It was 5 pm. He still had an hour.

Amitabh Bachchan performed a ritual every Sunday at 6 pm. That is, whenever he was in Mumbai. He would come out of his bungalow in Juhu, and wave to a crowd – a crowd, which was always gathered there on Sunday evenings, waiting for *darshan* of their beloved Bollywood hero. Nobody knew how or when this ritual began, but without fail, every Sunday at 6 pm, Amitabh could be seen stepping out of his bungalow gates and waving to the crowd. Amrit hoped Amitabh was in town. He got dressed, raced down the steps, brought the RX100 engine to life, and zoomed off towards Juhu.

There was a large crowd gathered. Police and private security men had formed a cordon around the main entrance to the bungalow, keeping the crowd back. Amrit wished he had come early, for now he was at the very back of a two hundred strong crowd, all shuffling to get into position to see the great Bachchan.

Shiv! That's Shiv!

Amrit noticed Shiv Shankar Pandey, dressed in a security guard's uniform, standing guard at the large wooden gate of Amitabh Bachchan's bungalow, instructing the crowd of onlookers to stand behind the cordon mark.

"Shiv Shankar Pandey!" Amrit screamed.

Shiv made eye contact with Amrit, and instantly recognised his classmate, waving to him from the crowd. Shiv waved back, a smile breaking across his face, and he gestured Amrit to come forward. Amrit complied, making his way through the crowd, jostling through a group of daily wage labourers, a pregnant woman, some school children, an elderly couple, a group of Japanese tourists, and finally emerged at the edge of the crowd, facing Shiv.

"Shiv Pandey! What is this? You ... in a security guard's uniform!"

"What to do Amrit *bhaiya*! Tough times make everything possible. I ran out of money. Going back to Benaras was not an option. I had burnt all my bridges there. So one day I stumbled into an employment bureau, who sent me to the office of this security guard company." Shiv pointed to the name and company logo on his shirt.

"The manager at the security guard company asked me what skills I had. So I recited some dialogues of Amitabh Bachchan to him. The manager laughed so hard that all the other people in the office came into his cabin. They asked him what had happened. The manager asked me to repeat the dialogues. So, I repeated the dialogues. Then everybody in the room laughed just as hard as the manager had. After calming down, the manager said, 'Post him at Amitabh Bachchan's bungalow.' And so, they posted me here. To do duty at Amitabh Bachchan's house."

Shiv took a long drag on a *bidi* he had lit.

"Still smoking?" Amrit exclaimed.

"Now smoking *bidis*. Cigarettes are too expensive on a guard's salary. Now I am not smoking to make my voice heavy. Now I am smoking out of habit. Besides, all the other guards smoke too. It bonds us together." Shiv smiled.

Amrit smiled back, a plastic, forced smile. He didn't feel like smiling. He felt like crying. This was no smiling matter. It was the tragic brutal end to one Bollywood dream. A dream that had started with Amitabh Bachchan's movies and had ended at the doorstep of Amitabh Bachchan's bungalow. Shiv Shankar Pandey was not the only one. There were thousands like him. They had ended up as taxi drivers, milkmen, shoeshine boys, petty hawkers, pickpockets – each according to their inclination, ability and luck. Amrit wondered if his Bollywood dream might end this way too. A shiver went down his spine.

"So, you're here to see Amitabh?" inquired Shiv. "I see him everyday," he threw the *bidi* down and put it out under his rubber slippers.

"Yes," is all Amrit could say, his mind wandering.

"Come, stand here. I'll put you in the best spot. From here, you can see him clearly." Shiv positioned Amrit in a spot just behind the guard's cabin, from where he had a clear view of the gate. Shiv was being a good friend. They were so different from each other, from such different backgrounds. Amrit was a software engineer who could be working writing code for the mainframe of a Fortune 500 company at this very moment if he wanted to. Shiv was a semi-literate from Benaras. Yet, they had so much in common. There was camaraderie between them that actors who have trained or worked together share. Like among soldiers who have fought shoulder to shoulder in a battle together, that bond is lifelong. It was evident in the way they looked at each other, the way they smiled at each other, the way in which Shiv had waved Amrit forward and given him a VIP viewing spot. Amrit would have done the same had the roles been reversed.

Though not surprised, Amrit was nevertheless deeply disturbed to see Shiv in a security guard's uniform. It was as if he had seen Shiv in a coffin. Something seemed to have died, even if it was just a dream – Shiv's dream. When strugglers first arrive in Mumbai, the big question on their minds is: *how* will I make it? As the struggle continues unfruitfully, the question then becomes: *will* I make it? And finally, when all hope is lost, the question becomes: *is* it worth continuing trying? For those who come to Mumbai with family consent and support, the world cuts you some slack when you are trying. As time passes, and no headway is made, the rope begins to tighten, the pressure from back home begins to mount, the countdown to the end begins. Thousands of strugglers follow this loop like clockwork every year in Mumbai. *Arrive-Struggle-Depart.* For others, like Shiv, who have burnt all their bridges from wherever they came and cannot got back, the loop becomes *Arrive-Struggle-Switch.* Switch to something else – that could be virtually anything – in Shiv's case it meant becoming a security guard.

There was an audible commotion in the crowd. Amitabh Bachchan had been spotted. The veteran Bollywood star stepped out of the massive wooden gates, wearing a comfortable looking kurta pyjama, and waved to the crowd with his multiple ring adorned left hand. Amitabh Bachchan is left handed – all his fans know that. He always held a gun in his left hand; threw his first punch from the left; and waved with his left hand. The crowd waved back, howled, cheered, whistled, clapped. Amitabh smiled. Then he turned and went back in, the large wooden doors closing behind him.

"Okay people, the show is over. Go home. Go home now." Shiv announced to the crowd, as he got busy dispersing them.

Shiv was now too far away from Amrit and looked embroiled in the important task of crowd dispersal. Amrit waited to make eye contact with Shiv, and when he did, he saluted him with his right hand. Shiv stood up erect, and like a soldier, saluted back, and then smiled.

"Hello, Amrit?"

"Yes." Amrit spoke into his mobile.

"Amrit, it's Ramu, from *Saas Ka Sindoor*. Remember me?"

"Yes, of course Ramuji! How are you?" Amrit recalled the AD from *Saas Ka Sindoor*. Ramu was one of the more clued-in ADs, who had once told Amrit he would go far.

"I am fine, Amrit. I have quit Jai Jai Productions." Ramu replied.

"Why?" Amrit asked.

"I got another opportunity; to be the first Assistant Director on a film project. Film is anyday better than television." Ramu explained.

"Oh that's great! Moving up the chain!" Amrit was happy for Ramu.

"Yes, thanks. Look, Amrit, the reason I'm calling you … we are looking for a new boy for our movie, a fresh face. I've seen your acting, and I've recommended your name to the producer. Can you come meet the producer? Now." There was an urgency in Ramu's voice.

Amrit thought for a moment. His thoughts briefly went to the night at Rajeev Chatterjee's den. But this was Ramu. He knew Ramu. This was okay.

"Okay, where?"

Within an hour Amrit was at the office of the producer.

"Please have a seat," the producer eyed Amrit from top to bottom.

"Amrit, Ramu tells me you are a very good actor," the producer continued. "He says he has seen you perform brilliantly."

"Thank you sir." Amrit beamed.

"Well, Amrit, I want a good actor for my movie. I can take you."

"I would love to work with you sir." Amrit was enthusiastic.

"However, there is one more thing, I don't know if Ramu told you about that?" The producer looked at Ramu. Ramu shook his head in a negative response.

"You see, Amrit, I would require you to put money in the film. Not much. Just one crore."

"I am sorry, I don't understand." Amrit was confused. Actors are supposed to get paid. The producer was asking *him* for money instead! Had he heard correctly?

"Amrit, it is straightforward. Nobody is going to give you a break in his movie. No matter how good an actor you are. If you want a break in films, you'll need to put up some of your own money, to co-produce the film. Here, you have an opportunity. I am only asking for one crore rupees. The film will cost six crores. So, you're only putting up one sixth, and you get a launch. Good deal!"

Amrit was silent. This is not what he was expecting to hear.

"Don't worry, it'll be money well spent. Once the movie is out, you'll be a star. You'll get other offers. You'll get the money back. And don't forget the money you'll get from endorsements, advertisements, brand ambassador contracts, star shows, ribbon cuttings, dandia appearances ... there are so many ways of getting your money back once you become a known face. Maybe you could even join politics. Who knows?"

"But sir, I don't have one crore rupees." Amrit said, looking down at his shoes.

"Then, I'm afraid, sunny boy, you're going to have to be doing television serials for the rest of your life."

With this, the producer got up, and signalled to Ramu to escort Amrit out.

Amrit walked out with his head hanging. Ramu put a hand around his shoulder, as if consoling him, as he walked him out to where Amrit's bike was parked.

"Amrit, I'm really sorry dude. I would really want you to be in the movie. I am powerless. The producer decides the casting. I could only suggest your name." Ramu justified himself.

"Ramuji, thanks. No problem. I know you did your best. Not your fault." Amrit said in a low, crackling tone.

Ramu sensed Amrit was deeply disappointed.

"Amrit, you're a damn good actor. Really, really good. This industry is so fucked up man." Ramu kicked a stone, which went and hit a sleeping dog, sending the poor mongrel into a whining scurry. "I mean ... look ... look at Riz, for example ... Sandy Khan's son. I mean ... the fellow really sucks. From no angle does he look like a hero. If it was not for his father, nobody would even look at him. My milkman is better looking than him. The fellow has a double chin, has to have a stubble on all the time just to hide it, is cross eyed, can't act ... and he's got five movies lined up ... five ... I mean ... *you* deserve to be a hero." Ramu stopped, facing Amrit, gesturing at Amrit with his eyes. "You've got it all ... the height, the body, the acting ... but ... but ... it's so fucked up man."

Ramu was genuinely distraught. He was truly hoping to have Amrit in his movie. He had seen Amrit's acting abilities. If he could, he would sign Amrit in a heartbeat.

"Bollywood works in strange ways," Ramu continued in a consoling tone. "Actors and actresses are 'launched,' as if they are satellites that are to be propelled into orbit by rockets. The rockets that propel these next-generation star-kids into orbit are custom-made films. Launch films are scripted keeping the hero and heroine to be launched in mind. If a newcomer male has to be launched, the script will be heavily weighed to showcase his talents. If he is a good dancer, there will be tons of songs picturised on him. If he is a bodybuilder action guy, there will be lots of action sequences reverse engineered into the movie. If the boy has a penchant for melodrama, expect a lot of that in the script. The aim is to make a star out of the lad by hook or by crook. Fathers, uncles and entire clans and networks are summoned and their resources marshalled for this task – the launch! The best of the best will be commissioned for the task. The best scriptwriters to write the script, the best lyricists to pen the songs, the best music director to give the music, the best cinematographer to shoot the film, the best foreign locales will be chosen for the shoot, the best designers, stylists, art directors, the best ... the works ... it's so fucked up man.... Even if the fellow doesn't know the ABC of acting, they will bloody make a star out of him. *Zabardasti.*"

Amrit nodded his head in acknowledgement. Riz would become a star, even though he did not know the ABC of acting. *ABC! Huh!* Amrit's mind was drifting ... back to another day at the acting academy ... *ABC...*

"Today, we will do an exercise that is called ABC. It combines what you have learnt so far and also tests your ability as an actor to think on your feet." Guruji announced to the class.

"As actors, you should be thinking creatures, using your own head even if you have been provided with a script and direction. The best actors are those who are not only talented, but also intelligent and can think on their feet. Today, I want to test that. The ABC exercise is an improvised scene between two actors. This scene could be happening anywhere, and the two actors playing it could be anyone. When the scene begins, there will be a conversation between the two actors. The rule of this exercise is that the conversation should begin with the alphabet 'A' and end with the alphabet 'Z,' going through all the alphabets from A to Z. So, for example, when the scene begins, when the first actor says a line which begins with 'A,' then the second actor has to say a line which begins with 'B,' and then the first actor will say a line which begins with 'C,' and then the second actor will say a line which begins with 'D,' and so on and so forth until you reach 'Z,' which is when the scene ends." Guruji made eye contact with every student.

"Through your conversation, you will have to define the scene, and act it out. Remember you are playing a character, and through this scene you will have to define that character. And, with your partner actor, you will also define the scene.

By the time the scene ends, the audience must know what the scene was about and who the two actors were and what their relationship was. It must be a complete scene. You have to be able to do this while keeping in mind that you have to strictly adhere to the A to Z rule. Tough? Not if you can think on your feet and on multiple tracks at the same time! Actors have to do that. At least the good actors do."

"Let's see … who should we start with … Riz … and Bhola…"

Riz and Bhola got up and came to the front of the class.

"Okay, both of you. You understand the rules of this ABC exercise?" Guruji asked.

"Yes sir," both replied.

"Good. Start. Action."

Riz and Bhola stood there staring at each other. Ten seconds passed. Twenty. Thirty. Still silence.

"Come on … Riz, Bhola, say something." Guruji could not take the silence any more. "Riz, you are from a distinguished acting family. Come on, show me what you're made of and what you've learnt at the Academy."

"Aaahh…. Ummmhhh…" mumbled Riz accidentally. Bhola took this as the start of the exercise and replied,

"Buddy, how are you?" patting Riz on the shoulder.

"Ouch … fuck you Bihari … why did you hit me so hard?" Riz rubbed the spot on the shoulder where Bhola had placed his heavy hand.

"Riz" Gurji shouted, "what comes after 'B' in the English alphabet?"

"Ummhh…" Riz was still rubbing his shoulder. Bhola was a strong man, but Riz was an exceptional weakling. Years of pampering had left him weak.

"C," replied Bhola, trying to help out his partner.

"That's right, 'C'," said Guruji, "then, Riz, why did you say 'Ouch,' which begins with 'O'? A, B, C; not A, B, O. Don't you know your ABCs?"

"Because he hit me and it hurt," said Riz, making a face at Bhola.

"Whenever you are on stage, or in front of the camera and a scene is going on, always stay in character, even if someone stabs you. The show must go on. Learn to stay focussed. Tomorrow you will be a movie star, people will say Riz was my student, I will have to hold my head in shame if you behave like this on the sets."

There was snickering from the class. Everyone knew Riz's family backing. He was a star kid. But everyone also knew that he was a total nincompoop when it came to acting. Acting may have been in his genes, but it certainly did not show.

"Sit down." Guruji said in disgust. Riz and Bhola sat down. Bhola was disappointed at getting such an inept partner and the exercise going badly. Riz still looked sullen and held the spot where Bhola had tapped him, less so because of any pain and more so to show that he had actually been hit, like a spoilt brat unwilling to accept his mistake.

"Meghna ... and Amrit ... you two." Guruji called out.

Meghna and Amrit sprung to their feet, thrilled at the chance.

"You two understand the rules of this ABC exercise?"

"Yes, sir," came confident replies in unison.

"Okay. Start. Action."

"Aah! Sweetheart, where have you been?" Amrit charged towards Meghna, with his arms spread, inviting a hug.

"Been busy. How are you?" replied Meghna, looking upset over something and avoiding Amrit's hug. The exercise was off to a flying start.

"Come to think of it, not too good without you darling." Amrit replied, noticing Meghna's mood.

"Do you really miss me that much?" inquired Meghna, still in the same upset mood.

"Ehh ... come on now ... what kind of question is that my love." Amrit tried to cheer her up.

"Forget it. There is no point asking you a direct question and expecting a direct answer." Meghna replied brooding over something.

"God! What is wrong with you darling? I have been away for a week on a family vacation with my wife and kids and this is the kind of welcome I get from you?" Amrit replied, slightly perturbed.

"How was the vacation?" Meghna asked in a matter of fact way.

"It was okay. Though I rather I could have taken you to the Bahamas instead. Just you and me, and the beautiful vast beaches ... sun and sand..." Amrit gesticulated with his hands, trying to convey the scenery.

"Just saying it or do you really mean it?" Meghna inquired, looking up at him.

"Katrina come here and give me a hug. I have been away from you for too long sweetie. I can't take this separation from you my love." Amrit extended his arms again, inviting a hug.

"Last time you said the same thing." Meghna didn't budge, still maintaining her icy tone.

"My god ... you have the memory of an elephant ... but the body of a swan..." with this Amrit put his hands around Meghna's neck.

"Now say that to your wife, huh!" Meghna said without moving and without responding to his gesture of affection, still icy.

"Oh! You're in some strange mood today." Amrit pulled his arms away from her, sounding unhappy at Meghna's lack of warmth.

"Perhaps…" said Meghna tersely.

"Quiet! I don't want us to talk," said Amrit putting a finger on Meghna's lips, and curling his arms around her, "I just want to hold you close to me and hear your heartbeat next to mine."

"Ratan," said Meghna looking straight into Amrit's eyes, "You are quite a player you know … and I have been thinking … I wish we had kept things just at the boss-secretary level."

"Stop it now Katrina! Enough is enough. You know I love you. I know I have been away from you, but I have been missing you all this while. Look into my eyes…"

There was a long silence. Meghna just continued staring into Amrit's eyes. Amrit felt she had lost the flow, forgotten what comes after 'S.' A quizzical look appeared in Meghna's eyes, which gave way to a look of panic. *Oh no! Meghna has forgotten what comes after S. T! Meghna – T!* Before the silence became too long for everyone to notice, Amrit decided to carry on with some nifty improvisation.

"Tears … I hate tears…" said Amrit as he wiped off imaginary tears from under Meghna's eyes. It was a good save.

"U…u…" said Meghna, breaking into a smile, "U are such a smooth-talking double-faced man…"

"Very good! This is what I get … huh … this is what I get in return for all that I do for you. I have given you a flat, a car, money … to hear this … this…" Amrit sounded hurt.

"Why can't you give me what you've given her?" implored Meghna. "You never intended to … did you Ratan? You just wanted me on the side … as your little mistress…. You only promised to make me your wife, but you really never intended to. You will always be married to her."

"Xtra…xtra…xtra…why does a woman always want extra? Never satisfied with what she has!" said Amrit in disgust.

Meghna didn't like this second grade treatment, and her face now showed anger.

"Yes … yes! I do want that something extra. I don't want your bloody flat, your bloody car, your bloody cash … I don't want to be your bloody whore…" Meghna stormed off in a rage. She walked out of the class. Amrit was left in the centre of the class. He stood there in silence for a while, wracking his brains for a word starting with 'Z.' It would be the last line of this ABC exercise. He wanted to make it a good one. Finally, he spoke.

"Zebra can't change its stripes, can it?" he said with a half-mischievous, half-sinister smile.

There was loud clapping and cheering from all the students. Guruji nodded in approval. Meghna, who had charged out of the class, returned on hearing the clapping, now smiling.

"Good! These two have picked up the ABC of acting," said Guruji, "while Riz, you have forgotten even your basic ABCs." Riz was still clasping his shoulder, and looked on, sulkingly.

Amrit smiled, a smile that tried to hide pain, and spoke softly to Ramu, "It's okay Ramuji. It's okay. It's the way the world is, I guess. Anyway, thanks for your help. I know you didn't have to do this. Thanks. Appreciate it!"

There was genuine gratitude in Amrit's words. He tried hard to sound upbeat. It wasn't Ramu's fault. As Ramu put it, it was a fucked up industry.

"Keep at it, Amrit. Don't give up. You have it in you." Ramu waved to Amrit, as he walked up to where his RX100 was parked. Amrit felt like talking to someone. He pulled out his cellphone and dialled Bhola's number. *This mobile number is either out of coverage area or switched off.* Amrit tried a few more times. Still the same pre-recorded message. *Where the hell is Bhola?*

CHAPTER 11

There was a massive traffic jam outside Andheri's Fame Adlabs multiplex movie theatre, as dozens of khakhi clad policemen and special commandos cordoned off the area, blocking traffic and allowing only VIP vehicles in. Amrit decided it was best to park his motorcycle far away and then walk up to the main entrance. Today was the premier of Riz Khan's debut movie, *Loverboy,* and a lot of high profile people were expected to be in attendance. Sandy Khan wanted this to be a grand event. After all, it was not everyday that his son's launch movie would be premiered. As a backup, though, the elder Khan had lined up five more releases for his son should this one bomb at the box office. Amrit jostled through a narrow gap between two media vans that were parked just where the red carpet began, and managed to slip through the crowd. The media contingent instantly began taking photographs. Amrit instinctively waved back to the flashbulbs. Amrit might not have been a movie star, but he surely looked like one, enough to confuse the photographers into taking a few snaps before realising their folly.

"Amrit!" Meghna called out to him from the other side of the metal detector. "This way."

Amrit made his way through the metal detector, showing his invitation pass to the security guards, and joined up with Meghna.

"Come fast, we were all waiting for you. The others are all seated upstairs. We need to be in our seats before the VIPs start arriving. Strict instructions from Sandy Khan."

Meghna took Amrit's hand and led him into the darkened cinema hall, and to their seats. They were ordinary seats, tucked away in the back corner of the five hundred-seater hall. Through the darkness, Amrit could tell that the hall was almost full, except for the first three rows, reserved for VIPs and special guests. Riz had kept his promise to his classmates from the Academy, and had invited them to his debut movie premier.

"I am so excited for Riz." Meghna said to Amrit, her diamond choker glittering in the dim lights, worn with matching diamond ear rings and a lovely black low-neck dress.

"Meghna, you look like you're dressed for the Oscars." Amrit flashed his dimples.

"Well, why not? There were press people outside, and a red carpet, didn't you notice? One never knows…" Meghna added in a hushed tone. She was really excited; as if it was her own movie that was premiering.

Suddenly, there was a flurry of activity on the red carpet that led to the front rows. A pack of press photographers and cameramen walked backwards as they filmed Sandy Khan, the Chairman of Govardhan Motion Pictures, politician Bandhoo Kumar, and a host of other celebrities as they made their way up the red carpet. Once they had settled down, another set of celebrities arrived. The cameramen let out bursts of flashes everytime they spotted a known face walk up the red carpet. Amrit held his breath as he saw the next couple walk up – it was Sapna, with Zaeed Zakaria! Amrit craned his neck forward and focused his eyes, though seated in the very back of the hall, it was hard for him to pick up everything that was going on. Sapna was dressed in a mermaid-like white flowing gown, worn with what looked like oversized pearl-drop earlobes, and a round pearl shaped egg in her hairbun. Zaeed Zakaria, looking dapper in a black tuxedo and gelled hair, led her down the red carpet towards their VIP seats in the front row. Amrit exhaled, then looked away. There was a loud bang as a brass orchestra that was positioned just below the stage began to play. Amrit tried to make out what the music was. The band was playing tunes from Sandy Khan's films.

"Ladies and gentleman!" A booming voice came over the hall's impressive sound system. The band had gone silent. A spotlight suddenly shone on what appeared to be a man standing with his back to the audience, next to a large object that was draped in a white silk cloth. The man turned around.

"Oh my god! It's producer-director Tapan Grover!" Meghna cried out like a little girl, as the man in the spotlight turned to face the audience. It indeed was Tapan Grover.

"Welcome to the premier of *Loverboy*, starring Sandy Khan…" There was loud applause. "And introducing, the one and only, the star of the next generation, the heartthrob of girls from Mumbai to Miami, and some boys…" Tapan snickered at his own joke. "Presenting, the newest addition to Bollywood's galaxy of stars, and my good friend, and son of Sandy uncle … Riz Khan!" The band played out a loud celebratory tune, as confetti began to rain down from the ceiling above. There was a loud firecracker explosion, and Riz Khan appeared from what looked like a hydraulic lift that emerged out of the stage floor. He was wearing a well-tailored three-piece suit, and had a multi-day stubble on his face. Riz smiled and waved to the crowds as he walked up to where Tapan was standing next to the mystery object.

"Ladies and gentlemen, here I give you … Riz Khan!" Tapan's words were drained out by the band. Tapan now signalled the band to be quiet.

"I would now like to request our chief guest for the evening, Shri Bandhoo Kumarji, leader of the Loktantra Party, and special patron of Bollywood, to please come up on stage." Bandhoo Kumar got up from his front row seat and walked up on to the stage, accompanied by Sandy Khan. Tapan Grover passed the mike to Bandhoo Kumar, who began to speak,

"Respected members of the audience, dignitaries, and fellow Indians. *Jai Hind!* It is a great honour to be here today. As a servant of the *peepull*, I am pleased to say that the *peepull* of India are proud of Bollywood. Not only in India, but all over the world, Bollywood has brought us Indians great glory. On behalf of the *peepull* of India, let me say, that we are proud of Bollywood, and all the Bollywood *peepull!*" There was a round of applause. Bandhoo Kumar continued, "Sandy Khan is like my brother, and young Riz I have seen grow up before my own eyes. He is like my own son. So today, on this very happy occasion of his first movie being released, I want to present him with a small gift from my side." Bandhoo Kumar signalled to a few stage hands who pulled the sheet off the mystery object.

"It is a platinum plated limited edition Rolls Royce Phantom car." Tapan Grover roared, as the silk sheet came off the vehicle.

There was a gasp from the audience.

"She's a real beauty!" Amrit exclaimed and let out a low whistle.

"Yeah!" Meghna agreed.

Bandhoo Kumar presented the keys of the Rolls Royce to Riz, and then they posed for photographs with the car.

"And now, ladies and gentlemen, what we've come here for – the movie – *Loverboy!* Sit back, relax, and enjoy!" Tapan Grover announced and walked off the stage. A few stage hands pushed the Rolls Royce into the wings, and the curtain on the screen began to be pulled up. The screen came alive, as the titles began to roll.

Loverboy
....
Starring: Sandy Khan
....
Introducing: Riz Khan
....

"Udita, you have to sleep with him. Do not argue." Bandhoo Kumar repeated in the face of Udita's opposition. During the movie, Bandhoo Kumar had text messaged Udita on her mobile to meet him in the hall's VIP men's toilet during the interval.

"Or else." Bandhoo Kumar pressed the PLAY button on his mobile DVD player, bringing to screen Udita's sex with Bhola caught on tape surreptitiously.

"What is wrong with debauchery. After all, if something feels so good, what's wrong with it? I believe in fornication – it gives me pleasure, money – two of my basic needs are met. To hell with society. I am not answerable to anyone. I like it and I am going to continue to do it."

Udita watched herself utter these lines before engaging in sex with Bhola.

"Stop!" She cried, anger and frustration welling inside her. Blackmail is a very powerful tool, and Bandhoo Kumar had already used it to make Udita sleep with three businessmen, two politicians and one foreign diplomat. She had become his personal call girl, to be used wherever and on whomever he wished.

"Mike Patel tells me your father is looking for a suitable boy for you to get married to. I've also heard he's a heart patient. What if I made a thousand copies of this video recording on DVDs and distributed it among the porn-movie sellers of Mumbai, and also sent one copy to your father?" Bandhoo Kumar suggested menacingly.

"What do you want me to do now?" Udita asked in desperation. Her father would certainly die of a heart attack if he ever laid eyes on this footage.

"As I said, there is this visiting foreign businessman. I want you to sleep with him. He's an important man. You have to make him happy. Understood?" Bandhoo Kumar signalled.

"Okay, I'll do it. But this is the last time. You will hand me the original video recording after this. Right?" Udita demanded.

"Yes, this is the last time. God promise. I will hand you the original video after this. Promise." Bandhoo Kumar pledged.

"That's what you said last time too ... with that diplomat. Every time you say that. But I swear to god, if you don't hand me the original video recording this time, I will…" Udita raised a finger at Bandhoo Kumar.

Bandhoo Kumar immediately grabbed Udita's hand and twisted her arm around, making her squeal in pain.

"Listen you girl, don't you ever threaten Bandhoo Kumar. You know who I am?" The veteran politician fumed with anger as he twisted Udita's arm further.

"In India, if you have money and power, you can get away with murder. Literally. What are *you*? I could snap my finger, like this," Bandhoo Kumar snapped his fingers. Overbearing onion and garlic vapours wafted from his breath and filled Udita's nasal passages. Udita was too stunned to complain. "You would vanish into thin air, nobody would know a thing. They would cut you up into a dozen pieces and feed them to crocodiles. Finish. No trace."

Bandhoo Kumar let go of Udita's arm. Udita felt a shiver run down her spine. She was shaking. Bandhoo Kumar was a seriously powerful politician; and powerful politicians in India are above the law. It's an inconvenient truth everyone in India knows about, yet can't seem to do anything to change. Caste, money and criminal politics in a country that is still largely illiterate ensure that the likes of Bandhoo Kumar would continue to stay in power in the world's largest post-colonial democratic experiment. Like a little inconsequential fly, Udita was sucked up into the midst of this unstoppable tornado of politics, corruption and crime that defines the polity of the modern Indian state. She was trapped. She really had no option but to comply with Bandhoo Kumar's orders. She wished she had never decided to step into the rotten treacherous world of Bollywood.

"*Saali randi! Ab jaa raha hun picture dekhne.*" Bandhoo Kumar spat out chewed paan into the sink and walked out of the men's toilet.

Cocktails were arranged in the lobby of the cinema hall after the show. Amrit sipped an iced tea as he stood looking at Bollywood's rich and famous. *What rubbish acting*, Amrit mused. *Loverboy is surely going to flop. Riz still can't act.*

"Meghna tells me you're a software programmer." Raman interrupted Amrit's thoughts, sipping from his glass of white wine.

"Yes." Amrit replied, still analysing Riz's performance in his mind, and thinking how he would have done the role if given a chance.

"So why did you decide to come to Bollywood? Same reason as Meghna's – to get famous?" Raman inquired, pointing to Meghna, who was boisterously mingling with the Page 3 crowd.

Amrit shook his head to say no. Suddenly he spotted someone he knew. It was Guruji, from the Anil Taneja Acting Academy, standing next to Anil Taneja, the businessman-owner of the Academy. Guruji had that look on his face … a look Amrit had seen before … Amrit tried to recall … His mind slipping back to the days at the Academy … to the day of the Bollywod Roulette exercise…

"Today, boys and girls," said Guruji, "we will do an exercise that is called Bollywood Roulette."

"I am sure most of you have been to a casino or seen or read about the game of roulette." Shiv looked back at Guruji absolutely puzzled. There are no casinos in Benaras.

"Well, if you haven't," said Guruji, looking at a confused Shiv, "just remember that the game of roulette is a game of chance and a game of luck."

"There is another version of the game of roulette," he continued, "known as Russian Roulette, which is played with a revolver and one bullet. A revolver has six chambers which can hold six bullets. In Russian Roulette, you put one bullet into a chamber, and then rotate the chambers randomly and close them, so that you don't know in which chamber the bullet is."

"Like Gabbar Singh did in the movie *Sholay* sir … the *kitnae aadmi thae* scene…" Shiv blurted out, finally getting what this roulette thing was about.

"Yes. Except that Gabbar had three bullets in six chambers. In Russian Roulette, you have only one bullet in six chambers. Better chances of survival." Guruji continued.

"This game we will play today, Bollywood Roulette, is similar to Russian Roulette. In that there is a revolver with six chambers, and I will put one bullet into a chamber, and then rotate the chambers randomly so that no one knows which chamber the bullet is in."

"And then," continued Guruji, "we will all sit around in a circle, and I will put the revolver to the head of someone. I will then ask that individual why I should not kill him or her. That individual has to answer to me, as best as he or she can, as to why I must spare him or her. If I am convinced by the reasons given, I will spare him or her, and move on to the next person. If I am not convinced with what he or she has to say, I will pull the trigger ... and then, depending on where the bullet is, that is, depending on luck, he or she will either survive or die."

Shiv started having hiccups, worried that he might get killed here. Passion for acting and becoming the next Amitabh Bachchan was fine, but he didn't want to go down like one of Gabbar's goons. The hiccups intensified. What was the need for this strange game, with a revolver and one bullet? He began to wonder if leaving Benaras was such a good idea.

"Relax," said Guruji noticing Shiv's condition. "The gun is a toy gun and the bullet is a fake, a blank. Just a dummy. Only bang, no blood."

Shiv felt better. He was not going to be martyred at the altar of the creative arts.

"So arrange yourself in a circle."

Everyone sat around in a circle.

"For me, this game of Bollywood Roulette is an ultimate test of your acting abilities. Steel is tested under fire, and actors are tested under pressure. As actors, you must put everything that you've got into each of your acting performances, as if your life depended on it. In the game of Bollywood Roulette, you life depends on how you perform. If you are able to act convincingly, you survive. If you can't be convincing, you are dead. Finished. Everything I have taught you so far boils down to this. Are you convincing? Your life depends on that. No matter how small your role is, treat it with respect. As a do or die situation. In Bollywood, in this brutal city of Mumbai, you might not get a second chance. You might, if you are lucky, and the chamber is empty when the trigger is pulled. But then, you might not be lucky, and the trigger might be pulled with the bullet right there, boom! End of story." Guruji walked around the circle, revolver in hand, into which he dropped a blank shot, spun the chamber vigorously, and cocked it into place, ready to fire.

"Meghna." Guruji said, placing the gun on Meghna's temple in a flash.

"Yes sir," replied a noticeably shaken Meghna. Even though the shot was a blank, a gun still felt uncomfortable to any head.

"Why should I let you live?" asked Guruji, casually.

"Sir, I am a wife, a daughter-in-law, a doctor, I have responsibilities. To myself, to my family, to society. Besides, I have been the most diligent student in your class and I wish to show the world what I've learnt here and make a mark for myself in the acting world of Bollywood." Meghna said quickly, but clearly and confidently.

"Hmmm..." Guruji murmured and moved away from her.

"Shiv!" The gun was now on Shiv's head.

"Sir ... sir ... why me sir.... Sir, I am going to be the next Amitabh Bachchan. Why kill me sir? I will become famous and tell everyone how great Guruji is."

"We already have one Amitabh Bachchan, why do we need another one?" Guruji said coolly, pulling back the hammer of the revolver.

"Bbbbuuttt sir ... why sir ... don't sir ... please sir ... don't sir..."

Click. Guruji had pulled the trigger as the hammer came down on a blank chamber.

"Lucky fellow. Highly unconvincing, but lucky. You might not be so lucky in real life."

With this Guruji moved on to Amrit, placing the gun on his temple.

"Sir, you can kill me if you want to. I am not afraid to die," said Amit looking straight ahead, pride in every word. "What I will be disappointed in is that I won't get a chance to fulfil what I am really passionate about. I will not get a chance to test myself against the best of the best in Bollywood. But if that be my destiny, then so be it. Man is not god, and god I wish not to displease. If it be god's will that I may perish now, then so be it." There was fire in Amrit's tone, as if a fearless warrior had just entered the fray, not caring a damn about his life.

"Hmm… passion…" Guruji said with a chuckle and moved on, without any reaction from Amrit, who continued to be in his trance.

"Sapna …do you match the same passion?" Guruji asked the ever-effervescent Sapna, playfully tilting his head to where Amrit was seated, alluding to the chemistry between her and Amrit, which was not hidden from Guruji's seasoned eyes.

Sapna smiled back, those eyes dancing playfully. She knew this was just another acting exercise, and wasn't nearly as serious about it as Amrit and Meghna.

"No sir, if we were all so serious about things we would be in such a boring world, no sir?" Sapna played on, pointing her eyes in Amrit and Meghna's direction, almost mocking their seriousness. Guruji smiled back. He liked humour, especially in tense situations.

"I will tell you why you shouldn't kill me. Because I am needed to relieve the tension. There is so much tension in this world, and I, Sapna, am needed to relieve that tension. I am needed to add masala." She continued playfully. "I am going to do a little dance to entertain all of you. If you like the dance, don't kill me. If you don't, then do. Okay?"

"Okay!" Guruji liked this.

"There is one condition, I don't want everyone to be so gloomy and sad. I want you to clap as I dance." Sapna was intent on lightning the mood.

"Like Basanti danced for Gabbar in the movie *Sholay*!" beamed Shiv, to which everyone laughed. Sapna had succeeded in thawing up the freeze. Guruji beamed back. And then to everyone's clapping, Sapna did a little Rajasthani dance in the middle of the circle. When she finished, she did a little bow, aimed more towards Amrit, making eye contact with him. It did the trick. It broke his trance. He smiled back, those dimples appearing, to which Sapna winked at him.

"Good. You deserve to live. The world needs you." Guruji spared Sapna.

Next, Guruji placed the revolver on Riz's head.

"You ... Mr. Khan ... do you want to live?"

Guruji tapped the gun on the star-son's head.

"Ouuch..." squealed Riz.

"Still stuck on Ouch ... Riz?" Guruji said, hearing which Bhola chuckled loudly, recalling the ABC exercise that Riz had bungled up with him in a similar manner.

"Yeah ... Of course I want to live ... to be a star ... the next Khan on the block ... Bollywood superstar ... yeah ... like my dad." Riz looked up at Guruji with an arrogant expression. For a few moments there was silence, and then Riz shrugged his shoulders and said, "Why ... isn't that reason enough?" Riz looked around the class for support. There was just disdain in everyone's eyes. Nobody respected him for what he was. If he did not have the family backing that he did, nobody would even glance at him a second time. Guruji read these thoughts in Riz's classmates' eyes.

"No. That is a very poor reason. I'm afraid, Mr. Khan, you will have to die." Guruji said, in a matter of fact way, trying hard to push the lad to react, a last-ditch effort to get some passion for acting out of him.

Riz stared back, blank. Finally, Guruji lost his patience, and pulled the trigger.

Bang!

"You are dead, Mr. Khan," announced Guruji. "Unfortunately, very shortly, Bollywood audiences will have to endure you as a new star." Meghna and Amrit looked at each other with a look that said it all. It is such an unfair world!

At that moment there was a knock on the door. Anil Taneja, the founder-owner of the Academy, walked in.

"What was that noise?" Anil Taneja asked Guruji.

"We were just playing Bollywood Roulette," said Guruji.

"Oh!" Anil Taneja broke out in a forced laugh. "So, who was the unlucky one? Who got killed?" Anil Taneja beamed as he looked around the class.

"Riz Khan," replied Guruji.

Anil Taneja's smile immediately dried up. Riz would be the last person in the class whom he'd want to see dead in a game of Bollywood Roulette. Riz was a horse worth betting on – he was going to be launched to stardom, and would eventually become a star – Anil Taneja had no doubt in his mind. His superstar father Sandy Khan would not rest till that happened. It was on the likes of Riz that the future business of the Academy depended. When Riz would go up on stage to receive an acting award at a Bollywood awards ceremony, which was anyway rigged, Anil Taneja would want him to mention the Academy in his 'thank-you' speech. Such thank-yous from past student stars is what kept the admission roster buzzing at the Academy. It was crucial to keeping the image going that the Academy was the only place to go to if you wanted to make it as an actor in Bollywood. A pissed-off Riz would be less likely to remember to thank the Academy in his speeches and interviews. It was crucial that Riz not leave the Academy with a bitter taste in his mouth. Business depended on it. Anil Taneja's mind was racing.

"Ha! Ha! Ha!" Anil Taneja put on a laughing mask as he clapped his hands loudly. "This is great news for Riz!"

Riz looked up, confused.

"You know, in the past, all those students who have died playing Bollywood Roulette, have ended up as stars in Bollywood. So, it is a great omen for you, Riz. Ha! Ha! Ha!"

Riz cheered up, unable to see through Anil Taneja's antics and actually believing him.

Guruji looked at Anil Taneja with a pained look on his face.

It's that same pained look on Guruji's face again, Amrit now remembered. Amrit could tell that Guruji was disappointed with Riz's performance in *Loverboy*. Anil Taneja, on the other hand, was grinning from ear to ear, standing next to Guruji sipping from his mug of beer. His prophecy had come true. Riz was officially a movie star now. He had bet on the right horse. Now, he just hoped and prayed that Riz would win the award for the best male actor in a debut role for *Loverboy* and thank Anil Taneja and the Academy profusely in his acceptance speech – that would set the admissions (and cash) register at the Academy on fire. Fantasising about his future fortunes, Anil Taneja eyed the proceedings with much greed, grabbing a second mug of beer from a waiter who passed by.

Just then Meghna arrived with Riz.

"Congratulations Riz." Raman said.

"Thanks." Riz said cheerfully.

"What did you think?" Riz asked Amrit.

"Not bad. But why did you have to keep a stubble throughout the movie? Didn't the plastic surgeon in Los Angeles get rid of the double chin?" Amrit asked.

Riz was unhappy with Amrit's question.

"I asked what you thought of my *acting*." Riz said tersely.

"You were copying your father too much. But I guess that's what the director must have wanted. A clone of Sandy Khan! In any case, acting was never your strong point even at the Academy." Amrit was in a belligerent mood.

Meghna's jaw dropped.

"Neither was dancing, nor fighting, nor ... I'm trying to think what your strong point is?" Amrit continued in the same vein.

Riz was stunned.

"His father." Guruji, who had been listening, joined in. "That's his strong point."

"Okay tell me, did Tapan Grover make a move on you ... did you have to indulge in butt-sacrifice?" Amrit continued his tirade. "Is he really gay? Did he make a homo out of you too?"

"Stop! Just stop okay!" Riz blurted out so loudly that people started staring at him. "Why are you guys always sniping at me, huh? Is it my fault that I am a star-son? That I was born to superstar Sandy Khan? Fine I know I have opportunities that you guys don't. But is that *my* fault? If you were in my position what would you do? Would you not gladly take the opportunities that were before you, as they are before me? Or would you say 'no, I'm going to make it on my own, to hell with my father and all his connections and all the strings that he can pull?' None of you would do that. *None of you!* You would do *exactly* what I'm doing. You would grab the opportunities. Hypocrites!"

Meghna tried to pacify Riz by putting an arm around him.

"Don't touch me!" Riz pushed Meghna way. "You are like them too ... don't I know ... secretly you abhor me too. I know. Is that what you grudge me, that I have opportunities and you don't? Is that why you despise me so much? Is that where your jealously and hatred of me stems from? Well, if that is the case, so be it. I don't care. You want to hate me and be jealous, fine, you go ahead and do it. I am not going to care. I have the opportunities, I'm lucky, but I intend to make full use of them. I might not be the best actor out of our class, I might not be the best looking, and yes, maybe if we were in a purely meritocratic world, one of you would have been where I am. But guess what, we don't live in a meritocratic world. It is a world where the king's son becomes the next king, and that's the way it has been for ages. And that's the way it will be. Better get used to it. I am being nice to you guys, you are my classmates, I like you, really, I do. But you guys are just jealous. *Just simply jealous*. It's despicable! My father is right, he says it is always lonely at the top. You really can never have friends. Fine, I can deal with that. Comes with the turf."

"Riz, relax, you're overreacting. *I* liked your performance in *Loverboy*." Raman tried to pacify him.

"I am sorry. I mean *we* are sorry. Perhaps we were too harsh on you." Meghna added. "And I mean this on behalf of everyone ... including Bhola, who is not here."

"By the way, where is Bhola?" Amrit asked, suddenly realising Bhola's absence.

"Don't you *know*? I thought you two were best friends." Riz quizzed.

"*Know* what? I went to his flat ... he's not there. Isn't picking up his phone too. I have no clue." Amrit had a confused look on his face. Was there something he didn't know?

"Bhola is dying. He's in ICU. It's the bodybuilding drugs he used to take. Gave him liver cancer. Serves the bloody Bihari right." Riz felt avenged.

Bhola was a horrifying sight as he lay there on the hospital bed. The chemotherapy and radiotherapy treatments to fight his late-stage liver cancer had caused his hair to fall – Bhola was totally bald now – and his skin had an unhealthy pale glow to it. Most shocking, however, was the state of his body. The rock-solid bodybuilder's frame was gone. In its place, Bhola had shrivelled to a thin emaciated skeleton, his skin dangling loosely everywhere, visible around his neck and arms. He had lost nearly hundred kilos of body mass. The visual impact of the transformation shocked Amrit.

Bhola recognised Amrit as he approached his bed, a bouquet of flowers in hand. Bhola put his hand out for Amrit to shake. Amrit took Bhola's outstretched hand. It felt weak and cold, not like the warm-blooded iron grip that it once was.

"Hello, my friend." Bhola spoke, with some difficulty.

Amrit burst into tears. He just couldn't believe it was the same Bhola. Bhola smiled as he noticed his former classmate, who had always struggled with crying, now facing him with watery eyes.

"So you do cry, Amrit from Amritsar! Guruji should have seen this. The acting trophy would have been yours!" Bhola said with a smile. Amrit noticed Bhola's gums were bleeding.

Amrit forced a smile, more tears filling his eyes. Years of steroid abuse had finally taken its toll on Bhola's health. The bodybuilding drugs had given him liver cancer, and it was now all but certain that Bhola was going to die. In a last ditch effort, the doctors had been pumping Bhola's body with toxic, cancer destroying chemicals and had been firing x-rays at his liver to contain the deadly spread of the cancer. They too knew that chemotherapy and radiotherapy might delay, but could not prevent, the now certain end. Bhola was a skeleton waiting to breathe his last.

"Bhola, you shouldn't have taken steroids." Amrit said, his voice choking. As soon as Amrit said it, he realised he shouldn't have.

There was pain in Bhola's eyes as he contemplated his past actions. Bhola had brought this upon himself. In a mad pursuit of his Bollywood ambitions, he had ended killing himself. He had pumped his body with drugs that had destroyed his liver. Tears appeared in Bhola's eyes as he stared in silence for some time.

"Amrit," Bhola said softly, as he played with Amrit's fingers, "You are from a good family ... get out of this rotten place before it is too late." Bhola looked right into Amrit's eyes, imploring him. Amrit nodded his head, as he swallowed.

A nurse arrived with a bedpan.

"Time for your ablutions," the nurse announced, manoeuvring the bedpan into place under Bhola's lifeless body. Amrit placed the bouquet of flowers on the bedside table. He couldn't bear to see a man once so supremely strong and glorious now unable to even take care of his most basic needs. Amrit couldn't even bear to say goodbye to Bhola. The thought that his friend would probably be dead in weeks, if not days, deeply troubled Amrit. He took one final look at Bhola and left, tears streaming down his cheeks.

CHAPTER 12

Amrit was at a stage when he would have tear-eruptions many times a day for no apparent reason at all. His eyes would fill up with tears and a lump would come in his throat. And then he would wipe his eyes, swallow and carry on.

Amrit took a gulp of whiskey from the bottle. The warm fluid went down his throat calming him. Alcohol weakened him and he wept even more. Tears swelling down heavy eyelids, slipping down unstoppably, warm and wet.

"Amrit, I would have given you the best actor trophy," Guruji had said, after announcing that Meghna had won the best actor trophy for their batch, "but you need to work on one particular aspect of your acting repertoire – the ability to cry. You need to learn to be able to cry. You are fantastic in every other department, better than Meghna, but this is your Achilles heel." Amrit had always struggled with scenes in which he was required to cry. He had always wondered why a grown man would ever cry. Now, he knew. A grown man cries when he feels powerless, boxed-in, unable to do anything. When the testosterone-driven male instincts of lashing out, physically or otherwise, seem inadequate – in fact, comically weak and worthless –

when all mental solutions are exhausted, and the man is emotionally drained – then those tears flow out. As much as he tried to hold them back, he was just wholly-grossly powerless at doing so. They would just keep flowing. It had become a general state of his overall being, a condition that Amrit had never known before. Grief, loss, frustration – these words don't fully capture the threshold crossed when those tear glands activate. When all the other muscles in Amrit's body failed him, his tear glands didn't. Strong men don't cry, he was told as a boy growing up in Amritsar. Today, the strongest of them was crying. The floodgates were open. He just couldn't help it. Grown men cry too. The strongest of them do too.

There was much to cause Amrit these tears. Bhola's approaching end; Amrit's unfulfilled Bollywood dreams; and then, there was Sapna. Amrit was sad not just because he had lost Sapna. He was sad because he knew deep down that even if Sapna returned to him, it would not be the same again. She had strayed; he had strayed. The purity and innocence had been lost. Even if love was reunited, it would not be as it was before. This depressed him further. It was a lost cause. There are paths you walk down that you can't reverse – they had both walked down parting ways. And from the looks of it, Sapna wasn't coming back to him in the first place. He sunk down deeper. He wished he could have it like in the films. Boy meets girl, both fall in love, and live happily ever after. Their story had got horribly complicated. Wish he could have that simplicity again. Amrit wished he had taken up Sapna's offer, when on so many occasions she had pleaded with him to drop everything and get married and settle down in Bangalore. Amrit wished he could go back to that point in time. He had been so stupid. And now he had lost her. But he couldn't seem to lose her in his thoughts.

"Amrit!" Meghna's voice came over the phone's speaker. "Did you go see Bhola? How is he?"

"Not good. He's dying." Amrit coughed as he struggled for words.

Meghna could hear sounds that sounded like sobbing.

"Amrit? Are you crying? *You?*" Meghna said.

There was silence from Amrit's side.

"Amrit. You don't sound too good to me. Listen, what's been going on with you? I heard about your *Saas Ka Sindoor* exit. And I know what's going on between you and Sapna. Look, Sapna wants to meet you." Meghna could hear Amrit clear his throat.

"Why?" Amrit asked, still sounding heavy.

"She will tell you tomorrow. I am shooting at Qayamat Studios in Bandra. Meet me around noon. I have a 7 am shift and should be done by noon. I'll get Sapna to come too. Will you be there?" Meghna implored.

There was more silence.

"Yes." Amrit finally answered.

"Good! See you there. And cheer up. Count your blessings, okay?" Meghna cajoled.

"Okay. Thanks Meghna. See you." Amrit said, hanging up the phone.

Amrit went and sat down by his bedroom window. Rain was pouring down. The monsoon season was in full swing. Amrit's thoughts drifted. He thought of Bhola. He couldn't believe it. *Bhola is dying!* He tried to push the thought of death away. Amrit looked up at the sky. The cloud cover was thick. Amrit thought of the time when he and Sapna were at the Bandra seafront. What a magical time it had been! How happy they were, in each other's arms, with the rain drenching them! Oh how he wished he could go back in time to that day! They had grown so apart. Yet, it still felt like yesterday. Amrit shut his eyes. He could see Sapna's face. Sapna dancing in the rain. Sapna in his arms. Her eyes ... Oh those hazel eyes! Amrit opened his eyes. The rain had intensified. Amrit could feel warmth swell in his eyes. Tears rushed down his cheeks uninvited. Guruji would indeed have been proud.

Amrit parked his motorcycle outside Qayamat Studios. The rain was heavy and Amrit kept his raincoat on. His mind kept going back to Bhola. Then he thought of Sapna. Amrit wasn't sure how his meeting with Sapna might go. Why did she want to meet him? There had been a lot of water under the bridge. Amrit decided to have a few drinks to fortify himself before he met Sapna. It was morning but it was still crowded at the Zen Bar and Lounge. There were many at the bar, sipping beer and spirits, and some on the dance floor, grooving to the techno tracks blaring out of the powerful speakers acoustically arranged around the dance floor. This was a favourite joint of college students, who would bunk classes to go drinking and dancing instead.

Amrit took off his raincoat and put it on the bar stool and ordered a double shot of vodka. In an instant, he gulped it down. *What would he say to Sapna? Could he ever forgive her?* Amrit downed two more shots of vodka. *Those eyes! How he loved those eyes!* Amrit had another shot. Amrit's thoughts once again drifted to the time when he and Sapna had gone to the Bandra seafront. But a lot had happened since that day. Amrit took another shot of vodka. *Zaeed Zakaria! That bastard!* Amrit's mind conjured up an image of the billionaire playboy in bed with Sapna. Amrit downed two shots. And then two more. Vodka only inflamed the storm brewing inside him. He had lost out on love. Sapna was with another man. He had lost out in his profession. His acting career was not going anywhere. In both love and in career, he thought he should have gotten there. His friend Bhola was on his deathbed. He thought of Riz – he must be shooting for his second movie. Such an unfair world! Amrit emptied another shot of vodka. There was tremendous unease within him. The storm brewing inside Amrit was threatening to erupt with the force of a volcano.

Amrit decided to hit the dance floor. He began grooving to the music. His body was loosened by the alcohol in his bloodstream. The music was synchronised to the blue laser lights aimed at the dance floor, painting a surreal environment. Amrit's body grooved to the music, his head and body moving to the beat. His mind was switched off but there were subconscious thoughts going on. He continued to move. The vodka had now completely worked its way into his body. The DJ changed the track to one with a faster tempo. Amrit's body started moving faster too, matching the beats blaring out of the speakers. Amrit was approaching a trance-like state, not in control of his body anymore. The rhythm of the music and the subconscious rhythm of his mind ruled his movements. His eyes shut, Amrit was in a world of his own. Flashes of Sapna's face and her mesmerising eyes kept coming to his mind. The blue lasers cut across the room like light-switchblades. The music became faster, working its way up to a crescendo. Amrit was moving faster. Faster. Faster. Suddenly there was a loud explosion. Amrit blurted out – a scream – loud and long. He was looking towards the roof of the discotheque, his eyes still shut, his arms spread wide, and screaming a loud primeval scream. The roof of the disco had ruptured, rain water pouring down on the dance floor like a waterfall. People ran helter skelter, as water poured in from above. Amrit pelted for a full two minutes, and then finally dropped to his knees and burst into tears. Water kept falling directly on him, drenching him, as Amrit remained knelt on the dance floor.

When Amrit cries, the whole world will cry, Bhola had once remarked. Today, the sky was indeed crying, letting go all its pent up heavy swells in an outpour as heavy as Amrit's. Not in tiny droplets here and there that prettily tip-tipped now and then, the kind you would enjoy watching from a window; but in sheet after sheet of furiously heavy torrents that just kept coming and coming in wave after wave, as if unleashed from a mysteriously inexhaustible source, bringing the whole world to a standstill. Every single man, woman, eunuch and child in this city that doesn't stop for anyone, had been held by their scruffs and commanded to a halt! – till the important business of purging, outpouring, cleansing – so long overdue, could take place.

Until today, school children across India were taught that the record for the highest rainfall in any single day anywhere in India stood at 838mm for Cherrapunji in the remote eastern Indian state of Meghalaya, a record that had stood since 1910. Today, that would change. Henceforth, school children will be taught that the highest amount of rainfall that ever fell anywhere in India was 943mm on this day, in Mumbai. Yes, in Mumbai. Not in some far-flung remote hilly town. Here, in Mumbai, bang in the centre of all the action. Today! What this record-altering statistic would not tell them is that the 943mm of unprecedented rainfall would cause an unprecedented flood in India's premier metropolis, wrecking havoc, destroying houses, shops, washing away entire buildings, turning roads and railtracks into fast flowing rivers, bringing down power lines and grids, drowning hundreds of people and causing hundreds of others – those who managed to survive – to be stranded away from home that night, scampering for shelter, as the rain continued to come down heavily all night long.

Even the animals were not spared from the wrath – dogs, cats, stray cattle, birds, creatures of the soil – all subject to the same treatment. After all, they too were Mumbaikars and had partaken of the largesse of this city. No excuses. Grey justice would not spare anyone today. The twin pincers of descending skies and ascending waters would today squeeze the light out of many lives. Justice would come randomly and swiftly. From billionaire stockbroker to roadside mongrel – they were all scurrying. It was a return to the primeval – each one for themselves, clinging on to anything they could, to survive this flood. Justice was meted out in strangely arbitrary ways. Water rising to nostril-level of a stray cow standing isolated on a pavement blinking its innocent large black eyes, as it drowned, accepting silent death as it came surely – second by second. The business magnate's sedan remained planted in the river that the road had become, water almost reaching the last six inches of its rolled up windows. The sophisticated electronic security system of the car had short-circuited, permanently jamming the doors and insuring that it will become the occupier's coffin. Death was only six inches away. Yet, the powerful and mighty magnate, struggling hard against the door, could do nothing about it. Effluence had overpowered influence today. Death came not in a faraway or unfamiliar land; it came right here, in Mumbai, in his own citadel. Death by clouds! "A business tycoon killed by the fluffy moisture stuff from the sky! Ha!" Amrit thought of a possible newspaper headline, as he waded through the waters in a state of delirium.

Today, the world seemed to have indeed gone crazy. Or perhaps, today was the only day that made sense. Had *he* caused it, wondered Amrit. Naah! But it sure was fun to watch! Today boundaries had been breached, barriers broken, hearts and skies ripped open. Hah! No more holding back. No more bottled up pain. Let it all flow. Amrit flung headlong into the water, and started swimming, free stroke, then turning around, doing a backstroke, then switching to free stroke, splashing around. He was reminded of his days as a little boy at the Gymkhana Club swimming pool in Amritsar. Oh, what fun it used to be! The joys of childhood! Flipping around in the crystal waters, splashing others in the pool, and then rubbing water out of the eyes which others had splashed water into in retaliation. The waters today were not crystal clear, they were dark, slurpy, with a viscosity of oil, and an intention and an agenda, not neutral. These waters meant business, and they went about doing it quietly and ruthlessly.

A large electric pole fell just ahead of Amrit, the electric wires immediately setting off a violent sparkling display on impact with the water. Amrit stopped for a moment and looked at the crackling and the blue bolts that seemed to have a life and pattern to themselves, dancing and whizzing to a beat that would normally cause fear. But today, somehow, they didn't. The short-circuiting display appeared strangely beautiful. Amrit straightened himself and watched, as the sparking finally died out, and the heavy electric pole went under, pulling the live wires with it, forming a type of suspension bridge of wires that rose out of the water like multiple fishing lines connected with the next pole, that still managed to stay anchored to the ground, standing defiantly erect. A bicycle floated through the currents and got tangled in the electric wires, instantly letting off another bout of high-voltage fireworks. The rubber tyres of the bicycle caught fire, giving out a smoke that reminded Amrit of the pattern made by smoke from burning incense sticks. Amrit folded his hands and bowed his head to the smoke in a strange recall of reverence, as if he was at an altar, praying. He was reminded of his grandmother, and how she would pray every morning. He missed her sorely today, at this very moment. More warmth filled his eyes. More water, everywhere. He felt cold in his legs. He decided to kick off, jump back in headlong for another swim, when he felt a vibration in his pocket. His mobile phone was ringing, on vibrate mode. Amazed that in spite of all this water, the damned instrument was still alive, Amrit chuckled as he pulled it out of his pocket.

It was Meghna calling. "Amrit," screamed Meghna. "Where the hell are you? Hello? Amrit?"

"Meghna.... I am swimming! Ha ha!" Amrit laughed an odd throaty laugh, clearing the phlegm that had built up in his passages.

"Are you okay? You sound drunk. I had told you to come to meet me at Qayamat Studios," rattled Meghna. "Listen, this phone may die anytime.... Do you know where the St. Michael Church is? Come there. I'm there. It's safe here. Come fast. It's dangerous out there."

"Okay okay," is all Amrit said. Maybe hearing a familiar voice, a voice he respected, brought back some sanity to his crazed bearings. Like a hypnotised obedient boy, he followed Meghna's instructions, turning right towards the hillock on which St. Michael's Church was situated. The waters had not gotten there, the natural elevation offering protection. An old church, established by Anglican Missionaries in 1812, who had tagged along here with the English imperialists, riding with them on their boats to wherever the Empire went, to spread the word of the Lord. There was a stoic solidity about the stone structure, standing steadfast like a beacon of hope in a sea of deluge. Justice was halted at its gates – years of penance and prayer had perhaps kept the vengeance-seeking floodwaters at bay with a strict 'Do Not Enter' sign.

As Amrit trudged towards the safety of St. Michael's, its large wooden cross hoisted over its clay-tiled roof was now visible in the distance, amid carnage all around. Everywhere Amrit looked, the flood had gone knocking. Shops were flooded, with waters lapping the counters, the wares floating about. Amrit covered his nose in a grimace as he crossed an overflowing garbage dump, the kind that are lined with white porcelain tiles and are the common receptacles of all the garbage from neighbourhoods – at least the solid household kind; the other flowing into the gutters, which, too, were now overflowing and mingling with the flood water in a show of liquid unity. The garbage dump was completely flooded in, with all sorts of stuff you would normally not like to look at, dispersed and put on individual display by the flood waters like in an art exhibition – a bright orange peel here, a plastic bag there, a marigold garland, packets of chips, egg shells, cucumber peel – this was all the best of the worst, floating on top, the creme de la creme muck, the real bad stuff, the heavy stuff, had stayed below, or dissolved and become part of this huge mass of grey-black oil slick of a flood that Amrit now waded through.

All the filth of Mumbai was out today. Every cranny, every nook, every rat hole, was now flooded, and its contents out. Those grey waters drew out Mumbai's deepest and dirtiest secrets. It poured and it poured and it poured non-stop. It flooded and it flooded. The heavens beat down rain in wave after incessant wave, shooting down millions of simultaneously fired shots of water pellets.

A shudder of disgust passed down Amrit's spine, his body quivered, his face grimacing further, as the stench from a floating dead rat entered his nostrils. As he felt his body making contact with this filthy water, he wished he could somehow not be here now. He wished he could somehow not have to touch this water. Living in Mumbai can make one forget how utterly filthy the city actually is. Unless, of course, the filth was stuck in your face, placed prominently under your nose, dissolved into one big molten curry of muck right up to your neck, like it was now. Generally, water is a very gracious medium. It hides. Taking in all that is bad and sinister and making it disappear, by still being water – familiar, good old water, the liquid of life. Today, even water had given up. It had been overwhelmed. There was just too much to hold; too much to dissolve; too much to make go away.

Amrit felt sick in his stomach, nauseated. Suddenly, he erupted in a vomit. Even before Amrit could see what had come out, the flood had hungrily gobbled it up, enveloping his ejections, making it its own now, part of the unified grey. Amrit felt better now, and he tried to move faster. He tried not to look at the garbage dump.

His head was still dizzy, his heart still pounding. Vodka buzzed in his head, making him feel he was in a dream – a strange dream, where he was walking through familiar-looking streets, which, for some strange reason, seemed to have been converted to grey rivers.

Amrit tried not to look down at the water. His eyes scanned the higher floors of the buildings, their roofs, and then his eyes stopped at a large hoarding. It was a typical Bollywood hoarding, painted in bright colours, angry faces, smiling faces, action sequences, explosions, titles. It was a hoarding announcing debutante actress Rupa Devi's newest Bollywood 'launch' movie, her third. The previous two had bombed at the box office. Next to it was another billboard, this one showing a garlanded Lalita Devi, Cabinet Minister, and Rupa Devi's mother, waving out to supporters at a large political rally in Mumbai's Shivaji Park. Amrit stopped there for a moment, alternating his gaze between the Bollywood poster featuring the daughter, and the political poster featuring the mother. He noticed that they actually looked quite similar – Rupa looked like a younger version of her mother. Amrit wondered if he could somehow switch the mother and the daughter in the two side-by-side billboards – placing Rupa in the political rally poster and the senior Devi in the movie poster. Amrit did an imaginary drag-and-drop using an imaginary mouse in his hand, and then made a 'click' sound with his tongue, having mentally completed the operation of switching mother and daughter in his mind's computer screen. Amrit laughed at his own mental joke, as he imagined the role reversal. If only the whole world was a computer screen, he could make so much happen. He could make this flood go away, by just highlighting and erasing the grey. What else would he change? Certainly give the whole city a fresh lick of paint. Would he use Photoshop or Corel Draw for that?

Amrit's thoughts were interrupted by a whizzing movement in the water. He felt as if a rope was slighting by his thigh. Amrit instinctively shot out an arm and grabbed it, pulling it out of the water to discover that it wasn't a rope. It was a muscular silver grey sea snake! It was an *Enhydrina schistosa*, or better known by fishermen in the area as the beaked sea snake, with venom eight times deadlier than that of the king cobra. Amrit eyed the curious creature, looking at its grey scales, so perfectly camouflaged with the water he lifted it out of. He had never seen a snake so up close, certainly not a sea snake. Amrit had gripped the large reptile just above its head, and looked straight into its button eyes, its mouth now open, fangs exposed. *Wow! What a beautiful creature!* Amrit was reminded of the snakes he had studied in the biology class in school, preserved in formaldehyde filled glass jars. They had all appeared frozen in time, inanimate, things from the past. The one he held in his hands now looked so alive, writhing and swinging, trying hard to free itself of Amrit's grip. As Amrit peered into the snake's eyes, he wished he could have a conversation with the snake. There was a melancholic sadness in the creature's dark eyes. Amrit wondered if snakes had the same emotions that humans did, whether this snake had ever felt the same way as he did right now. The snake had its mouth fully open, moist fangs exposed, as Amrit's tight grip squeezed its head. Amrit felt as if the snake was screaming, but somehow, someone had pressed the mute button on a TV remote control, making the snake's scream inaudible. The picture was there, but there was no sound, as the snake blared its fangs in angry silence. "I'll let you go now, my friend." Amrit said and lowered the snake gently into the water. There was a flutter of activity and the snake quickly swum off, disappearing deep into the grey, leaving just a fast closing ripple where it had entered the water.

At the base of the little road that led to the hillock on which St. Michael's Church stood, there was a large gushing drain spewing a powerful flow, which, a few feet sunk in, was today, overwhelmed by the amount of liquid, and overflowing on to the road. Amrit noticed something familiar stuck in the drain.

Well well well! What do we have here! Is it not Inspector Gaitunde!

Amrit made his way to the mouth of the drain, in which was stuck the khaki clad body of Inspector Gaitunde, caught awkwardly in the flow. Gaitunde was still wearing his silver tinted Ray Ban sunglasses, but his body seemed to be limp, his head tossed back, the police uniform drenched, water gushing over his legs and arms. Amrit grabbed Gaitunde's body from the shoulders, and pulled the Inspector out. It was difficult at first, but then Amrit applied pressure, and managed to pull Gaitunde free from whatever had got him stuck so awkwardly in the drain. As Amrit pulled him out, he noticed a knife stuck in Gaitunde's back, his khaki police uniform shirt marked in deep red concentric circles around where the knife was lodged. Gaitunde had been stabbed and dumped into the drain.

"Inspector Gaitunde! Jai Maharashtra!" Amrit slapped Gaitunde's face, the silver rimmed glasses still in place. "A friend of yours did this to you?"

"You are very quiet today, Inspector *saab!* What's the matter? Look! Look at all the pollution around. Aren't you going to book someone for pollution today? Look at your Mumbai city today … it's a bloody flooded sewer … pollution … pollution! Pollution my ass! You only cared about how much bribe money you could make! Ha ha ha!" Amrit laughed a delirious laugh.

"Okay … don't talk to me. But … are you carrying your *stuff* today too?" Amrit lifted Gaitunde's silver glares, and winked at him. Gaitunde's eyes were closed. "You look pretty bad … but let's see if you have the *stuff, re*." Amrit unbuttoned Gaitunde's shirt pocket.

"*Voila!* Here it is!" Amrit pulled out the stash of white powder.

"You wouldn't mind if I borrowed some, would you?" Gaitunde did not respond. Amrit took a large pinch of cocaine out of the pouch, put it to his nose, and sniffed hard. The powder was still dry, and potent, thanks to Gaitunde's careful double zip-lock packing. The cocaine hit Amrit's head. He sniffed a little more. He felt a surge race through his body, as the drug dissolved into his blood and made it to his heart and then was pumped to his brain. Amrit returned the pack to Gaitunde's pocket. Amrit noticed the revolver holster on Gaitunde's belt. He pulled out the gun. Cocaine had now hit the neuroreceptors in Amrit's brain.

"Ha ha ha! Thanks for the toy! You carry on with your duty Inspector! I will give you a three gun salute." Amrit let go of the body, which flowed into the sewer, and disappeared into the drain below. *Bang! Bang! Bang!* Amrit raised the revolver into the air in his left hand and let off three shots, while he brought his right hand to his forehead and made a military salute in honour of the uniformed Gaitunde.

"Jai Maharashtra!" Amrit saluted, and then made a bugle sound with his mouth, as he stood there at attention as if he were a young soldier saluting a fallen war hero. Gaitunde's body flowed with the current and disappeared into the drain below. Funeral over, Amrit raised the revolver high in the air, and set a course for St. Michael's Church. The world was spinning around him. The cocaine only exacerbated his delirium and took it to another level. Amrit continued playing the military bugle tune with his mouth as he wobbled his way up to St. Michael's.

When Amrit walked into the church, in addition to Meghna and Sapna, he was surprised to find his former classmate Udita Usgaonkar and politician Bandhoo Kumar, seated on the front row bench facing the pulpit, as if waiting for a sermon to begin. Unknown to most, Bandhoo Kumar owned a shack on the beach, a stone's throw from St. Michael's Church. He had called Udita to the shack today, with the intention of sleeping with her, and with a promise that this would be the very last thing she would have to do before Bandhoo Kumar would hand her the original copy of her notorious sex video he was blackmailing her with. The unexpected heavy rains had flooded the love-shack, cutting short Bandhoo Kumar's carnal designs, forcing them to evacuate his love quarters and trek up the hillock from the beach to the relative safety of St. Michael's. As was always the case whenever Bandhoo Kumar went to his seaside sex cabin, even today he had deliberately not brought his contingent of machine-gun toting security guards that trailed him almost everywhere else. Anonymity in his amorous acts was important for Bandhoo Kumar to maintain his façade. Today, however, he hoped he had made an exception. He hated being trapped like this, in this strange church, with these strange people. Bandhoo Kumar knocked his cellphone once more, trying desperately to make a call. If he could get through, he would call in a chopper to have himself airlifted. The cellphone did not come alive. Water had destroyed its circuit. Bandhoo Kumar had tried using Meghna's phone, but that too was not working any more. Bandhoo Kumar could do nothing but wait for the waters to subside.

"Well! Today is a day full of surprises!" Amrit exclaimed as he saw the front-row audience. "Who do we have here? Shri Bandhoo Kumarji, senior politician and leader of the Loktantra Party! How fortuitous! Udita! You look sexy as ever! Dr. Meghna! And Her Royal Highness Miss Sapna – Bollywood star! What an assortment!" Amrit chuckled funnily.

"Amrit, where did you get that gun? Put it down. What is wrong with you?" Meghna commanded, as Amrit casually pointed the revolver at everyone.

"Shut up Meghna, or I will blow your brains out. I don't take instructions from anyone." Amrit said. Meghna had never seen Amrit behave so rudely. There was certainly something wrong. Amrit pointed the revolver straight at Meghna's head.

"What is wrong with you Amrit?" Meghna tried again.
Bang!
Amrit fired a shot in the air. It had a chilling effect on everyone. This was no toy gun. It was a government issue police revolver. Meghna decided to keep shut. Amrit seemed capable of anything right now.

Amrit walked along the front row bench, waving the revolver in his hand.

Bandhoo Kumar was markedly uncomfortable with this crazed lad armed with a gun, and finally spoke up.

"Look, young man, I don't know what your problem is, but don't you know who I am? I am a very powerful man. Put that pistol down. If you try anything against me, it won't be good. I'm warning you!"

"Well hello hello! Look who has decided to take charge now! Shri Bandhoo Kumarji, leader of the Loktantra Party, the party that promises the betterment of the people and the country! I know who you are. I voted for your party." Bandhoo Kumar smiled.

"But you and your party lied, you son of a bitch! You see that flood out there? You bastards talk of economic development, of making Mumbai into Shanghai, huh? It's bloody Venice out there – and that too a very shitty Venice." Bandhoo Kumar tried to make a grab at the revolver in Amrit's hand. Amrit must have been high, but he was still alert. Amrit immediately saw Bandhoo's move and took evasive action, pulling the gun away, and then retaliated by landing a gentle blow on Bandhoo Kumar's nose. Bandhoo Kumar's nose started bleeding, as he rolled back in pain. The blow was deliberately kept at low intensity, just a little pat of reprimand. A full strength one from Amrit would have knocked out Bandhoo Kumar completely.

"You try that again and I swear I'll kill you. I want some answers from you, you swine." Amrit warned Bandhoo Kumar. "So tell me, where's all that money gone that we tax payers paid? Why does my country look the way it does today, Mr. Politician? Why is Singapore, Malaysia, even bloody China – so bloody ahead of us – when they started much later on their march of economic development? Where is the infrastructure that you promised? The drains, the sewers, the roads, the everybloody thing that you promised? Why is my country still Third World?"

Bandhoo Kumar sat in silence. He didn't know what to say before this madman wielding a gun. He'd already given him a bloody nose. Bandhoo wished his security guards were with him at this moment. He was never without his security cover. Without the commandos, he felt vulnerable, naked, facing this angry young man who seemed to be out of his mind. Bandhoo Kumar calculated that his best bet would be not to say anything.

"Ahhh ... I know where all the public money has gone! It's in your bloody Swiss bank account, isn't it, Bandhoo Kumarji? All the tax payers' money that should have gone into public works so that we don't have a shit-hole of a city which is, if you have noticed, spilling over today, huh?" Amrit said angrily as he knocked the muzzle of the revolver against Bandhoo Kumar's head, as if to try to knock some sense into the veteran politician.

"Look here, whatever your name is, I am warning you again. You can't blame me like this, malign my good name, with these baseless allegations. You will face dire consequences; you could go to jail, even worse. You can't do this to an honest public figure. I have dedicated my whole life to serving India." Bandhoo Kumar said in a virtuous, school-teacher preachy tone, as if he were in a television chat show, trying to respond to an allegation.

Thuh! Amrit spat on Bandhoo Kumar's face. He waited for Bandhoo to wipe his face clean with the cuff of his kurta, and then looked straight into the politician's eyes and spoke.

"There is hot young blood flowing in my veins. I don't fear death, certainly not at the hands of a scoundrel like you. You threaten me again, and swear to god I will wring your throat like that of a chicken."

Bandhoo Kumar shivered. There was rage in Amrit's eyes. Bandhoo Kumar decided to look down and avoid making any further eye contact with Amrit.

"I just had an idea!" Amrit's eyes brightened.

"Do you remember the game of Bollywood Roulette? The one we played in the Academy." Bandhoo Kumar was the only one who didn't know what Amrit was talking about. Amrit opened the chamber of the revolver, took one live round and put it in his pocket, and threw all the other rounds out of the window. He then showed the live round to everyone, "it's a real bullet!" Amrit placed the live round into a chamber and rotated it vigorously, and then snapped the chamber back in place. The revolver was now ready with one bullet in some unknown chamber.

"What … what is this?" Bandhoo Kumar asked, confused.

"It is called Bollywood Roulette. It's a game of chance. You have so much interest in Bollywood and in Bollywood actors, I think you ought to play this game too, Shri Bandhoo Kumarji! It's very simple. Just like Russian Roulette. I will ask you a question. If you give me a convincing answer, I will not pull the trigger. If I am not convinced by your reply, I will pull the trigger. Whether you live or die, then, is purely dependent on your luck – depending on where the bullet is. Easy, no?"

Amrit walked along the front row, brandishing the revolver, passing Sapna, Meghna, Udita and Bandhoo Kumar.

"Let's start with our distinguished chief guest for the evening, Shri Bandhoo Kumarji." Amrit pointed the gun straight at Bandhoo Kumar's head. "Why … why should I let you live, you pig? Look how fat you've become…and

I bet you still want more, don't you, you hungry swine! Why should I let you live?" Amrit dug the revolver into Bandhoo's scalp.

"I am very, very sorry. I have done a lot of bad deeds. Like I made this poor girl, Udita, have sex and then taped it, here, on this tape." Bandhoo Kumar showed the tape. "It was such a shameful thing to do. I need to be made to suffer for that. I need to be made to repent. Death is too easy a punishment. I need to be exposed in front of the whole nation. My face needs to be blackened with boot polish, a garland of shoes put around my neck, and I ought to be paraded on a donkey through the streets of Mumbai. I have destroyed this girl's life. And that of so many others. I have done so many wrongs. Oh! Please ... please give me a chance to repent. Please, I beg of you. I will give you all my money. Everything in the Swiss bank, everything." Bandhoo Kumar folded his hands before Amrit.

"Wow! Bandhoo Kumarji, you should have been an actor! You are so good at acting! Anything for self-preservation, isn't it? You chameleon, I know what you're made of. You didn't mean a word of what you just said. Let destiny decide whether you ought to live or not. You see, in this game of Bollywood Roulette, luck plays a very important part. Let's see what luck has in store for you." Amrit began squeezing the revolver's trigger. Then, after some thought, Amrit pulled the gun away.

"But before I pull the trigger, I want to give you one last chance to repent. I'll let you pray. Do you ever pray, Bandhoo Kumar?" Amrit looked at Bandhoo's eyes. "No you don't. You son of a bitch! Well, today you will. I'll make you pray. You will pray for all those who have died today in the flood. A lot of that blood is on your hands.

You will pray for them. You will pray for atonement, for all the sins you have committed."

Amrit moved to the pulpit and picked up the leather bound Bible that was lying there, open midway from the last sermon, and dropped it into Bandhoo Kumar's lap.

"Read." Amrit commanded.

Bandhoo Kumar hesitated.

"I know it is a Bible. I know you're not a Christian. You say you are a secularist, don't you; I've heard your speeches on TV. So it shouldn't matter ... *Bible, Quran, Gita, Guru Granth Sahib*... same thing. C'mon, read."

Bandhoo Kumar hesitated again. Amrit dug the gun's barrel into Bandhoo Kumar's head.

"Okay okay ... don't fire." Bandhoo Kumar looked down at the open page and started reading:

> *Luke 17:25: But first must he suffer many things, and be rejected of this generation*
>
> *26: And as it was in the days of Noe, so shall it be also in the days of the son of man.*
>
> *27: They did eat, they drank, they married wives, they were given in marriage, until the day that Noe entered into the ark, and the flood came, and destroyed them all.*
>
> *28: Likewise also as it was in the days of Lot; they did eat, they drank, they bought, they sold, they planted, they builded;*
>
> *29: But the same day that Lot went out of Sodom it rained fire and brimstone from heaven, and destroyed all.*
>
> *30: Even thus shall it be in the day when the son of man is revealed.*

"Amen! Enough repentance. Now we will play, ladies and gentlemen, Bollywood Roulette!" Amrit said in a sinister tone.

The chambers of the revolver began turning, as Amrit slowly applied pressure on the trigger, the barrel pointing dead into Bandhoo Kumar's head.

Click!

Bandhoo Kumar gave out a gasp of relief. So did Meghna. Sapna was still looking down.

"You lucky son of a bitch … you lucky … story of your life, you filthy shit … ha ha ha ha!" Amrit went into raptures, tickled by a strange humour about the whole situation, which seemed understandable only to him. Today everything appeared funny to Amrit. Everybody else in the room was dead serious, pushed to the edge seeing a madman-like possessed Amrit. By pulling the trigger on Bandhoo Kumar, he had proved that he was not himself today. *Amrit could never do this! Amrit! No! But he just had!* Meghna sat still, wishing she could take Amrit to see a psychiatrist right now. *He needs help! Poor soul!* Amrit was now settling down from the convulsions of laughter, and turned his attention to pick the next unwilling player in his game of Bollywood Roulette.

"Amrit! Stop this! Please!" cried Meghna, half afraid and half unbelieving that this was the same Amrit. Amrit glanced at Meghna and pointed the gun at her, tilting his head and smiling demonically at her.

"Shhhh … your turn will come too." There was a seriousness in Amrit's eyes, like those of a cornered tiger, a look that said *do not stop me or else*. Amrit looked capable of doing anything right now. Anything. And with a revolver with a live bullet in his hand, that anything could be to anyone.

Amrit walked up and down the front row, taking his time to pick the next person.

"Sapna! The star! The latest arm candy of Zaeed Zakaria! Would you care to play, your royal highness?" Amrit put the gun on her head. Sapna continued to look down, staring straight ahead, lost in her thoughts. "Oh I'm sorry Miss, or shall I call your *Mistress*, you are so quiet and silent now. How come? You're so bubbly and vivacious on the screen! And in those Page 3 pictures and interviews! C'mon, amuse us little mortals a bit here! Like you once did in class." Amrit said in a steely voice. "You will have to play, whether you like it or not. It doesn't matter that you're a big star. Or that you have a billionaire boyfriend. Look ... even Bandhoo Kumarji played ... and he's a celeb too! He's on Page 3 more than you are. Look what a good sport he was."

Sapna continued to look down, not reacting. It infuriated Amrit further. She was ignoring him, not taking his threat seriously. He pointed the gun at Sapna's head, held it there in outstretched hands, as he took aim. He felt warmth swelling in his eyes, as he took aim at her head, that hair, that profile, bringing back vague memories. Then the thought of Zaeed Zakaria came back, and the warmth turned to bitterness. "Why should I let you live?" Amrit announced. Amrit pulled the hammer of the gun back, and everyone could hear the clicking sound. *He can't do that! No! Not to Sapna!* Meghna was petrified. Amrit put his finger around the trigger, and began squeezing gently, Sapna's profile was straight in the sights of the revolver. Just then, Sapna raised her head, and looked straight at Amrit. Her eyes were moist. Amrit hesitated. *Those eyes!* They still did something to him. Sapna began speaking, her eyes locked with Amrit's.

"In moments of solitude, I think of you. I think of the magical moments I have spent with you, like the time we went to Madh Island…"

Meghna looked up. Amrit's expression changed. Sapna's eyes were growing wet. Amrit felt a rising warmth in his eyes too, which he couldn't seem to push back. Sapna continued.

"And the time we got drenched in the rain at the Bandra seafront. How happy I was, in your arms … how completely at home I felt in them … as if I belonged there … as if they were made especially for me. In you, Amrit, I thought I had found happiness, and security … and then…"

Tears streamed down Sapna's cheeks, as she blinked and looked away. Amrit felt a lump in his throat. Tears ran down his cheeks too. There was no need for glycerine today. Then Sapna looked back at Amrit, and spoke again.

"If you want to point the revolver, don't point it at my head, point it at my belly – because in my belly lives proof of our love. Amrit, I am pregnant with your child. That is what I wanted to say to you."

Amrit let out a gasp! His eyes were overflowing, his lungs heavy. Tears were incessantly streaming down Sapna's cheeks like rivers flowing down pearl white valleys. Amrit suddenly came back to his senses. The tears washed away the alcohol and the cocaine, and Amrit was suddenly fine again. His head was splitting, as he held his head in his hands. *What the hell was wrong with me? Oh shit! Amrit, what are you doing!* Amrit looked at Meghna, with apology filled in his eyes. *What had overcome me!* Meghna could see the return of the kind and gentle Amrit she had known, and nodded and smiled, as if to say, *Welcome back! It's okay.* Amrit turned his gaze to Sapna, who was still sobbing. *How could he have pointed a gun at Sapna? She was pregnant with his child!* Amrit despised his behaviour.

Amrit felt a big blow to his head, and for a moment lost his equilibrium. Bandhoo Kumar had snuck up on him and struck him on the head with the *Bible*, the only thing he could find. The gun dropped from Amrit's hand, and Bandhoo Kumar picked it up. Bandhoo Kumar now pointed the gun straight at Amrit. Sapna got up too.

"You sister-fucking lad, you were going to bring Bandhoo Kumar to justice. Do you know *who* you are dealing with? When I was your age, I had already murdered dozens of men and raped twice that many women. No court in the land has ever been able to bring me to justice, and *you* will!" taunted Bandhoo Kumar, revolver pointed straight at Amrit.

"What *filmi naatak* is going on here? *Wah wah!*" Bandhoo Kumar snickered, as he looked at Sapna. "Are you sure it's *his* baby … not Zaeed Zakaria's? You filmi *laundiyas* are very *chaaloo!*"

Amrit wiped the tears from his eyes and tried to get a grip on the situation. Bandhoo Kumar was pointing a gun, which still had a live round somewhere in it, at him. He tried to position himself so that he could make a quick move on the gun. Bandhoo Kumar, sensing Amrit's intentions, cried out, "Don't you try to move, you son of a bitch. I'll blow your brains out if you do," as he took a few steps back, out of reach of Amrit.

"Now *you* say your prayers." Bandhoo Kumar took aim at Amrit's chest. "Goodbye." With this Bandhoo

Kumar pulled the trigger. In a flash, Sapna moved across, and placed herself between Bandhoo Kumar and Amrit. *Click!* The gun did not fire. It was an empty chamber. Sapna was now right in front of Amrit. *Bang!* Bandhoo Kumar pulled the trigger again, this time, the gun fired.

Sapna fell to the ground. Amrit collapsed too. The bullet had hit Sapna in the chest, puncturing her rib cage. The bullet had then left Sapna's back, and entered Amrit's shoulder, where it had finally lodged itself. Sapna fell back, and into Amrit's arms, as they both collapsed to the ground. They were now in each other's arms, their eyes locked. "Why did you do that, Sapna? Why?" Amrit asked, tears running down his cheeks.

"Because I love you Amrit. Always have. Always will. I don't want to bring a child into this world without his father." Sapna said, gasping for breath. Amrit winced, and cried as he wrapped his arms around her. "Oh Sapna … Sapna! I love you so much … Oh god … what have you done. This is not how it was supposed to be." Sapna put her finger on his mouth. "Shhh…" and then she moved her finger from Amrit's lips to where dimples would appear on his cheeks. "Where have my dimples gone? I want to see my dimples," she said, barely audible. Amrit smiled. The dimples appeared and Sapna poked her finger into them. Strength was draining out of her, her finger barely able to reach Amrit's cheek. "Ouch! It hurts. You still have long nails." Amrit exclaimed, tears streaming down his cheeks. "My macho man." Sapna's eyes went motionless as she became unconscious. Meghna rushed to Sapna.

"Sapna! Sapna!" Meghna tried desperately to revive her. Thankfully, there was still a pulse. Meghna took off her *dupatta* and wrapped it around Sapna's wound, to stem the bleeding. Then, she turned to Amrit, who was also bleeding profusely from where the bullet had hit him. "Hang in there Amrit! You're a strong lad. Don't you die on me." Meghna examined Amrit's wound. She desperately needed to get the bullet out, or it would poison him to death.

Bandhoo Kumar still held the revolver in his hand, but it was, like him, impotent; unable of doing any further harm. Udita, who had been watching, lunged forward at Bandhoo, going for the tape in his kurta pocket. Bandhoo Kumar dropped the revolver, grabbed Udita's hair and pulled her away from his kurta, and gave her a tight slap across her face. Udita was thrown back by the blow, her hair now dishevelled. She again leapt at Bandhoo, desperate for the tape. Bandhoo grabbed her hair with both hands now, upset at her persistence. Udita let out a groan, as she felt her hair pulled by Bandhoo's hands.

"Bitch! You bitch! I will parade you naked on Marine Drive, you slut." Udita shrieked in pain as Bandhoo Kumar tightened his grip on her hair, pulling hard at her scalp as she stared at him. There was anger in Udita's eyes as she glared at the politician. This monster of a man had ruined her life, and that of so many others. Bandhoo Kumar looked back at her, his eyes red with anger and diabetic blood pressure. He tightened his grip further.

"You are showing me eyes, you two paisa whore. Showing *me* eyes." Bandhoo Kumar tugged further. Udita was now in pain, as she tried with both hands to loosen Bandhoo Kumar's hold on her open mane.

"Let her go, Bandhoo Kumar." Meghna implored. "Please let her go."

Bandhoo Kumar ignored Meghna, continuing to grip Udita by her hair. Suddenly Udita felt something poke her in her breast. It was her six inch pencil-like metallic hair pin, which had held her hair in place in a neat bun, and which had fallen from her hair and lodged itself in her blouse; its sharp, dagger-like end piercing her flesh. Udita had an idea. She looked at Bandhoo once again.

"You evil man," Udita said, looking straight into Bandhoo Kumar's monstrous eyes. Before Bandhoo Kumar could react with another slap or a tighter tug on her hair, Udita retrieved the hair pin from her blouse and thrust it with all her might into Bandhoo Kumar's neck. "Die." Bandhoo Kumar's eyes became bigger, as he felt the thrust of the dagger-like hair pin penetrate his neck. The pin had struck its mark, rupturing Bandhoo Kumar's jugular vein and immediately sending spurts of blood gushing onto Udita's face like a spray from a punctured hosepipe. Bandhoo Kumar's grip on Udita's hair loosened, and he brought his hands to his neck, trying to stop the blood from gushing out. Meghna immediately leapt, placing a hand over Bandhoo Kumar's neck, asking him to lie down. Sworn to a Hippocratic oath she had once taken, she was obliged to try and save him. Though in her heart she felt anger and hatred towards this murderous man, she kept her hand planted over the politician's neck. The dilemma was to be shortlived, for the doctor in her soon deduced that Bandhoo Kumar could not be saved. In an operation theatre, with life saving equipment, there was an outside chance. Here, certainly not. Udita had dealt him a mortal blow. With every beat of his heart, blood squirted out from the veteran politician's neck in an incessant stream. With each passing second, Bandhoo Kumar was losing his strength and drifting towards certain death. Meghna took his pulse. It was fading. Within a few more seconds, it had stopped. Meghna returned to where she had placed Amrit and Sapna on a bench, seated upright to minimise the blood loss. She desperately needed to get them to a hospital, or else they too would meet the same end as Bandhoo Kumar's.

Just then Udita stood up, with tape in hand, readying to leave. "Where are you going?" Meghna asked Udita, as she applied pressure on Sapna and Amrit's wounds. Udita didn't reply, she just looked at Meghna. Meghna noticed that Udita's face looked very different today. It was pockmarked. Her eyes looked different too. The rain had washed away all the foundation, the mascara and all the other makeup that Udita always had on her face. Today, for the first time, seen without makeup, she looked very different. She looked extraordinarily simple. Like any lower middle class Maharashtrian girl who could be spotted on a local train or on a Mumbai bus. This was the original Udita from the Railway Colony in Virar.

"I am going," said Udita as she strode out. "Wait! Don't! Udita!" Meghna watched as Udita sprinted out, videotape in hand. Meghna watched as Udita's figure disappeared into the dark night. For a moment she felt she should follow her, but then realised it would be foolish. Maybe instinctively she knew where Udita was headed.

As Udita stepped into the water, she let go of the tape, which was hungrily swallowed by the grey monster. The grey monster was still hungry, and was willing to devour anything it could. It was pitch dark now. The electricity had been cut off. The cloud cover had cut out any light that might have come from the stars and the moon. The rain was still pelting down. Udita continued walking, submerging further as she continued her march. The water level rose, first to her waist, then to her chest, then further, until it was just below her nostrils. Udita did not know how to swim. The first time she had worn a swimming costume was for a modelling shoot, where she was made to pose next to a bottle of hair oil. Today, she would go for her first and last swim. She took another step, the waters lapped up her face, and she sunk in. The grey monster took her in, happily welcoming her. She was now fully immersed, swallowed up, without trace, her watery grave left unmarked, save for a mild ripple, which too soon disappeared.

Meghna sat helpless, unable to do much. Both Sapna and Amrit were drifting in and out of consciousness, blood oozing out of their gunshot wounds. *I need to get them to a hospital! Fast!* Meghna worried about the bleeding as she went to the window. She could hear the violent rain beating down on the roof. St. Michael's Church was like an island in a sea of rising floodwater, slowly but surely being encroached upon by the grey monster. Meghna picked up the last burning candle and took it with her to the window. The warm yellow glow from the candle seemed reassuring. It gave her warmth on a cold night. She placed the candle on the ledge, carefully choosing a spot shielded from the rain and the wind.

Time passed slowly. Water lapped around Meghna's ankles now. The rain had not stopped and the floodwaters were rising. She had never seen Mumbai so dark before. *Where had all this darkness come from? From water? Water!* A substance so benign and life giving. *It* had turned dark tonight? Assaulting the city from the skies and the ocean, spreading its dark tentacles everywhere.

"Is anybody there?" Meghna heard a distant, authoritative voice from outside the window. She peered out of the ledge and noticed a powerful searchlight and what appeared to be a man on an inflated rubber boat holding a megaphone.

"This is the Indian Navy. We are here to help you."

"Here!" Meghna cried out, almost choking, and then cried out again, "Here! Help! Help!"

The searchlight shone directly on her face, blinding her momentarily. Then, the man with the megaphone replied, "We see you. We are coming!"

The boat veered outside the window, positioned there by the sailors so that Meghna could step off the window ledge and straight on to the boat.

"Come on down, ma'am. Step into the boat. Don't worry, we'll hold you."

"I have two wounded patients here. They need urgent medical attention." Meghna added.

"Don't worry ma'am," the sailor with the megaphone replied in a stern military voice. The other sailor pulled himself up over the ledge and came in through the window.

"I'll carry them on to the boat ma'am." The sailor announced. "Here, please put this on." He handed Meghna a life jacket.

Meghna tightened the makeshift bandages as she helped the sailor lift Amrit and Sapna over the windowsill and into the boat.

"Don't worry ma'am, we're headed to a hospital."

The boat moved on, the sailor with the megaphone repeating his calls to survivors as they sailed forth. Meghna was blanking out, her mind running amok. She could hardly hear the man with the megaphone. Her thoughts went back to the days at the acting academy, to Guruji's lessons, to the good times they had had…

"Ma'am! Ma'am! We've reached!" The sailor blurted out as the rescue boat now pulled up near a hospital, where all the survivors were being ferried. It was still pitch dark, and Meghna could not make out much, as two ward boys carried Sapna and Amrit off on stretchers.

"Take them to the OT." Meghna ordered the ward boys to take Amrit and Sapna to the operation theatre.

Meghna followed as the ward boys rushed towards the hospital building, and then stopped outside a locked door and placed Sapna and Amrit's stretchers outside the door of what was the operation theatre.

"Why are you leaving them here?" Meghna asked.

"Madam, there is no doctor. The operation theatre is closed. We will leave them here till a doctor comes."

"Open the OT. Now!" Meghna screamed at the ward boys. "I'm a doctor. Hurry up! Get the instruments ready. I'll do the operation." Sapna and Amrit were now in critical condition; there was no time to waste.

The ward boys complied – the OT was opened – and they wheeled Sapna and Amrit on to the surgery beds.

Many hours later, Meghna walked out to the veranda, and came to rest against the large archways that opened on to the west, with a view of the ocean beyond. She had managed to save Amrit and Sapna, who were still in the OT.

Amrit felt a sharp pain on his shoulder as he regained consciousness, the effects of the anaesthesia wearing off. He looked around, and found Sapna lying on the bed adjacent to his. She was staring at him.

"Wake up, *oye* Amrit from Amritsar!" Sapna said, as she saw him regain consciousness.

Amrit noticed the wound on Sapna's chest, which had been stitched by Meghna. Sapna winced in pain.

"Are you okay?" Amrit asked.

"Amrit, before I die, I want to tell you something. I never slept with Zaeed Zakaria. You were the only man…" Sapna winced a little more, the pain from the wound unbearable, and closed her eyes.

"Nobody is going to die." Meghna announced as she walked into the operation theatre. "Both of you are out of danger. And so is your baby. Just relax and rest. You've lost a lot of blood."

"Sapna!" Amrit cleared his throat.

"What?" Sapna replied, through the pain.

"I know you're a princess and I'm a commoner … but … will you marry me?" Amrit asked.

Sapna opened her eyes. They were filled with tears. Not from pain, but from joy.

"Of course I will," she broke into a smile.

Meghna walked out of the operation theatre, with a smile on her face. Her body ached. She pulled the stethoscope off her shoulder and massaged the back of her neck. It had been a long night for her – saving Amrit and Sapna had not been easy – and the fresh air invigorated her. It was almost midday. Meghna stood there, with her hands resting on the parapet. In the distance, a crack was appearing in the grey-black cloud cover that had engulfed Mumbai like a thick blanket for the last twenty-four hours. A few rays of the sun were also visible through the crack in the clouds. Meghna felt exhausted – physically and mentally – but her thoughts were elsewhere. She stood there for some time, her mind darting here and there. The last few hours had flown by. After operating on Amrit and

Sapna, Meghna had performed numerous other surgeries. A constant stream of patients was still being brought in – cases of drowning, electrocution, injuries, even snakebite. Her presence at the hospital was making a difference. Meghna turned around to go back in. Just then, she realised that an elderly woman, perhaps in her seventies, wearing a well-worn sari over a shrivelled, frail body, one end of her sari, her *pallu,* covering her head, was eyeing Meghna carefully. Meghna turned towards the old woman and placed a gentle, sympathetic hand around her shoulders.

"*Amma,* are you okay? Do you need anything?" Meghna said in a concerned tone.

The old woman continued to examine Meghna's face carefully with her foggy eyes, then raised a shaky finger and pointed it towards Meghna's face.

"You … you…. I have seen you … somewhere…" the old lady was struggling with her memory, trying hard to recall, her eyes squinting as she had evidently recognised Meghna from her TV show.

"You come in TV serial, *na*!" The old woman's face lit up, as she seemed to have now placed Meghna. "I have seen you on TV! You are a TV star! No?" The old lady was excited, but still not fully sure, her memory and eyesight weakened by age.

"No, *amma*. That's not me. I'm just a doctor." Meghna took a deep breath, and looked out, the crack in the sky was now widening, more sunlight pouring in, and then she looked back at the old lady.

"Just an ordinary doctor." Meghna put the stethoscope around her neck and returned to the operation theatre.

EPILOGUE

A swarm of flies was buzzing around a pile of human faeces. Another pile was a few inches away, with another corresponding swarm of flies hovering above it; and then another pile a few inches away, and then another. The entire rail tracks were pockmarked with human droppings rained in place randomly from the open toilets of the train coaches that passed above. A lone dog was walking the tracks of Mumbai's Victoria Terminus Station, occasionally taking a bite out of a pile here and a nibble out of one there – seeking nutrition from the undigested foodstuff from the intestines of the passengers who relieved themselves in the toilet compartments a few feet above. A little cloud of flies went buzzing up in a storm as the mongrel meandered over the tracks, descending back to the track once the canine marauder had passed. The dog had much to choose from. A gourmet of human droppings surrounded him all along the half-mile long platform. Though the Indian Railways, which still used open toilets in its coaches, had put up notices requesting passengers not to defecate at train stations to avoid shitty tracks at platforms, the advice was clearly not working. Most passengers, being illiterate, could probably not get the message; and those who did, didn't give a shit. This was tragedy of the commons at its worst. The Indian Railways – flagged off in 1853, right here at this spot, called Bori Bunder then, and subsequently, in 1888, remodelled into a newly constructed Gothic-style massive edifice proudly rechristened after the Queen of the Empire, Victoria – was today many things to many people. It was the largest employer of humans in the world; and the largest employer of flies in the universe. It was a relic of the bygone British Empire in India; and the skeleton of steel that now precariously binds and holds together a modern nation of a billion people, ferrying them from one part to another.

To most Indians, Victoria Terminus, fondly referred to as just 'VT', is a symbol of hope, bringing them to Mumbai—to India's golden city, the financial capital, the place to find a job, the place to make it big, the place to realise the Indian Dream. The place where thousands had come with nothing in their pockets and had become rich, made it big, realised their dreams – they had all passed through the gates of VT. Fuelled by those success stories, real or imaginary, aspirants poured in from all over India, in search of a better life, fleeing persecution, fleeing hopelessness, or just to exercise the right granted to them by the Indian Constitution, to live wherever they wanted within the Republic of India, freely as they chose. To all those hopefuls who arrived in Mumbai by the iron carriage, whatever be their previous motivations and whatever be their onward dreams, this railway station named after a dead English empress was the gateway to that dream. It was the last stop on the journey from where they were coming, and the first stop on the journey to where they were going.

The mongrel stopped feeding and looked up. He could hear the approaching train in the distance. It was time to vacate the tracks or be slaughtered by the two hundred-tonne electric locomotive that hauled the Tagore Express into Victoria Terminus. The flies, however, stayed on. There was a distant sharp note from the railway engine that grabbed everyone's attention on Platform No.13. A cheap loudspeaker hung loosely from the asbestos roof above, blaring out audio advertisements for all and sundry – advertisements for biscuits, for a local hotel for travellers, for a sexologist who cured 'hidden diseases,' for a job placement agency, for a marriage bureau, for a toothpaste – now switched from advertisement mode to announcement mode. "Train TKOL Tagore Express from Howrah Junction via Tatanagar, Bilaspur, Raipur, Nagpur, and Wardha Junction is now arriving at Platform No. 13." There was commotion on the platform. Coolies in their red tunics and with brass emblems tied around their arms, a uniform unchanged since the days of the Raj, were in motion everywhere, getting into position to jump into the moving train and reach their potential customers first. The first coolie to reach a passenger was most likely to get hired to carry the luggage out of the carriage, up the stairs and out to the main exit. Competition among coolies was fierce. Friends and relatives of passengers jostled here and there to position themselves at the right disembarkation points. As the engine cruised forward, at a slow but determined pace, pulling in the passenger-laden carriages behind it, there was a sudden storm of flies onto the platform. All hands instinctively covered their faces as the flies struggled to find new perches. Through a cloud of flies, people waded through, making last minute adjustments in their positions, hands still covering mouths and faces. The train was now coming to a halt and it let out a final shrill whistle that had the effect of disturbing the flies once again, sending them into another frenzied cloud. The coolies were already in, experts at jumping into moving carriages. Flies, coolies, passengers, relatives, touts, pickpockets, policemen, pimps, hawkers all mingled together in a noisy, dense commotion concentrated on the edge of Platform No. 13.

Gaurav was finally in Mumbai. He peered outside the grilled window of his compartment and took in a whiff of Mumbai air. He instinctively withdrew back in. Sea breeze mingled with the smell of fish mingled with a thousand different odours filled his nostrils. It wasn't pleasant. He would get used to it. Everybody in Mumbai does. Undeterred, Gaurav gathered his belongings and made his way out of the compartment. A middle-aged overweight woman in a polyester sari stood blocking his way, as she tried to get her second large tin box down from the top berth she had occupied for the last one thousand kilometres. Her first, larger tin box was on the floor, blocking Gaurav's exit out of the compartment. Gaurav had spent the last eighteen hours in this compartment, and was impatient. "Aunty, move, move please!" he blurted out impatiently to the lady. Aunty was not budging; the tin box was heavy. Gaurav realised that if he was going to have any chance of making it to the exit of this compartment before the train started its journey from Mumbai's Victoria Terminus back to Kolkata, he would have to help Aunty bring the box down. So, Gaurav extended a hand and together he and Aunty just about managed to bring the tin box down. Gaurav saw an opening – he quickly jumped over the tin boxes and was at the mouth of the exit in a flash. Here, unfortunately, there was another obstruction. A fully laden coolie was stuck halfway between the door, waiting to embark with his customer's luggage. Half inside, half outside, he stood precariously balanced carrying a large black suitcase on his head, two large nylon garment bags flung around his torso, a thermos flask in his left hand, with which he also held on to the railing, and a massive olive-green holdall in his right hand. This was a major obstacle. Gaurav had two options. Either he backtracked and let the coolie into the carriage. Or, he acted aggressively and bulldozed his way out of the carriage door, taking the coolie out with him. Gaurav had to make a split-second decision. The coolie was heaving forward – swinging in and out of the door like an overloaded human pendulum – with every passing moment his centre of gravity was shifting forward. Gaurav decided to go with option two. Aunty had already exhausted all the patience he had left in him after the 18-hour journey from Kolkata to Mumbai – and to Bollywood stardom!

Out charged Gaurav, like a rugby player, his bags held ahead of him to act like logs, as he rammed through with the zeal of a medieval soldier on the charge. The coolie was all protests. He had no choice. Gaurav was a big lad; and he had a determined look in his eyes. The coolie backtracked onto Platform No.13, pushed off by a charging Gaurav. Gaurav finally laid feet on Mumbai soil, spread out his arms into the air, and let out a victorious cry. Yeah! He was finally here. In Bombay. Sorry Mumbai. Whatever. In the city of dreams. In the city of Bollywood.

In the city that would make him a star. A Bollywood star! *Yeah!* Gaurav took out a piece of crumpled paper from his trouser pocket, and read the address of the place to where he had to go:

> *Anil Taneja Acting Academy*
> *212A Mhada Colony*
> *Andheri (West), Mumbai*